INSIDE THE PERIMETER
SCAVENGERS OF THE DEAD

ALAN SPENCER

ACKNOWLEGMENTS

A slew of people have made it their goal to keep me going as a writer, namely my wonderful wife, Megan, who has been my editor and biggest fan ever since reading my awful first novel entitled "Zombie Crisis"; this stinker will forever be buried deep in the files of my laptop. I also wanted to thank my family for their unyielding support; without them, I literally wouldn't be here. Finally, I'd like to give a hearty shout out to Tim Marquitz, Jason Wendleton, S.E. Cox, and every single person out there who still currently reads horror fiction. Without you, these books are wasted trees.

OTHER LIVING DEAD PRESS BOOKS
JUST BEFORE NIGHT: A ZOMBIE ANTHOLOGY
ETERNAL NIGHT: A VAMPIRE ANTHOLOGY
BLOOD RAGE & DEAD RAGE (BOOK 1& 2 OF THE RAGE VIRUS SERIES)
DEAD MOURNING, BOOK OF THE DEAD: A ZOMBIE ANTHOLOGY
LOVE IS DEAD: A ZOMBIE ANTHOLOGY, BOOK OF THE DEAD 2: NOT DEAD YET
DEAD HISTORY: A ZOMBIE ANTHOLOGY
END OF DAYS: AN APOCALYPTIC ANTHOLOGY VOLUME 1 & 2
DEAD HOUSE: A ZOMBIE GHOST STORY
THE ZOMBIE IN THE BASEMENT (FOR ALL AGES)
THE LAZARUS CULTURE, DEAD WORLDS: UNDEAD STORIES VOLUMES 1- 5
FAMILY OF THE DEAD, REVOLUTION OF THE DEAD
RANDY AND WALTER: PORTRAIT OF TWO KILLERS
KINGDOM OF THE DEAD, THE MONSTER UNDER THE BED
DEAD TALES: SHORT STORIES TO DIE FOR, THE WAR AGAINST THEM
ROAD KILL: A ZOMBIE TALE, DEADFREEZE, DEADFALL, DARK PLACES
SOUL EATER, THE DARK, RISE OF THE DEAD, DEAD END: A ZOMBIE NOVEL,
VISIONS OF THE DEAD, THE CHRONICLES OF JACK PRIMUS

THE DEADWATER SERIES
DEADWATER, DEADWATER: Expanded Edition
DEADRAIN, DEADCITY, DEADWAVE, DEAD HARVEST, DEAD UNION,
DEAD VALLEY, DEAD TOWN, DEAD SALVATION, DEAD ARMY (coming soon)

COMING SOON
BOOK OF THE DEAD 4: DEAD RISING, THE BOOK OF CANNIBALS VOLUME 1 & 2
END OF DAYS: AN APOCALYPTIC ANTHOLOGY VOLUME 3
CHILDREN OF THE VOID (FOR ALL AGES)

INSIDE THE PERIMETER: SCAVENGERS OF THE DEAD

Copyright © 2010 by Spencer Wendleton & Living Dead Press
ISBN   Softcover   ISBN 13: 978-1-935458-50-0   ISBN 10: 1-935458-50-7

All rights reserved. No part of this book may be reproduced or transmitted in any form or by any means, electronic or mechanical, including photocopying, recording, or by any information storage and retrieval system, without permission in writing from the copyright owner.

This is a work of fiction. Names, characters, places and incidents either are the product of the author's imagination or are used fictitiously, and any resemblance to any actual persons, living or dead, events, or locales is entirely coincidental. This book was printed in the United States of America. For more info on obtaining additional copies of this book, contact: www.livingdeadpress.com

Edited by Anthony Giangregorio

PROLOGUE

Gary Fortner kept himself hidden in the cover of darkness, knowing if he was sighted by his pursuers, he'd be dead instantly. The skulking enemies were there one moment and gone the next, their stalking methods strangely confident and planned.

Creating more distance from them, he kept participating in the twisted game of cat and mouse. He crept into the unknown woods, finding odd tools scattered between huddles of trees and bends in the terrain: an axe head, a pair of bloodied gardening shears, a gore-smeared mallet, and so many knives and steel edges, all broken and abused.

The sight of them increased Gary's stride to scout somewhere to hide and catch his breath.

This was indeed a chopping block, he kept thinking to himself, skirting around a pile of human entrails, each piece ranging from fresh to deep decomposition. Running harder now after taking in the fetid sight, he nearly tripped in reaction at the next grotesque item ahead: a naked torso of a man sliced from the pelvis down and laid out on a sizeable rock. What was stranger was how the pelvic stump was cleanly severed.

Who could enact such violence? he thought, knowing it would take a table saw or a mechanical machine to inflict such a deep precise wound. He looked closer, noting that the toes were plucked from the severed legs; a kneecap also removed from the left leg, leaving a concave hole of bloody soup. The remains appeared to be the end result of a torture orgy, but he had a strong premonition there was something more behind the mess than a gore-hound getting off in the woods.

Gary scanned the horizon again, recounting what had brought him here. He had woken minutes ago propped against an oak tree, the dense miles surrounding him giving no indication of where he'd been dumped or where he should go next or why he was here. Groggy-headed, he knew he'd been drugged and left for dead. Getting up, he then smelled the tang of rotting flesh in the air.

Then he heard the closing in of footsteps, the shuffle and abrupt stop of movement, and the moans and breaths of air escaping clotted throats, a macabre pining for their prey.

Who put him here?

The question kept cycling in his mind, as he climbed over a series of jagged rocks, where he met more of the same crowded stretches of trees.

He'd been in jail for two years, finishing his term for robbing a bank with his piece-of-shit brother-in-law. They hadn't escaped the parking lot before the squad cars circled them. With the evidence piled up against him, Gary took the plea bargain for seven years with the possibility of parole. But how he was transported from jail to these woods was a mystery. He was asleep in his prison bunk last night, and now, he was here, running from unknown assassins that stank of sun-baked meat and spilled blood.

Suddenly, brain-piercing pain flooded his body, beginning with his right leg, and he lost his footing upon the wrenching clink of metal. His entire body clenched for a split-second before going limp and collapsing; he was useless against the electric wave of agony emanating in his right foot.

He looked down with tears in his eyes to see the bear trap was now a bleeding set of teeth, his foot jammed in it tightly. He couldn't pivot his body forward to separate the trap.

He unleashed the rawest stream of curses in his personal history, pounding the earth and growling and weeping as the pain only increased. Every panic button in his body was pressed; fear for his life, fear of bleeding to death, and fear of an agonizing demise, all worked against him in his moment of helplessness.

There was a whistling sound for a second and then, without seeing it happen before it occurred, a steel pole was driven through his chest with a hollow, wet whistle. The impact knocked him flat, his shoulders digging into the earth beneath him. As he stared up at the night sky, his body going into shock, he bled fervently from his sternum, his life's blood dripping onto the decaying bed of leaves and branches beneath him.

The crunch of footsteps came to his ears and then two dead hands twisted the pole he was impaled on, forcing it deeper into the earth; pieces of its greasy flesh came off on the weapon in the process, coating the pole in threads.

An insect-eaten skull stared down at Gary, callously turning its head in mock curiosity as Gary belched and vomited, aspirating the blood flooding into his lungs.

Unable to move, Gary could only watch in horror as the other living dead people—walking post-mortem anomalies—filed out from their hiding places wielding metal implements that reflected the moonlight overhead.

They surrounded him, a half dozen or more, and began to dissect him piece-by-piece. As Gary begged for mercy from the pain he was in, the purpose of their violence unknown to him, he almost welcomed it when an axe split open his belly and a machete spliced his skull in two.

CHAPTER 1

Boyd Broman was scheduled to be driven out of Hutchinson Penitentiary for reasons unknown to him. What new prison he'd be transferred to, he wasn't notified. What state—his best guess would be wrong.

Jerry Wright, Boyd's lawyer, failed to divulge the details about the switch and had been unavailable to take his calls. He was ushered from his job folding laundry in the sub-level basement and then promptly delivered to a dark armored car outside the barbed gates by two non-county officials without a hint as to why.

He sat alone in his seat for over an hour, itching at his wrist shackles, as the vehicle coasted down a lone barren road. Boyd didn't catch a single road or highway sign during the trip, though he kept watching for any indication as to where he was being delivered. That's why he was lucky when the driver finally broke the silence, reading into Boyd's apprehension through the rearview concave mirror. The man was in his early twenties, a rosy cheeked and buzz-cut good ol' boy who hadn't seen enough real combat to question his directives.

"You're lucky in a way, Mr. Broman. Those criminals would've murdered you in lock-up. All ex-cops face that danger behind bars, right? At least in this *other* place, you'll have a real fighting chance to live."

Boyd failed to grasp the driver's vague explanation and fired back, "What do you mean, I'll have a fighting chance? Everybody's closed-lipped. First my lawyer, then the warden, and now my driver won't say anything." He lifted his arms up, rattling the chains. "Somebody better start speaking up or else I'm gonna lose it."

The driver was offended, as if the nugget of information he'd given was generous and spouted off, "That's too bad, because I'm done talking. I shouldn't have said anything in the first place. You're just like the rest of them, antsy and stupid. Just sit tight, shut your mouth, and you'll find out everything you need to know soon enough."

The law enforcement vehicle didn't carry a badge decal or county number now that he was thinking about it.

Were there even government tags on either side of the bumpers? he wondered. Why would they go through the trouble of transferring him to another prison so quickly? It would take months of paperwork to approve such a measure. Chief Edward Hill of the Crawford County Precinct said that Boyd had developed a sixth sense during his thirteen years on the police force as a detective. Anytime something bad was about to occur, Boyd suffered a migraine.

And right now his skull buzzed.

His front to mask his anxiety dissolved, and Boyd demanded, "Would you just tell me where the hell you're taking me?"

The driver didn't reply, indifferent to Boyd's stress. Though the man kept staunching sweat from his forehead with the back of his hand, the man's nerves were creeping up on him, too.

The man's uniform was solid military green without rank. No badge or decorations either. *Who does he work for?*

Almost three hours had passed before they suddenly made another turn, this time traveling deeper into the forming dense woods. The terrain had changed from paved road to a rocky, jouncing dirt path. Three towers came into visibility after minutes of passing the same trees and foliage endlessly stocked on the horizon. Armed men guarded the tops with sub-machine guns, the men staring down at the armored vehicle unaffected by its routine appearance.

After another mile, the vehicle car hooked a left, and they slowed to ten miles an hour, soon reaching a fence topped with barbed wire. The woods had been cleared again, a wide expanse of space opening up without an intruding nature.

Another prison, Boyd realized, cursing under his breath.

The driver pulled up beside a security checkpoint—a booth—where he signed a waiver and gained approval to enter. The entrance parted and revealed another pair of gates, these higher and laced with thicker barbed mesh, the jagged reams promoting entrapment. Closing in on the new gate, the driver was on high alert, his eyes roaming the landscape, bulbous and paranoid.

The gate opened by sensor-activation, and they drove through it, now looking on at the perimeter of an unknown base. The concrete barrier walls were twenty or thirty feet high, impossibly high, each side of the giant square spanning for miles. It was like standing outside a baseball stadium, the seats and field invisible from the parking lot.

This wasn't a prison, Boyd realized, it couldn't be that simple.

The vehicle moved south of the base. They continued alongside the tall-standing concrete wall with no destination in sight. Excruciating minutes passed, and the driver stopped outside of a wrought-iron gate built into the concrete barrier.

The driver kept the engine running, and he turned to face Boyd. "This is it, Broman. Brace yourself." The driver stepped out, opening the side door and unlocked Boyd's shackles. Training a Glock pistol on him, he insisted, "You're going to follow me, and don't try anything."

Boyd had no choice but to acquiesce to the commands, the muzzle digging into his back. They walked to the gate, the driver punching a code into the security panel. The lock disengaged, the door edging open with a dis-inviting creak.

"In a way, you're set free." The driver urged him towards the door by waving the gun at it. "I wish you the best of luck. Play it smart from here on out. Now get in there."

"What's inside?" Boyd refused to obey the commands, grinding his heels into the earth and putting on the brakes. "I'm not taking a goddamn step until you tell me what this place is."

"I don't know how to answer that question, and even if I could, I'm not supposed to do anything except make sure you get inside. Just walk straight and follow the concrete path. Keep it simple. You'll spot an old brick station a quarter of a mile up ahead; you can't miss it. Go inside. That's all I can tell you." Under his breath, *"That's all they told me to tell you."*

Boyd was nudged in the back again, and this time his resistance was answered by a swift kick behind the legs, sending him onto his knees and hands like a dog. Then he was dragged by the arm through the threshold, the man showing surprising strength in that quick moment. "Now get in there!"

Landing on his side, Boyd was slow getting up. He attempted to charge the door, but it had slammed closed.

He was too late.

"What the hell is this?" Boyd clutched the iron bars, desperate for release. The three weeks he slept in a prison cell was difficult, yet that form of incarceration was clearly unlike what lay behind the door. He could be walking into an orchestrated trap. Perhaps the government was testing a new weapon, and he was the guinea pig? He imagined walking down the stairs and a giant laser beam searing through his midsection and cutting him in half. "What's behind that door at the bottom of the stairs? Please, tell me anything. You can't just leave me here."

"Turn around, Mr. Broman."

Boyd didn't move.

The gun was pressed to his temple through the gate. "Turn around, *now*."

"You going to shoot me?"

"I could, but that means I'd have to clean up after myself. Brains are a bitch to clean up. The spatter alone..."

"I wouldn't want to inconvenience you, huh? You've got a life, right? A wife and maybe a kid and another on the way, but me, I'm stuck here. I should do as you say, so you can go back to your happy existence, is that right?"

The driver's face softened, and he sighed, leveling with him, "This is a chance for you to reclaim your life. All I can do is point you in the right direction. The rest is up to you. Many men better than you have been turned away for this opportunity. Take full advantage of it. Go to the station in the courtyard; you'll be told more later."

Boyd studied his surroundings, namely the concrete stairs that carried down for three flights below to the final gate between him and the facility. Leaves and piles of broken dogwood limbs littered each tier. Boyd suspected nobody came through to clean up.

"Mr. Broman, there's nowhere for you to go except inside. I suggest you do as I say and head straight for the station." Giving him a stern face, he metamorphosed back into a government-type goon. "They pulled a lot of strings to get you in here. Start appreciating it."

Boyd spun around to face him again and gave one final entreaty to release him, but the driver had retreated back to the car, running all out. The man sped down the road, denying Boyd any further exchanges and leaving him in a cloud of gritty dust.

He glanced at the surveillance camera directly above him and flipped it off.

On the ground, Boyd spied the Glock resting against the gate. He reached through, picking it up. He stood for a few minutes and decided there was no other option but to enter the unknown. The final door automatically unlocked at his approach and swung open. What waited at the bottom? The question added fuel to his building migraine.

He cradled the gun, liking the way it felt in his grip. The wind kicked up a heap of leaves, the dry scrape of them mincing in his ears. It was the only sound for miles. No footsteps or hushed voices, he was the only living person here for all he knew.

And there's no real way to know for sure until you walk inside.

He crept down the first series of steps, softly pressing his feet down so as not to make noise. He held his breath, his pulse suddenly pounding, his instincts telling him to run in the other direction and not to enter at any cost.

Boyd looked up at the sky, the sun radiant and delivering blistery heat. Pausing a moment, he thought how someone had created this enclosure, whether it was local law enforcement or military or higher up. Freed from prison, he was here to do a job, and with the gun in his hand, the fact couldn't be more obvious.

He completed the last set of stairs and waited at the threshold of the door. He expected a line of officers on the other side, but instead, a hill greeted him unmarked by human life. Power lines hovered in the distance. A concrete path was crudely built into the crabgrass, the squares already breaking and helter-skelter.

Stepping through the final gate, he edged up the hill to catch a glimpse of where he'd been abandoned. A post office came first, and the series of cars parked outside the building were charred, fire-eaten frames. The strip of stores: Jones Prescription Drugs, Cosmic Bowling, Carlson's Shoe Repair, and Sun Market Grocery were of the same decimated condition—looted and defaced. He kept to the concrete path as the driver instructed and cleared those obstacles to a circle drive.

He was about to call out to someone, but thought against it. He didn't understand the situation, and the gun confirmed this wasn't a safe place to be careless.

He passed a flag pole around an island of grass adjacent to the post office. The flag was upside down. *If an entire town's in trouble, why the hell am I here?*

A tan bricked structure was positioned about a quarter of a mile from his standpoint. There was no sign marking the building located where the straight-away ended. A road winded out of the courtyard to a series of houses, three or four blocks of residential property. But no one lived there anymore, and the concrete borders indicated everything other than civilian property.

Boyd continued walking towards the station, taking every universal precaution known to a cop. He clutched the Glock and surveyed his surroundings again: the broken windows of the grocery store, the huddled shells of fire-ravaged vehicles, and a water fountain in the center of the courtyard with a cherub on a perch, the inside of the fountain colored with green algae and scummy-black water.

No sign of anybody yet.

He inspected the ground and stopped walking.

He turned his head to the side, shocked, his skin now covered in an uncomfortable heat. He backed up a step, gasping under his breath.

A severed hand lay in the grass.

The stump had been cut clean from the wrist. And it twitched as if alerted by his presence. The fingers arched a spider's legs and pivoted its bulk towards him. The skin was a rotten blue-black. Sections of the bone were revealed from the softened tissue, wilted and puckered from the sun's heat. The fingernails were yellowed and blood encrusted. The details rushed in at him when the hand crawled after him, the fingers becoming legs, the extremity now an enemy. He wasted no time sprinting from the strange, living hand, still distrusting himself and what he believed he was seeing. His sense of equilibrium was lost, the ground under his feet tilting. He opened and closed his eyes to pull himself out of a dizzy fit; he couldn't afford to weaken his defenses now.

Boyd was a few strides from reaching the station, far away from the scurrying appendage now. The windows were boarded up from the inside, but the front door was open and begged him to enter.

Before entering, he caught movement in his peripheral vision. A figure stood in the courtyard, but it didn't move, frozen and fixed on him. A man. He was in tattered clothing, his face a dirty smear.

"Hey, what's your name?" Boyd waited for an answer, but he didn't get one. The figure's chest sucked in, and he heard a grunt. "Where are we? Say something?"

The man tilted his head back, perhaps on the verge of words, though nothing came out. "My name's Boyd Broman, and I don't know why I'm here. Please tell me who you are."

The man let out an earsplitting shriek and launched itself across the courtyard and closed the space between them with a knife clutched in each hand, pulling them from thin air. In one hand, the blade was titled upwards to the sky, and the other was pointing to the ground.

The man unleashed another condor shriek, coming in closer.

His shirt was in rags, the pants the same, but it was what Boyd mistook for clothes that caused him to recoil. Flesh dangled from the man's body like loose flaps of skin. The outermost covering was fresh, but beneath the patchy surface, diagonal strips of decayed skin were sewn into place. Boyd had seen dead men at crime scenes, and this man's skin was darker, at least a few weeks old, perhaps aged a month or even a year. The last thing he noted were the eyes, and how they appeared fresh and not sunken or clouded; the rates of decay on the body left many contradictions.

Without warning, the figure hurled a knife. It landed between Boyd's feet, sinking an inch into the dirt.

A putrid waft turned Boyd's empty stomach, sauntering up to him in the air.

The figure arched its other hand to launch the next knife.

Boyd took aim, and with marksman's speed, fired a round into the man's shoulder, rendering the arm useless, the limb blown off the body.

INSIDE THE PERIMETER

From the body came a crunch of bone and burst of blackened blood. Boyd didn't waste time asking the man questions. He cleared the door, retreating into the station, and swiftly closed it behind him.

Outside, the dead man picked up the shot off arm. Shoving the tender meat through the clothes hangers shaped into hooks jutting out from the affected stump, he jammed the appendage through the pinions and locked the arm back into place.

CHAPTER 2

Boyd checked outside by peering through the building's windows to see that the aggressor had disappeared. Strange, he thought, how the decayed man had vocal cords to yell and how he moved at a living man's speed. And why did the man try to knife him? Maybe it was the gun that scared him, but it was pointed at the ground until the knife was thrown. He had been no threat to the man.

Relieved for the time being, he spent the rest of the time securing the station. In the lobby, an American flag was wadded up on the floor in front of the check-in desk, a chalkboard cracked and riddled with bullet holes. He counted five ruined computers, now broken heaps on the floor, suffering a brutal technological death. Multiple puddles of dried blood colored the bare floor, but no bodies; the only vestiges were shreds of clothing, resembling the same green fabric the driver who had brought him here had worn.

Finding nothing else, Boyd checked the hallway and entered an office, the only window obstructed by a large bookshelf. He read the titles strewn on the floor, mostly encyclopedias and books on anatomy, anatomical design, and molecular biology.

"This isn't a police station," he muttered, staunching the sweat trailing down the side of his head with the sleeves of his shirt. "No police station I've seen, anyway."

He yelled out when a phone rang, startled. It sat on the floor in the corner as if placed there to avoid damage. He rushed to pick it up, recovering from the shock of the ringer. He almost dropped it, his hands vibrating and trembling so hard. Boyd refused to let go of his gun or avert his eyes from the hallway in case the man outside ventured after him again.

He posed the question flatly, unsure who he was addressing. "Hello?"

"Boyd Broman?"

INSIDE THE PERIMETER

Boyd didn't recognize the voice. He waited a moment and then answered, "Yes, who's this? And explain to me why a rotting man just attacked me?"

"You weren't hurt," the man answered coolly, downplaying the threat. "In fact, you handled yourself quite well—a lot better than many of our own. This is the deal, Mr. Broman, even though you're not in a position to say no. It doesn't matter what attacked you, and it doesn't matter who they are. Only one person matters, and that's Hayden Grubaugh."

He felt dizzy, a feverish weakness penetrating him. His chest went hollow, and he experienced that tilting, sinking feeling again.

But Hayden Grubaugh's dead. Jesus Christ, what's he got to do with anything?

"T...t...that cannibal was killed in prison. Hayden died of a cranial hemorrhage; his cellmates slammed his head into the floor until he died. He was killed; it was all over the news." Boyd stammered, denying the statement, though believing it could still be true.

"Any cannibal's death would be, Mr. Broman. Hayden's been in this complex since then, and he's very much alive. He never died. But we thought he would've been, well, *dispatched* by now."

"Why is he in this place to begin with? It looks like a small town that's been shot to pieces, except there's no one around aside from the dead man that attacked me." Boyd forgot to take a breath, spitting it all out. "That dead man, are there more like him out there?"

A shuffle and a pair of voices argued on the other line, and then the speaker returned. "Like I said, they don't matter. You defended yourself well. I have faith you can handle anything we have to throw at you here." The man then turned serious and spoke harshly. "Hayden's our main concern. He's been causing problems within the complex, and we can't risk sending anyone after him that isn't familiar with the kind of man he is. You arrested him, Detective, and you're the perfect man to bring him back to us."

"If you threw him in here, then why are you so desperate to get him back?"

"Investigators have found more of his murdered victims, and we want to question him. Now that he's dead on paper, we can use whatever tactics we choose to bleed the information from him. Most of what they found were the bodies Hayden stored in his uncle's rental storage unit in Jefferson City, Missouri, all sealed in plastic bags. Hayden's uncle died two weeks ago, and then the storage unit was opened and six bodies were uncovered with some of their parts missing. They suffered clean cuts on the fleshier parts of their bodies. Hayden must've eaten them like he did the others."

Boyd nodded, remembering. Hayden Grubaugh was forever engrained in his memory. Boyd aided another fellow detective in apprehending the man who was later deemed the 'Pittsburgh Alley Cannibal.' Hayden only attacked females, and they were of the bar scene or hooker variety. He didn't rape the women, but instead, paid them to leave their strip club or the alley in his Bronco truck. From there, he fed them alcoholic beverages, namely red wine, to sweeten their blood, along with the sleeping narcotic Norzepam. Once they were unconscious, he injected an air bubble into their veins and killed them. Hayden severed the body into pieces at his apartment, sorted the organs, and combined them with oregano, cilantro, paprika, bay leaves, garlic, diced onion, cumin, hot peppers, green tomatoes, and other ingredients, and boiled them at his brother's Italian restaurant after hours. The murderer grinded down the bones in the industrial garbage disposal and hosed the kitchen floor of blood, and it wasn't until there was a plumbing problem in the eatery and a plumber discovered gobs of human hair, teeth, and broken bones wedged in the pipes, that Hayden was investigated.

Why Hayden was kept in this concrete fortress and what problems he could be causing immediately concerned Boyd. "You've got all this security, so why make me track him down? I'm sure it was the county's worst nightmare filling out the paperwork to bust me out of jail," Boyd said.

"We arranged for your name to be cleared of your crime if you return Hayden to us, Detective. Your wife, kids, your community, even your fellow officers will accept you back again—and might I mention, your pension will be doubled. You can earn your father's pride from Heaven. He didn't get to see you graduate from the police academy because you were only six when he died. It's a shame your ordeal had to happen, what landed you in prison. It was a tricky situation, I know."

Boyd ignored the last statement and focused on one thing. "What do you know about my father?"

"Enough to know he was the reason you became a cop, and later, a detective. I have interview notes when you were accepted into the academy." Boyd heard the sound of pages being turned. "Ah, this is cute." He now talked like a six year old. "It says you wanted to be the kid of a cop that visited schools and warned kids not to take drugs or join gangs. You were old enough to see your father give a talk at your elementary school before he passed on. It warms the heart to hear that, Boyd."

"Fuck you! Let's talk in person. Show me your face! Tell me this shit face-to-face!"

"Okay, enough buddy-buddy talk, I got it, so calm down and hear me out. I'm offering you your life back. That's the deal. Besides, Hayden needs to be questioned quickly. He could have more bodies than we know about, and that's something you can care about, Mr. Broman. You helped arrest him. You pulled night watch at the strip clubs, and didn't Hayden shoot you in the ribs? Shattered two of them on impact, and you still were able to put him in cuffs and deliver him to the station. You're one tough S.O.B."

Boyd imagined having his family back and his job on the force the way it was before he was arrested for involuntary manslaughter. He quickly shoved the bitter incident in the back of his mind to focus on the conversation. The questions remained: why was Hayden here and why couldn't they track him down themselves? They had cameras, the facility, the barbed gates, and men in the towers surveying the area. This was military, he was convinced of it, so why not send a group of them to apprehend Hayden instead?

"You're not telling me everything," he said.

"And so it is, Mr. Broman. Take it or leave it, your only escape is compliance. The dead man outside, yes, there's more of them. You can handle it. I can't waste resources on tracking a man down like Hayden, and besides, your precinct wanted you to be set free. You were the district attorney's example to other cops not to play hero off-duty and now's your chance to escape prison. Just apprehend Hayden and everything can go back to how it was."

"You're lying," Boyd said accusingly, offended at how obvious the deception was. "If the precinct wanted me free, I wouldn't have been convicted of that bullshit charge."

"Believe what you want, but you have no choice," the voice said.

Boyd concentrated on what he needed to understand to survive if he wanted his life to return to normalcy. The man had a point; he didn't have a choice.

"So what do I do with Hayden when I find him? How big is this place?"

"Don't worry about that. Arrest Hayden, take him alive, and bring him to the gate you were dropped off at. We'll be watching and waiting for your arrival. Make it fast. And watch your back." The man hung up.

Boyd stared at the phone and waited for a dial tone to call an outside number, but the line was dead. No noise, it was as if someone had pulled the plug the moment the conversation was over.

Whatever he was forced into, Boyd knew he was trapped. And until he captured Hayden, there was no other option but to comply.

CHAPTER 3

"*I* hear they might be promoting you to lead detective, wink, wink."

"You're not supposed to say 'wink wink,' are you?"

"That's how impressive you are. I get to actually say it."

Boyd listened to Joey Louis, his childhood friend and fellow detective at his precinct, rattle on about his future prospects as the party in his honor continued. He returned from the hospital just yesterday, recovering from the twin gunshots to the ribs he received via Hayden's unregistered .45 Messingham. The doctor had asked him if he wanted to keep the hunks of steel post-removal. "You cops like souvenirs. Put it in a jar on your mantle."

Boyd declined, deciding not to give Karen another reminder of how dangerous his job could be. In his living room, over twenty people from the precinct were enjoying cake and ice cream as people chatted about the Pittsburgh Alley Cannibal, the man he'd put behind bars. Karen was busy preparing more punch and replenishing people's longneck beers with fresh ones. His children were at their Aunt Sue's. Karen wanted to celebrate his accomplishment, but talk of cannibalism and murder wasn't kid friendly.

She worked her way through the throng of blue and white balloons and the table of gifts to the backyard, disappearing again on another hostess errand, busily cooking hamburgers and hot dogs on the grill.

Joey spoke up again, always a cheery man asking cheery questions. "How was it meeting the mayor? I hear he's a blunt kind-of-guy."

Boyd laughed, tipping back the bottle and filling his mouth with ice cold beer. "Ferman shook my hand while I was still in recovery. I wish I could've been better dressed; the hospital gown isn't very snazzy. It's good he didn't come when I had my back turned; he would've had the best view of my ass, slopes and grassy knolls and perhaps even the profile of my balls." He clinked longnecks with Joey, chuckling hard. "No, no, he was a nice guy. He said he was grateful, and quoting him, 'That son-of-a-bitch is finally off the streets and on his way to the electric chair.'"

Joey seconded Ferman's quote. "I think everybody in the room shares those same sentiments. Let the creepy greaseball fry."

"Yeah, but there's a price to pay. I missed a lot of time with Karen and the kids going on stakeouts to nudie clubs, watching the parking lots for anybody looking like a cannibal killer pervert. Everybody marching in and out of Club 87 or The Red Closet or half the other strip joints in that area all fit that cannibal's profile."

"I'm just glad you're okay, Boyd."

It was every cop's worst nightmare not only being shot at, but to actually take a hit. Karen feared for his life from the beginning of participating in a cannibal killer stakeout, but this had been the first time he'd been wounded. She hadn't slept soundly for a week after it happened, and it showed, though she was perky today having guests to serve and praises to share.

Boyd looked on at her through the backyard window, flipping meats, grateful for such a wonderful wife. "I hope Karen will make it through this okay."

"I've been shot before too, Boyd," Joey said. "And let me tell you, they move on in time. The first time is always the hardest. Wives think everybody's gunning for you after that, but once you come home again and again without a scratch, life goes on. Trust me."

His friend Andrew Hardy shook his hand and so did Nora Johnson and Kim Davis, each who had been on the case. "Damn fine job." "Way to bust his ass. One less psycho to deal with." "Unless the courts fuck us over." "It's not everyday a cannibal killer makes the headlines. Wasn't Dahmer the last sicko to make the news?" "Dahmer ain't no Hayden Grubaugh, that's for goddamn certain! He's worlds beyond Dahmer."

The three moved on, leaving Joey and him alone after congratulating him again on his bravery.

Boyd couldn't help but ask Joey one more time. "You really think I'll make lead detective?"

INSIDE THE PERIMETER

Joey winked. "We'll see, buddy, we'll see…"

Boyd checked the clip in the Glock; the driver had given him a half-loaded gun. *That bastard, at least give me what I need to capture a lunatic cannibal.*

His train of thought ended when the dead man from outside punched a hole through the door and twisted the knob, throwing it open and stomping into the room. The creature had both arms, the one he'd shot previously now bent but still able to function, the fingers turning into a wet, greasy fist.

The wretched smell attacked him like a putrid perfume. He noted the organs through the patchy skin were kept firmly in place by staples, stitches, and reams of nylon cord. Rib bones protruded, warped and broken, some larger than others, ranging from ivory white to rust-orange. The face was a patchwork of skin grafts from black, white, and Hispanic flesh. More stitches and staples comprised the skeletal features, the skull visible through tufts of hair of different colors: red, brown, black, and blonde, the strands matted, frayed and oily. Boyd compared the dead man to a salvaged car, a rough working prototype of the original. It couldn't be real, but when Boyd gagged again on the dead man's stench, the fact couldn't be denied.

Boyd took aim to the head and fired. A dangerous assailant—a dead assailant in this case—couldn't be reckoned with, Boyd had learned through police training.

The bullet shattered the left lobe of the dead man's skull, but instead of brains and blood, shards of bone exploded. The figure was unaffected by the damage; beneath the skin, a housing of extra bones protected the brain, nailed in place.

But how?

Boyd reserved his bullets and questions and rushed into the hall and bypassed the dead man at his back in pursuit. Outside, the sunlight re-ignited his headache. He sprinted through a parking lot and ran full speed towards a diner. In the broken slats of windows and boarded up entries, he sensed movements within the darkened nooks. Behind him, at the pharmacy, post office, and bowling alley, the shapes of people materialized and were aroused from their hideaways.

There were dozens, maybe more, he couldn't waste time counting.

The clap of shoes against asphalt forced him to make a decision. The Glock couldn't kill them. No building was clear to enter, so his only escape would be the gutter.

The figure clutched a knife poised to throw, Boyd noted in his peripheral. The sun made clear the dent on its skull, which was white as the inside of a jaw breaker.

Boyd ducked into the gutter's opening, uncertain of what could be waiting below, but it was a better alternative than facing the mob of dead beings slowly approaching him. He splashed into ice-cold water below, the level up to his knees. A light on the wall flickered, the plastic fixture shedding green light from the mold covering it. The blather and shrieks of many voices echoed down to him. They were coming.

He sloshed through the water, the stream a brown-green sludge. A gangrene odor thickened the air, the tunnel a septic open wound. An overhead walkway was located around the turn of a corner. He climbed up the short ladder and was able to flee faster, but to where, Boyd was clueless.

Anywhere but backwards is fine by me.

The way was darker the further he trudged. Water trickled from tunnels and networks, pipes and drains that trailed to unknown corners. The new splashing of feet echoed in the tunnel, the shouts and blood-curdling shrieks—larynxes crushed and vocal cords worn thin—compelled him into fleeing even faster. He jogged six steps when something wet curled around his ankle to yank him down into the water below the walkway. It was a skeletal hand, the phalanges unhinging once they clasped his foot. They rattled and clanked onto the walkway like hollow porcelain.

Boyd narrowed his focus on what struggled to stay afloat in the water. A skeleton frame, a piece of moving flotsam and jetsam, shifted. The mandible and jaw clicked to mimic sound, but there was no throat, tongue, muscle tissue, or skin to comprise a body. It reminded him of the skeleton in his high school anatomy class, except this time, it was missing its legs.

INSIDE THE PERIMETER

What enabled it to function, he wondered, as he kicked it square in the jaw bone and sent it flying back into the water.

The hordes of monstrous taunts were seconds behind him, a myriad collection of pipes being dislodged by venomous tools.

The moans and wails were haunting, causing a chill to run down his back.

Boyd scanned the wall for a way out or a place to hide, the tunnel accesses blocked with metal grates. He faced a dead end. Turning around, the shadows were contorted by the looming shapes conspiring to crowd him. He double-checked his options and located a step-ladder leading back up to the street. He cleared the steps and nearly lost his footing when he shoved the manhole upwards, grunting from the weight of the cover.

Crawling topside and pushing the cover back into place, he was now in a different part of town, two blocks from the diner and the station. A convenience store and a string of restaurants were nearby. An unmarked three-story building was located to the far left of him, a border between the residential area and town center.

One restaurant in particular caught his attention by the acrid smoke exuding from the chimney. At Mariatelli's Restaurant, the windows were boarded up like everywhere else. The outdoor dining area was decorated with umbrella-draped tables, the remains of burnt corpses still sitting in the chairs. Black birds pecked at the corpses, stealing morsels, the bodies damaged beyond recognition and rendered to carrion. They had been tied in place with metal wire, the winged assassins now having a field day. The smoke billowing from the chimney reeked of cooking flesh.

It has to be Hayden.

Boyd rushed to the restaurant, prepared to confront Hayden, but the front doors were locked. The windows were secure with wooden planks, tables, and chairs. The side entrance and the back door were also locked.

No way inside.

He could climb up to the roof and find an alternative access, but his time to plan a break-in had lapsed. The manhole behind him rattled onto the street and hunched bodies poured out from the sewer. In seconds, they'd reach him.

Boyd fled to the closest place that looked safe, a three-story building. The front entrance was blocked, but after racing down the left end of it, an open side window was clear of any form of barricade. He crawled in and shortly afterwards, the streets were filled with the dead.

CHAPTER 4

Hayden Grubaugh had learned from Richard Massy that smoking the flesh was the best way to prepare human meat. Richard had been a next-door neighbor in his apartment complex in downtown Pittsburgh.

Vegetable oil ruins the natural fatty tissues already in the human body, his mentor had explained to him. *It'd be like eating a hamburger dipped in peanut oil and slathered in bacon fat. Besides, there's better ways to splurge the taste buds than Americanized recipes. You're not a stay-at-home mom, you're an aficionado.*

Hayden was standing in the empty kitchen of Mariatelli's with a cleaver clasped in his hand, wearing a blood-stained apron around his rotund midsection that read, **Kiss Me I'm Italian**.

Always have your garnishes and spices ready before preparation, Richard's voice thrummed. *And wash those hands. Use common sense.*

"The sauce comes next," Hayden sang under his breath. "My sauce is always best."

Don't get ahead of yourself, Hayden, Richard scolded in his head.

The man taught him many things since the age of seventeen. Richard had learned his cooking techniques from his father who lived in Russia when the region was suffering from the affects of The Cold War. The man ate human flesh because it was economically sound; the price of meat was outrageous even at the street markets. It was a necessity that turned into a convenient habit, though Richard later explained that his father was a murderer, compelled by his finely cultivated taste for human flesh to the point the killing also became a lucrative trade among the vendor markets.

Hayden selected a combination of marinara and barbeque sauce, mustard, brown sugar, onion and garlic powder, pesto, and mixed them into a large sauce pan. He then added a splash of bottled lemon juice for zest.

The sauce was complete.

Don't forget the red wine, Hayden. It's good for the heart and keeps the flavor robust.

He did so, obeying the voice, pouring a dash of red wine into the pan.

"Ah, now the fun part," he announced, speaking to the naked woman bound to the table behind him with rope. Her head was secured in a vise; no chance of escape unless she wanted to rip her head off first. "You're next, ma'am."

First remove the arms and legs from the torso; the torso's your soft spot filled with the most meat. The organs can be used for soup, but more importantly, the tender meat comes from the ribs. Succulent.

Hayden lifted the cleaver, leveled the edge, and the blade sliced through the shoulder with a driving hammer's force. The limb flopped onto the floor, the arms and muscles flexing and bending to somehow return itself to the body. He ground the heel of his boot into the forearm to anchor it down. "Now hold still."

The woman gagged on her tongue, the pain so excruciating she couldn't scream.

Hayden hacked her legs off from the hips, taking six swings each, and let them collapse onto the floor. They kicked and flailed, unable to rise into a standing position, trying again and again despite failure. Blood splashed on the floor due to their efforts, blood wasted, blood he could've used for the sauce.

Shit.

Determined to keep the meal cooking despite the mistake he made, he wrenched out the organs and slopped them onto a cooking sheet. There were coils and coils of long and small intestines, many of them of varying sizes that didn't belong to the woman; they had also been stitched into one another like unending snakes. She'd borrowed them from others, he knew. That's what they did to survive, and the process by which they fashioned new bones and tissue to their bodies was amazing.

Hayden rendered free the ribs with pinch clamps and a hammer, cracking them like lobster legs, then he heaped them onto another cooking sheet. He'd bake them in the oven at 450 degrees for twenty minutes, seasoning them first. Next, Hayden lopped off the corpse's breasts with sawing motions. The flesh was checkered white, tan, and green, and the nipples resembled blackened Hershey's kisses.

He sawed her head off at the neck, pressing both palms on the dulling edge of the blade to do so, leaning in to break through the spine. Foam and crimson dribbled from both corners of her lips upon the dissection as strange sounds escaped her mouth.

Her midsection, now without legs, banged itself onto the table while the arms hid under the shelf of pots and pans in the corner. Her legs had crawled across the kitchen, leaving behind a glistening red trail.

"Damn it," Hayden growled, reaching his breaking point. "You're going into the freezer. I can't do anything with you bastards after I cut you up. You keep moving and hiding."

The cold kept their movements at bay in the freezer, but even after covered in ice and then thawed, the pieces regained life.

"The doors are locked, and you can't escape," Hayden hissed, spitting into the woman's face. "It's because you know where you're going, isn't it?"

He paused at the glint of metal between her tuffs of red hair behind each ear.

Screws.

"Great, not more of those."

Hayden fished out the screwdriver from his back pocket and began removing them. The woman had bolted her skull together; it wasn't the shape of a normal skull, but instead a large oval. Broken pieces of tin and steel were added to secure the brain. He'd bashed many of them over the head with a crowbar with minimal damage. Hayden didn't have a gun, so he didn't know how well the layers of bones stood up against the punishment of a bullet.

It's essential you remove the brains immediately, otherwise they're one of the first to go bad. The melanin sheath dries up and flakes and ruins the tender meat underneath.

And shave the head, Hayden. Hair is a nuisance.

"No time, Richard...I'm sorry."

Ah, I'm very disappointed in you. I expect good things of you. I always have.

Hayden wiped the tears from his eyes and sniffled. "If you were here, you'd know—you'd know what it's like to work with decayed meats. I have to use brutish tactics to secure food. I'm not in civilization anymore. I don't know where the hell I am, Richard. Be patient with me, please."

The last screw issued a hermetic pop upon removal. The skull cap unhinged and broke in two halves, unveiling the prized meat within. He was amazed at the freshness of the brains. The color, the melanin sheath, the blood, the sheen between each cranial ridge, it was as if from a living source. "Nothing rotten about this meat," he bragged to himself. "It'll make a good soup. If I add enough tomato powder and garlic, it'll be perfect."

When he was finished cooking, Hayden seated himself in the nicer region of the restaurant, a back area with no windows and the door entrances draped with red silk sheets to ensure privacy. He faced a wall with a mock painting of Sandro Botticelli's *Birth of Venus*, Venus' body naked and proud as her red hair flowed about her shoulders. The rest of the original painting was replaced with a garden stock picture of ripe tomatoes hanging plump from vines. It was that moment he praised the force greater than him—whether it be God or the justice system, he wasn't sure who to address the thank you card to—for putting him here. Society had locked him up for what Richard taught him to be, and in prison, he would've eventually been killed for seeking out human flesh. This was the only place he could be himself. And that kind of happiness was impossible to find in any society.

There's nothing to be ashamed of, Richard's voice beamed, bestowing confidence upon him. God, the law, and your parents, don't know what makes you happy. Only you do, Hayden. The way you eat with me, I know it brings you joy. And the process, you like that, too. Blood doesn't scare you, screams don't scare you, bodies don't scare you. Nothing scares you.

But there was something different in these bodies he was now forced to eat. The flesh tasted odd. The seasoning covered it up for the most part, but the twang in the aftertaste remained. The blood was the same, but the muscle and skin, it didn't taste natural. It was rotting, and he'd tasted expired meat before at the price of losing his bowels for two weeks straight. The difference was that inside the perimeter the expired meat didn't make him sick. Their meat wasn't poisonous no matter how putrid or rotten it had become. He couldn't place why, and as long as it stayed that way, he could care less.

He placed a burgundy table napkin across his lap. His plate was stocked with six ribs—each nine inches long—and on the side, a soup of boiled brains in a blood and tomato sauce. He missed having access to fresh vegetables as he could've added a garden salad to the meal.

My doctor once told me there are four rules to a healthy life. Exercise four times a week, sleep eight hours a day, drink a glass of wine to flush out the toxins in the body with dinner, and eat only what you can find from outdoors—no processed foods. Hey, I followed my doctor's orders, he thought.

As he began to dine, the moans from outside shook him from his meal, and tonight he noticed, they were louder than usual.

Someone was out there.

And they were *alive*.

CHAPTER 5

Chris Jones had been awake for two days straight, and he presently sought a place to sleep safely. The delivery rooms within the hospital were ransacked, with no supplies or food. He discovered an employee's lounge, and inside was a refrigerator with a can of fruit cocktail, a bottle of expired milk, and a pizza that was spreading black mold. In the freezer, he discovered a carton of ice cream with a two-inch crust of ice. He ate it despite the way the ice cream tasted.

But hunger was second on his list of priorities.

He needed a syringe.

The day they drove him to this facility from Pelican Bay, he had enough heroine on him to shoot up twice, and after two days of being here, he had one hit left. He had used food trucks to smuggle drugs and other things of value into Pelican Bay. Wardens, guards, prisoners, even cafeteria workers, served as his outside help. Heroine, cocaine, cigarettes, porno magazines, alcohol, he was in control of what came in and out of Pelican Bay. And that's why he was shipped out. When the guards were high on marijuana and the prisoners were mellow and able to forget their confinement and punishments, it defeated the purpose of being a prisoner, his personal trump to the system.

He had been chased into the hospital by three of the creatures. One had an axe, the other a chain in each hand, and the last, a wooden plank. He somehow escaped them, turning enough corners, running up stairs, hiding and sneaking about the halls without making a sound. Chris had bypassed another creature on the second floor, though this one was easy to evade since the woman used a pair of crutches to compensate for her left leg that was severed from the knee down.

The problem was when she'd cried out to him, a piercing scream that set his teeth on edge.

Her shrieks had urged others from their hiding places. Dozens were after him now, coming out of the shadows, drawn to the noise, but once he reached the third floor, he locked the entrance and all the exit doors. He hid in a nearby supply closet, barricading the door with a metal shelf stocked with cleaning supplies. Standing still, hunkered with a knife he claimed from a toolbox in his clutches, he heard the elevator ding softly.

They were on their way up.

He removed the top of his prison smock, drenched with sweat, and rested against the far wall while pondering what could be his final moments.

Nothing happened for minutes. An hour.

He drifted asleep.

Disoriented, drawn from a deep slumber after an unknown period of time, something shifted above him and caused dust to fall on him from the ceiling. Snapping fully awake with a jolt, the ceiling caved in, and the light panel shattered on the way down to cover him in bits of plastic and rolls of insulation. He didn't have a chance to fight back; both his hands were pinned to the wall by knives in a wrist crucifixion. When he moved, jolts of electric agony triggered nerve endings and kept him in place; he was trapped. He couldn't spit out words or pleas, the wounds too intense to act beyond the pain. With his eyes open and quivering, he scrutinized his attacker, a man in baggy overalls a size too big; obviously not his original clothing. His face was sunken at the mouth. No mandible, jaw, or teeth, the inside of his mouth nothing but a gaping hole with a tongue.

The dead man studied Chris for a few more seconds before he removed a paint chipper from his belt.

Chris was punched in the mouth with the tool. The man was now sawing, stabbing, carving, and gouging to an unknown end. The process was excruciating, and Chris mewled and spat crimson slush, thrashing to escape, for it to stop; the knives stuck through his wrists refusing to release him. The blood loss paralyzed him and all he could do was watch the deformed man remove the shelf that blocked the door.

Oh, God, no...God no! he screamed in his head.

Dozens of bodies piled in with raised bludgeons ranging from planks of woods, to crowbars, to bricks and broken concrete. Many others were armed with scissors, the blades snipping and shredding the air in practice for carving human flesh. Scalpels gleamed in putrescent hands, promising razor-sharp precision helmed by infirm minds. Electric bone saws whirred, and a dentist's drill whined, sending gooseflesh and horror through Chris' body, as the spinning blades churned in the direction of his dissection. Before the new group was upon him, the original attacker stared Chris down, grinning crudely, now with a new jaw and set of teeth.

CHAPTER 6

*K*aren met him between the double-paned Plexiglas booth and regarded him with heavy, doleful eyes. Raising two kids and dealing with the turmoil of losing her husband had aged her prematurely, and now the strawberry blonde hair was giving to strands of gray. She wore a thin smile when their eyes met; it was labored, but genuine.

"I can't stop thinking about how this feels so wrong," she had said the last time they met between the Plexiglas. "I feel like I'm a part of a big scandal. You shouldn't be behind bars. Your co-workers keep saying the same thing, and your lawyer keeps saying we can appeal—and we did—but beyond that, we're stuck. I would do anything to have you back home. You saved our lives; why can't they understand that you were trying to apprehend Samuel, not kill him. It was an accident, a goddamn accident."

This was her second, in-person visit, and Boyd was at a loss for words. He was relieved when Karen decided to speak up again. "Paula Barr says she's going to help me start a website, and I've started collecting signatures. We can petition your appeal faster through the courts. Joey is raising money to get you a better lawyer. Your old partner said he'll find someone to take you all the way to the Supreme Court, if that's what it takes."

"Joey," Boyd sighed. "He's a good man. Let's hope they don't forget about me the longer I'm collecting dust in here. They may bury me under the system and forget about me. I may never get out of here."

"Don't talk like that," Karen insisted, placing her palm on the Plexiglas barrier. "I'm not leaving you, and I'm not quitting until you're free. I love you. This is wrong. You're not a killer."

He changed subjects, wishing to talk about life outside these walls. "How are the kids doing?"

The flare in her eyes from talking about websites, petitions and lawyers vanished. "They miss you." That's all she could say. She didn't want to paint a picture of Shannon and Mindy without *a father. And Karen had mentioned how it felt like when she had to constantly defend him at church, at work, and to her friends that aimed to tarnish his character, believing the news and their spin on his story.*

"Promise me you won't stay unhappy," Boyd insisted, "if things don't go my way, if I don't get my appeal. I'm looking at you, and I can tell you're sad. You can't handle years of this. No one can. I want you to be happy."

"I'm happy trying to save you," she said, adamantly refusing to follow into his line of thinking. "You can't get rid of me."

"That's good to hear," Boyd said, though in the back of his mind, he was concerned for her mental well-being in the long-term. "Because I'd miss you. You and the kids are the only things keeping me going."

"Then keep going," Karen said, every word honest. "That's all we can do for now. Just keep on going."

Boyd kept low to the carpeted floor and counted as forty bodies lurched about on the street. He'd calmed himself down by picturing his wife; her voice and her face, everything about her instilled comfort even in a terrible situation.

Among the walking corpses outside, some could have mimicked genuine life if it weren't for the graft lines across their faces and their rigor mortis gait. Others were less convincing, the deteriorated bodies practically skeletons. They used car bumpers as wheelchairs and wooden planks for crutches, their points of flexion fastened together by rope and human tissue. They carried weapons: knives, axes, crowbars, shovels, tire-irons, fists of glass, concrete cinder blocks, bricks, and human femurs and vertebrae, the rotting lot resembling primitive warriors.

Boyd couldn't stand to watch them any longer. Doing so, he realized where he was now. The rows of books, it was a library. It was strange how the place wasn't in shambles other than the blockades at the entrances; the single window was the only place unprotected.

He darted between the shelves and double checked for safety. There were no puddles of blood, torn clothing, or remains. It didn't smell fecund like it did outside.

He again questioned if this was a government facility. The framework was a small town, not military. He wouldn't be surprised to find a school house perhaps a block or two from this location. The burnt out cars by the postal station, the bowling alley, the restaurants, it didn't boast of military presence, though the driver of the armored car adorned in green fatigues inspired him to speculate otherwise.

He was careful upon opening the double doors ahead of him. Crossing the threshold, he edged down the steps, observing no other signs of blood or an attack. The howl of a scream rang out from across the street, halting him. There was no way to pinpoint if it was human or one of them, but it sounded different than what he'd heard before; it had to be human. It could be anything, he contradicted himself, and if it was human, he couldn't save them.

Thinking back to the dead people outside, he tried to pin their existence down. They tore human bodies apart and salvaged the pieces; there was something advanced in that process. The fact they were dead and walking was miraculous in itself, but their continued survival was another step in an unbelievable direction. Something had been created within these walls, and Boyd was forced to battle it within the perimeter. How many more people had crossed the barbed walls and been killed? How many were ex-convicts, and what other kinds of people were considered worthy of being placed in here besides him?

Boyd searched the next level below, the floor dedicated to audio-related items: books on tape, music, and an entire section of computers sectioned off by cubicles. He checked the men's and women's restrooms, and when both turned up empty, he stayed in the men's bathroom—strange for him to feel the need to respect the privacy of the women's bathroom, he thought—and tested the sinks. The water worked, and he washed his face with the pink-lavender scented soap from the dispenser. His brown hair was tussled and in strands above his eyes, his skin greasy with a hobo's sheen. His green eyes were bloodshot and irritated and weighed down by fatigue.

Thirsty, he lapped water from the sink and talked to himself. "Where do you go from here, big guy? Alone in this place, and you have to capture one man, and you have a pretty good idea he's across the street. It's almost night, so what are you waiting for?"

Boyd picked up the Glock, pointing the muzzle down into the sink. He listened and heard no movement outside the bathroom. It wasn't safe to assume any corner was clear, and it was best not to stay in one place for too long. The library lights were on. Military or government affiliated, they were using electricity. He wondered if he'd find a phone; the way the conversation earlier ended at the police station, there would be no outgoing lines.

He was back to the beginning of the dilemma.

Capture Hayden Grubaugh.

They're not going to let you go. You'd be a fool to believe any of their promises.

"But you have a bargaining tool," he said, smiling in the mirror. "He's your hostage. It has to get you something, at least more answers."

He almost waited for the face in the mirror to begin talking without his consent, to explain things for him, but of course that didn't happen. He chuckled at himself for talking to his reflection.

Tonight, pursuing the cannibal wasn't as simple as locating him. Hayden had been aggressive with the authorities upon his arrest less than a year ago. He remembered Hayden's apartment being reminiscent to Jeffrey Dahmer's, with human parts stored in the freezer. Hayden had disposed many of his bodies by transporting them to rental storage units and keeping them in sealed, airtight plastic bags. He remembered talking to one of the crime scene techs, Chris Abrams, who reported to Boyd that upon searching the apartment, two severed heads were found sitting in the kitchen sink, thawing out, as well as a bathtub full of removed innards that Hayden had been stuffing into black garbage bags for later disposal. The ideas of it was as chilling as being in somewhat close proximity to that brand of serial killer. And according to the phone conversation earlier, the authorities happened upon more of Hayden's murders. Considering the cannibal had lived this long among the fiends in the town, Hayden no doubt was prepared to watch his back and it wouldn't be an easy task apprehending him.

Boyd descended the last set of stairs to locate the basement and hopefully, a back door. Arriving below, he reached the entrance of the library. The check-out desk was unoccupied, but behind a bookshelf, the wall paper was slaked in dried blood, the beige carpets the same.

But no bodies.

Boyd ambled through a section dedicated to microfilm. He walked between tables and high-standing metal shelves and caught a shadow skirt down a back hallway.

"Who's there? Hey—who was that?"

He peeked around the edge of the shelf to see a long hallway with three offices. As he moved down it, he saw the doors were closed. Each door had a small window and he saw the blinds were drawn. At the last door's window, the blinds swung back and forth, as if someone had entered the room in a hurry.

"I'm not one of those things," Boyd called out, praying another human being was in here with him. "I swear it. I'm alive. I'm talking to you, aren't I?"

The words came out jilted, his throat hesitant to make noise. He tried the door, and the knob didn't turn.

If someone's in there, they're not going to let you inside.

Before he could knock or call out again, the door was thrown open and something sprayed him in the face.

Blinded, slipping backwards and landing onto the floor, he was now covered in something wet, thick and cold. The Glock slipped from his hands as he wiped his face clean. He cleared his eyes in time to catch a woman clutching a fire extinguisher about to level it over his head.

He covered his head with his hands and yelled, *"Stop!"*

The woman's mouth opened in shock and an apology formed in her eyes. Boyd picked up his gun, and before he could say a word, she pulled him into the office, closing the door and locking it.

"Did they see you?" she asked in a hushed whisper.

He cleaned the mess from his face with his shirt. "No...no, they didn't. They sure as hell tried to get me, though."

He studied the woman. Her brunette hair was drawn back into a rough ponytail. She wore a gray button-up shirt, the sleeves and fabric dirty. Her red skirt was in tatters, stretched and pulled and crusted in many colors of soil and human grease. She looked to be in shape, though she carried an extra twenty pounds. An unkempt odor exuded from her, but it came from him, too, a combination of fear and sweat.

"Thank God there's someone else alive around here," she said, giving him the same once-over. "My name's Cindy Piper, what's yours?"

"Boyd Broman," he replied, forgoing shaking hands. "It used to be Detective Broman."

Relief washed over her ragged features. Her eyes brightened, as she said, "You're here to take me away, aren't you? Away from this place, I mean. Thank God for you, *oh, thank God.*"

Boyd didn't want to ruin her relief. He placed his hand on her shoulder, kindly telling her, "I'm sorry, but I'm in the same predicament you're in, Cindy. I was almost killed myself out there. Who put *you* in here?"

Cindy cast him a scowl, bitterly disappointed, and threw his question right back at him. "Who put you in here?"

Boyd was afraid to tell her his history and what brought him to prison. It wouldn't do him any good to lie, he reasoned. They were two people alone. In a population of two, it would be harder to judge the other—or so he hoped that philosophy proved true in Cindy's case.

"There's a lot I don't know, Cindy, but this is what I do understand. I was transferred from Hutchinson Correctional Facility. Does the name Boyd Broman mean anything to you? Think about it."

Cindy's pale face turned whiter, a shade next to bloodless. "I thought you looked familiar. You were all over the news; your trial, the murder...*your death.*"

He was stabbed in the chest, his skin suddenly numb and cold. Boyd braced himself against the office desk to keep standing. "My death?"

Hayden Grubaugh was reported dead in the news and Hayden was supposedly in the facility. Why wouldn't they do the same to him? Boyd's hope for freedom was false, and he knew that, but what was he being set-up for? Would they leave him in this hellhole after he returned Hayden to them, or did they have different ideas?

"How did I die?" The question half-amused him after living down the shock of being a dead man. "How did I become a ghost?"

"You hung yourself in your cell," Cindy whispered. "A prisoner arranged for you to get a rope, and you took your life. I saw your mug shot on TV, and it looks just like you." She shifted to the opposite side of the room and stared at the Glock. "You're not going to kill me, are you?"

Boyd placed the gun on the desk and scoffed at the idea. "You take it if it makes you happy. I'm not who you think I am, and if you don't believe it, I guess I can't blame you. I'm going to say it whether you understand it or not. A man named Samuel Tyson broke into my house. He tied up my wife and my two girls, ten and twelve, and I swear to you he was about to shoot them in my basement, but I scared him away. I recognized Samuel from recent police postings. He'd committed three robberies in the past two months in a similar fashion. He would tie the families up, rob the place at his leisure, and then shoot them dead before he left.

"I didn't want him to escape, so I chased him out, but I followed him in my car. I stayed on his tail, and when we reached the highway, the man hit his brakes. Samuel's car fishtailed; we were both going seventy miles an hour, at least. I crashed into his back end and his car flipped three times. He was thrown from the vehicle, and Jesus Christ, before my car could stop, my front wheels crushed him. It was an accident, and I agree with part of the verdict, Cindy. I had no right to tail him, and I should've called the police since I was off-duty, but I didn't want him to get away. The bastard would've done it to another family if he'd escaped. He would have killed again.

"I was scared for Karen and the kids, and I was angry, too. I can't explain what came over me, but the verdict shouldn't have sent me to prison. Okay, maybe a few years and probation, but not twenty years without parole. And because Crawford County has been under fire for recent police brutality allegations, the judge was harsh sentencing me. The media changed what happened into *me* speeding up my car and rolling over Samuel ten times to ensure he was dead under my tires. None of it's true, Cindy.

"I lost my wife and kids, and now my life. I don't want sympathy; I want understanding. My trial and hearing came so fast, it's unreal how the system worked double time to shove my ass into prison and then into this place. And if you don't believe what I'm telling you, then think about what we're doing here and why the system lied to everyone about my death."

Boyd cleared the tears from his eyes. He'd recounted the story to his lawyer, the judge, and every media person, and this time, the words struck true to Cindy.

And there was a reason for that, he soon learned.

Boyd continued his story, "I entered this place through a wrought-iron gate with concrete walls as barriers. A black armored car drove me through several gates. The driver forced me to enter the facility, and he handed me a gun. The driver told me to find what I thought was an old police station, a straight shot on the sidewalk that led into town square. I entered the station after being attacked by one of those dead people out there. Soon, a phone rings. I pick it up, and it's a man telling me that Hayden Grubaugh, a cannibal killer, is here, and if I want my name to be cleared, I have to deliver him to the front gate into custody. More of his bodies have been found, and the police want to question him. I'm here to capture him."

Cindy was in front of the window, but she didn't adjust the blinds to look out. "I guess you want to know why I'm here too, then, huh? It's only fair, and what else are we doing besides buying time? This place is driving me crazy, Boyd…whoever you are. And considering our circumstances, I wouldn't be surprised if the world thinks I'm dead as well. Yes, I believed what they said about you and that you maliciously ran down Samuel Tyson in the papers, but your wife was interviewed, and she defended you tooth and nail. Your fellow officers defended you, too. They said you were upholding the law as a public servant, and that you weren't acting as a criminal or a murderer. I guess it doesn't matter whether we're guilty of what we've been accused of or not sometimes. The courts decide right or wrong."

"You said *we*?" Boyd sat on the office chair. "Were you thrown into prison?"

"No," Cindy sighed, undoing her ponytail. "My case wasn't blown up for public consumption. I dated Brett Anderson, the Crawford County district attorney. It was more of a fling on the side for Brett since he was married, and I should've realized he wouldn't leave his wife for me. His reputation can't be ruined even if it deserves to be. We dated, and I might sound like a whore like you sounded like a killer—and I believe you, now that I can weigh our circumstances together—but I thought I had a chance with him. I was in love, and it made me stupid. I kept sleeping with him and hoped he'd change his mind about us.

"Our relationship was fine until my period was late. I go to the doctor's, and he seals my fate. I tell Brett, and he immediately drives me to the abortion clinic—it was performed in a doctor's house, might I add. Once the operation was completed, a set of men lugged me into a Jeep. They drive for what felt like hours, but before I can do anything, they pull out a syringe and inject me with a sedative. I woke up in this building. I was sitting in this office. There were directions on a pad of paper telling me where to find food and to stay out of sight. I've been here for eight days, and those instructions are the only reason I'm still alive right now.

"The note also warned me not to look out the window or venture outside, and of course, I did. I pulled aside these blinds, and outside, I saw them roam. Those dead people. There's things I've also seen in this building, things I have to show you. Your story alone, Boyd, wouldn't have convinced me that what you're saying is the truth, but I know something very wrong is going on here, something not even the government or military can control, and we've both been thrown into it. Our situations coincide, don't they?"

Boyd was alerted by the mention of a person or persons at the helm of this facility. Did Cindy know who was in charge? The mention of Brett Anderson confirmed that this was military or government, perhaps it was only state-level.

"Do you know who put this together?" he asked.

"There's something you need to see first," she replied, eying the door. "I've been too scared to check it out myself. It might answer your question."

Boyd was puzzled, but he was happy to find a person who finally believed the explanation of his crime. They were both victims of circumstance. Why someone would throw Cindy into the facility made him press the question further. "Did you know something that Brett didn't want you talking about to anyone else?"

Cindy bit her lip. "I shouldn't have been nosy, but on his cell phone, there were numbers in his directory that were definitely from the government. I called one number, just curious, and the person answered to the name of "Red Heron." I asked him who it was, and he said it was an old buddy from the marines. Brett kept a lot of his life private. In fact, I never saw his work office. I was his secretary on the job, and I took calls, but I never saw Brett's *real* office."

"Or found out what he could be doing as a side job, huh?" Boyd balled up his fists. "Does this make you wonder how many people have been falsely reported dead; how many cases like ours? There are piles of street clothes and shredded military uniforms scattered about this town. We weren't the first ones in here."

They both grew quiet for a time, and then a foul stink was detected in the air. A window in the corner of the office was partly cracked open. Boyd went over and peered out of the slit, careful not to be seen from outside, and found he had a perfect view of the restaurant. Smoke billowed out the back of the building in a gray cloud.

"What is it, Boyd?" she asked.

He pointed out the window at the restaurant. "You see that smoke? I think Hayden's in there. I'm sure you noticed the charred leftovers of bodies tied up in chairs in front. The man's a cannibal, and I'm sure he's living up to his name. I guess he's a ghost like me. A man like Hayden, he'd prefer to disappear."

Cindy's face bent in disgust. "He ate those strippers, right?"

"Yeah, I arrested the man. That's why they sent me to capture him. Why send anyone else? My situation is rather unique since Samuel Tyson's death. I'm exploitable."

"Just like a woman after an abortion," Cindy sneered, near tears. "Forget them, they've won their battle. We're stuck here. There's no use lamenting about something we can't fix."

Boyd shook his head, disagreeing. "No, we're escaping. I'm not staying here to die and neither are you. When I get out, since whoever put us here has killed me off, I'll show everyone what's going on in this place and these murdering creatures will be destroyed, and we'll get our lives back." He took her hands into his, "*We'll* get our lives back."

"I just hope our efforts will produce a happy ending." Cindy picked up the fire extinguisher—her weapon. "You take your gun, I trust you. I have something interesting to show you. I hope you're brave enough to crawl inside and find out what's on the other end."

Boyd watched her face and hoped she'd clarify her statement, but she led him out of the office to a short staircase without doing so. He was directed to a short hall. A door was open at the front, and looking inside, he saw it was a break room. There was a refrigerator, soda machine, and a vending machine that was half empty. Cindy stepped into the room, wanting him to follow.

"Are you hungry?" She pointed at the vending machine. "You've got some quick energy in there, or if you're interested in something more fulfilling, there's canned goods in the cupboard—mostly baked beans and Spam."

He shook his head. "I can't eat right now, my insides are in a knot."

Cindy popped open the fridge. "And I forgot to mention, there's stockpiles of beer. Here, take a bottle. Anyone who managed to survive out there long enough to find me deserves a strong drink."

Boyd accepted the bottle of Killian's Irish Red. It was cold enough to ease his throat, but his mind remained in turmoil. He was a dead man. That meant his wife was consoling his death and trying to move on. Was there a funeral? He imagined a small group of people at a cemetery plot and wondered what was really inside his coffin. It saddened him that their last memory of him was as a criminal.

He guzzled half his beer without realizing it.

Cindy was already finished with hers. "There's harder stuff in the cupboards as well. You might turn to that later, 'cause I sure have."

"My uncle taught me how to stay calm in bad situations," Boyd offered, turning the cold bottle over in his hand. "Uncle Ryan served four tours in Vietnam. He said you have to have a view of death. A stance. How can you fear it or conquer it if you don't have an opinion of the other side?"

"What did your uncle think death was?"

"He said it was a cycle of your favorite memories."

Cindy's brow bent, skeptical of the idea. "Like a greatest hits of memories?"

"Exactly. That's what I think death is. So knowing that, all I have to look forward to is the best if I die."

"I'm screwed; I'm an agnostic." She turned and went to the doorway, then pointed down the hallway, continuing the tour after a short stint of silence. "There's a bathroom, even a shower, but there's one room in the very back that I want you to check out." Her lips quivered, her gaze magnetized to the door at the end of the hallway.

The mention of bathrooms and the stockpiles of food, he analyzed the purpose of the library. The town set-up was very convincing, even the houses. He imagined everyone in town was slaughtered by the things, but how could that go unnoticed? It'd be easier to convince the world that Boyd Broman and Cindy Piper were dead, but to do the same for an entire town? Why was the library like an outpost or a survival station?

Boyd raised the Glock. "Should I be on the alert to shoot something?"

"I honestly don't know."

"Then what's in there that concerns you so much?"

"You'll see."

Boyd grunted low enough that Cindy didn't hear him. He approached the closed door, apprehensive to the task. It wasn't boarded up. No blood or shredded clothing.

"Have you been in the room yet?"

Cindy hesitated to answer. "I opened the door and thought it was more supplies, but I was wrong. Way wrong. I couldn't be ready for what was in there, not even after seeing those people outside."

"So you haven't seen one of them up close?"

Cindy furiously shook her head. "No, have you?"

Boyd glared at her a moment. "One of them threw a knife at me. I shot it in the arm and head, but it still came for me. I'm not sure if anything can kill those things except maybe burning them. I believe Hayden's across the street at that Italian restaurant. He's rigged charred corpses on the patio dining tables. I think he's using the bodies to scare others away from trying to break in, like corpse scarecrows. If we had something flammable, we'd be in a better position to fight them."

"I guess we're screwed for now." Cindy was still shocked that he'd survived an encounter with one of the dead. "I'm surprised they haven't come in after me yet. I assume they know I'm in here. God knows what they really think or don't. What can a rotting pile of flesh comprehend? I've had their presence in my mind constantly. Every night, I wake up every half hour to double check if the door is still locked and nothing's in the hallway. I still haven't been able to take a shower in this place."

"We're not staying much longer," Boyd advised her. "Even if they lied to me when they said I'd go free when I captured Hayden, the exchange would involve a confrontation, and I'll be damned if they're going to leave us to die. Someone has to let the world know this place exists. We're somewhere outside of Pittsburgh, I know that from the drive over here, but I can't say for sure where. I do know we're still in the United States and that means there are people out there who can help us if they know we're here."

Boyd was talking to procrastinate. He didn't want Cindy to learn he was scared to open the door even though he assumed she knew that much already. "How far did you get inside? What's it like?"

Cindy shrugged her shoulders. "I couldn't walk in. It was a small room. It's hard to see to the back. You'll know what I mean when you go in."

Boyd paused at the door. "You can stand back if you want."

Cindy turned the knob while smiling. "I wouldn't have it any other way."

CHAPTER 7

Ryan Briers was one of the few I ate in retribution, Richard once told Hayden. *He was a mechanic that worked on my piece-of-shit Ford truck. Ryan broke my headlights in the process of installing a new air-conditioning unit; ask me how that happens, I don't know. He charged me for the headlights despite my arguments. He even keyed my doors. I followed him home and rammed his bumper into a set of trees on an empty back road. From there, I drugged him, and the rest is culinary history. That man really upset me. People who willingly screw people over deserve the worst death. The ultimate revenge, Hayden, is to eat a man and shit him out. It's the most insulting thing you can do to another person. And that's just what I did to Ryan Briers.*

Hayden ventured through the back gate to a house behind the restaurant. The structure was a two-story Victorian house. Inside, he planned to relax in a warm sudsy bath. His favorite thing to do as a teenager was to drink and bathe. The warm water was like returning to the birth canal.

Lurking forward, the grass reached up to his knees. The chirp of locusts pursued him to the back porch. Walking up onto the patio, the back door was unlocked, and he stepped inside. He clutched a five-inch blade from the steak knife set he'd left on the kitchen counter. Armed, he wasn't worried about his safety. The sight of dozens of the figures scampering to hide from him emboldened him. They wouldn't dare hurt him.

Hayden crept into the darkness and entered the kitchen. Then he traced his hands down the hallway wall and found the edge of a staircase. The creak of every step made him wince; he was still afraid of them, he admitted. They could be anywhere, thinking anything, and ready to turn on him at a moment's notice.

Arriving at the bottom of the steps, he found the basement door closed, the way he'd left it during his visit last night. He swung it open, stepped inside, and locked it behind him. The abode belonged to a restaurant mogul judging by the contents of the desk in the corner. The drawers were organized with folders containing requisitions and progress reports from McDonald's, Big Boy Burger, Taco Bell among a collection of other fast food chains. The Italian restaurant nearby must've been a bored, rich man's experimental venture.

Chemical additives and preservatives, I abhor the fast food industry, Richard proclaimed whenever they walked the sidewalks of Crawford Center, just outside of Pittsburgh, a popular stretch of strip malls and fast food restaurants.

Hayden, don't get hooked on that junk. Why would someone add sugar to a beef patty? Imagine what else they put in that shit? It all tastes the same, the millions they've served, every damn burger tastes exactly the same. The way I cook my meats, every cut is similar, but distinctive, and I know what's in it. The same goes with humans.

I had a run in with a large hooker, close to three-hundred pounds. I was short on cash at the time, and she was willing to service me for a twenty dollar bill.

A slow night, she said. I put the flesh from her triceps on a skillet, and it turned to grease. That phrase 'you are what you eat' is true, Hayden.

Hayden entered a back room with a washer and dryer while the mental oration filled his head. At the end of the room, a bathtub was hidden behind a set of clear shower curtains. He stripped naked and drew a steaming hot bath. The soap was running low, but there was plenty of herbal shampoo; his favorite was hemp-based and strawberry scented. He soaked after drawing the bath, the curtain draped for habitual privacy.

And what would the dead cretins think of you naked? Hayden thought. *Stare at you like a voyeur? Would they enjoy it? Can they get hard-ons? Can the dead get wet? If their blood flows, it's a possibility.*

He didn't have much information about the dead people skulking outside. He'd dissected them and tasted their flesh, but how they moved about while being dead, well, he was surprised he didn't think too much about it. He was surviving, and as long as he had something to eat, it didn't matter what made them tick. The dead hunted for meat, but they didn't eat flesh. He once caught a woman at the back of the post office with eight different pairs of breasts inside a garbage dumpster, and each day, she'd change them out for the set least covered in flies and maggots. Their existence was elusive as it was harrowing, and he was convinced of the sound of the din of guttural baying from outside.

He pulled the plug, draining the tub, and rose to his feet, unable to relax as blood rushed from his head back down to his legs. The wine added to the fog in his eyes; a circulatory overload. He touched the curtain, but a hand reared it back for him instead. He didn't have time to register the intruder before it wrapped its arms around him and shoved his face back down into the water. Hayden scrambled to gain leverage, but the thing was on his back with its bare bone knees pressing against both shoulder blades.

He swallowed a mouthful of soapy water; the thing was going to drown him before the tub could drain completely! A hand clutched the back of his neck and submerged his face deeper into the water, unyielding to his resistance to escape. Hayden collected his strength, tensing up his muscles, and issued a banshee cry of fear and desperation.

Hayden launched backwards, using his back to throw the figure off-balance. The dead man fumbled backwards, slamming into the floor. Before it could get up, Hayden put his feet together and stomped on the corpse's head. Chalk breaking against slate, the skull merely cracked. Rust-colored fluids leaked from the top of the head, oozing out in a thin gruel trail.

"I'm going to break your head open and scatter those brains!" Hayden laughed, channeling vehemence into every syllable. "*How dare you come in here!*"

Hayden repeated the attack, slamming his feet onto its head, and after eight repetitions, the skull imploded with a hollow pumpkin's *pop*.

Still naked, he lifted the body that was trying to fit the broken bits of brain matter back into its skull and lugged it through the back door by its arms. He crossed the fence and trudged into the front yard. He counted two dozen dead beings standing on the sidewalks and streets, others hiding behind bushes and trees, cowering from him. Demons in the night, buzzards ready to feast on a fallen animal, they were parasites. But unlike normal parasites, they were frightened. The glint of eyes, the stillness of faces, they didn't move or charge him.

"You've seen me and what I do to your kind!" he yelled as he lobbed the body onto the front lawn. "I'll show no mercy on you. I'll slaughter you just to collect more pieces to eat. *I'll cut your fucking heads off for fun!*"

Hayden's heart beat faster. He shivered, naked in the cold, but the darkness hid his vulnerability. The dead things watched the damaged corpse stumble and walk on two legs, but its movements were jittery. Seconds later, the dead man flopped back onto the ground, its arms and legs unable to communicate proper movement, the body wanting to shift in four different directions at once.

"You protect your brains, don't you? It's all you have, isn't it? Somehow, you keep them fresh. The command center works, but the rest of you keeps going to shit. You're stinking up the air with your rotting bodies. You're not human, and you'll never be again!" He watched them warily.

They didn't budge at his words.

He wasn't sure what to do next, so he breathed in and out to calm himself. They could attack him, and they would win, but none of them acted on their natural violent impulse. They were afraid, and whether they could overtake him or not, they digressed. The war was a mental war, and he was their intellectual superior.

Hayden marched through the backyard, into the house, and collected his clothes from the bathroom, then retreated back into the restaurant. Once again safe in his fortress, he grabbed the nearest bottle of liquor which turned out to be Peso, Peruvian wine, and swigged it heartily. The attack had come out of nowhere, and if they decided to try it again, he wasn't sure he could counter it in the same way. He knew he had gotten lucky. If there had been more than one...

He continued to drink, disturbed by the night's events.

They weren't as afraid of him as he had believed. The attack was a question of his character, of his ability to survive. He considered the possibilities to strike back, but he was too shaken to think rationally. For now, he was content on staying safe. And drunk.

It wasn't until later in the night that he was disturbed again.

CHAPTER 8

*B*oyd had taken a shower after working the late patrol shift the previous night. It was seven in the morning after he toweled dry and he was ready to fall asleep. Shannon and Mindy were off for their summer vacation and they normally slept-in until nine, but today was an exception—and not a good one.

Karen had left for work a half an hour ago; she worked part-time as a dental assistant.

He entered his bedroom and noticed Shannon had taken his police belt off the top of the bureau and splayed it on the floor. Mindy, the more inquisitive child, had removed a clip from his holster and held it up to the light, fascinated by the gleam of the bullet at the end. Shannon followed her sister's lead and clutched his pepper spray. She fingered the nozzle.

"Put those down right now!" Boyd's heart panged and raced as he lunged to claim the items of interest.

The two girls yipped and backed away from the belt, denying their fascination with it.

You were careless. You left it out. I should've locked it up in the closet like I always do.

He'd heard of kids finding guns in unlocked parts of the house and getting shot or shooting someone by accident. Frustrated, but keeping himself in check, he moved to the girls, completing the distance between him and the belt. Mindy tried to run for the door, but he caught her by the arm. Softening his tone and belittling his authoritative stance, he said, "Now wait, girls. Let's talk."

"It was her idea," Shannon insisted, pointing at her sister. "I said to leave it alone. She wouldn't listen to me. I said we'd get in trouble."

"You big baby," Mindy scolded, crossing her arms. "You always tell. Tattle-tale, tattle-tale—I hate you!"

"Now both of you be quiet." Boyd took back what they'd taken. "You're curious about my belt, so I'll show you what everything is, *but you have to promise me never to touch it again. No touching it under any circumstances. Promise me."*

They promised.

He de-mystified the pepper spray by spraying it into the bathroom sink. He unloaded the clips, letting them hold the bullets. Then they held his baton and cuffs. The real spectacle he showed them was the .28 police revolver.

Once unloaded, he allowed each of them to hold it. During the show-and-tell, he thanked God they hadn't hurt themselves.

As nervous now as when his children had found his police belt, Boyd opened the door into the unknown room. Inside, was the last image he expected to see; he was a flinch from pulling the trigger. He expected a body to lunge out at him, but the room was quiet, deathly still. It was a janitor's closet, but so long and narrow that he couldn't see to the back—not through the hundreds of strings stapled into the walls laced with razors. It was a cobweb of sharp edges and make-shift barbs.

"I think someone set these up, and once they were done, they stayed back there to protect themselves," Cindy guessed, peeking around him and into the room. "I've looked hard in there, and I didn't notice it at first, but if you get on the floor and look, there's a pair of feet. They're not moving."

Boyd lowered himself to his knees. He stared through the strings of razors about seven inches up from the floor. The lights flickered on their last moments of life. He spotted a pair of black boots; they stuck out from behind a utility shelf.

"So you want me to crawl to the other side and find out who that is?"

Cindy averted her eyes, avoiding his scrutiny. "I won't blame you if you don't, but it might help us figure this place out better."

He swallowed a breath of air to stall. The room didn't smell, and the owner of the boots didn't move. He decided to call out, "Hey, are you okay in there?" He looked back at her with a crooked smile. "I had to try."

He crawled onto his haunches, convinced he had to investigate.

"Be careful," Cindy said as she watched him lay flat on the floor. "Those razors are sharp."

Crawling into room, his back brushed up against the strings, and the back of his neck was nicked. The sting was doubled by the sweat beading from his skin. "Damn it."

"You're almost there," she encouraged him. "Three more feet. Watch out, I don't know what's back there."

And neither do I.

A razor sliced into his scalp. "Christ, this sucks!"

I better not need stitches. Whoever did this had the right idea. Nobody would be crazy enough to sneak through here except for me.

He finally cleared the gauntlet. He turned his head in each direction to assure his safety, and gasped at what was slumped behind a shelf of cleaning supplies. A green uniform, black boots, and a beret, all of it covering a skeleton. The flesh was gone. No internal organs. The abdominal cavities were ransacked and the vent on the opposite wall was open.

After all that work and one hole in the wall got you killed.

There was an M-16 still in the bony grip. He searched the pockets and retrieved two clips and a grenade. A walkie-talkie was clasped in the skeleton's bare phalange-grip. Boyd spoke into it, the device issuing a sharp crackle.

"Is anyone out there?" He read the man's name badge. "This is Lieutenant Meyers. I need assistance ASAP."

No response.

"Who the hell are you talking to?" Cindy called out, confused. "What's back there? Who is Meyers?"

"Just a second," he said then continued speaking into the walkie. "Please, I'm Lieutenant Meyers, I need help. I'm injured, can anyone send assistance?"

Finally he gave up. He slid the walkie towards Cindy. "Keep track of that, will you? I've found a bag of bones that belong to a Lieutenant Meyers. I also have a better weapon."

He slid the rifle and two clips at her. "I'm coming back. Give me a second."

INSIDE THE PERIMETER

He returned to the hallway, this time successfully avoiding the razors. Cindy wielded the M-16 with confidence. "It's a nice gun. I like it."

"I'd prefer we didn't have to use it, but it's a big possibility." He pointed at the walkie in her other hand. "I tried to call using the lieutenant's name, but no one's answering. There's just static."

Cindy guided him back to the break room. She opened the cupboard and produced a bottle of vodka. "I don't have shot glasses, but drinking it straight from the bottle works the same."

Boyd was second to drink after her, the stuff burning down his throat and relaxing his headache. Cindy placed a cloth over his head and another at his neck and had him hold it down tight.

"That should stop the bleeding. The cuts aren't deep. The blood makes it worse than it really is."

"That makes me feel much better."

"Sorry." She studied him with soft eyes. "So what do we do next?"

"Hayden's still out there." He paused, unsure of what to do about the man and the deal that was offered him. The contract wasn't binding on their side of things, whoever the dealmaker proved to be. "It's come down to Hayden and me, really. I want to see their faces and know who exactly is running things. I have a rifle and a handgun, and a grenade, too. I can put up a fight if they try and abandon us."

He pulled the grenade out of his pocket and showed her.

"Wow, that's great," Cindy laughed. She was tipsy and was taking another drink. "Blow someone right to hell with that thing." Then she creased her brow and said. "Wait a second; couldn't you use the grenade to blow up the wall surrounding this place or something similar so we could escape from here?"

He shook his head. "No, even if the grenade did take down a part of the wall, the first thing I'm doing is going home. If they want me, they'll know right where to find me."

"You could run," she said.

He shook his head. "Not without my family. I need to do this if I want to get my life back."

"But is that really the right thing to do? It's like you want to wage a war with an enemy we haven't seen. They control everything around here, whoever they are."

"So, why can't we fight them?" Boyd clenched his fists; his buzz was turning against him. "What are you gonna do? Are you content in making that office your bedroom for the rest of your life? And that's if those things out there don't break in here and turn you into an organ donor. Lieutenant Meyers was attacked through an opening in the ceiling. They could be in here right now and we wouldn't even know it. Hayden survived this long out there and so can we. I have to see my wife again, and I will."

Cindy frowned, unconvinced. "You're a dead man, and I'm probably dead, too. They made it a point to be rid of us by tossing us in here. We both got mixed up with the wrong people."

"Don't give up yet," he insisted, taking the bottle out of her hands so she couldn't take another nip. "I'm sure there're more guys to fall in love with beyond that district attorney asshole. Good people. We're both good people, and as long as we believe it, someone else will eventually. We're war-criminals without rights or even a single phone call. We're on the wrong end of the Patriot Act, Cindy. Hell, we don't even know where we are. Do you want someone else to be taken advantage of, too? I died on paper, and you can't punish a criminal again once they've died, right? It's double jeopardy. What law says you can put a dead man on trial again or lock him in prison? I have a wife and kids, Cindy, who thinks I'm dead, and their memory of me is not very flattering. You don't want that for yourself before you've even started a life."

Cindy's lips trembled and she stifled tears, the truth sinking in fast. "I don't have those wonderful things you have, Boyd. I've never been in a relationship long enough to start a family. I always wanted a daughter, probably two so they can pick on each other and get into trouble. That's what children are put on this earth to do; annoy us until we grow old, and then they can change our diapers and refill our prescriptions when we're in the rest home."

He questioned her nugget of life wisdom. "You're not even thirty yet, are you?"

"Twenty-seven." She slugged down another shot, nabbing the bottle before he could protect it. "Bottoms up."

"It's not too late," he reasoned with her. "Hey, listen. You're an attractive woman, and you've held up well by yourself in this place. You've kept your cool, and unlike a certain lieutenant who boarded himself up in a room full of razors on strings, you've already beat the kind of people who've put us here. We simply have to dig ourselves out."

"I still don't see how we'll escape."

"Hayden's the key, like I said. They want him in questioning for the bodies they've found recently connected to him, so they need him, Cindy. We give them hell when we find them, whoever they are. Guns and everything, okay? I can't predict what will happen, but it's our only option. As long as we have something they want, we can use it to our advantage."

Cindy nodded. "But I'm scared of what's out there. Those things will kill us both."

Boyd recalled shooting the figure at the abandoned police station twice, and it still lunged after him. The grenade would do the job, but he'd need more than just one. It would take cunning and sneaking around to be safe, not weaponry.

"We'll have to hide and move at night. It's still dark outside; I think I'm going to check out the restaurant across from us, even if it's just to catch a glimpse of Hayden. I want to know what he's doing."

"I'm going with you," she insisted, concerned. "I've been alone for too long. I can't stand it anymore. And what if you didn't come back?"

"You'll be risking your life out there," he argued, making sure she could handle herself in a tense situation. "Are you prepared to fight?"

"I think so." She replaced the cap on the vodka bottle. "I'd rather be with you. I hate being locked up in here. And I have noticed that restaurant across from us before you got here. I keep smelling burning flesh. Are you telling me Hayden's eating those things?"

"It wouldn't surprise me."

Cindy handed him the M-16. "I think we should trade. The handgun works better for me."

"We can't use the guns unless we absolutely have to," he reiterated, accepting the exchange. "The moment those things hear us, they'll swarm us. It started with one out there, and when the thing shrieked and garbled a bunch of nonsense, dozens of them came out of the woodwork. Like I said, we have to keep to the shadows and stay quiet. We don't know much about them, but they're smarter than they appear. It's like they can communicate with each other. I don't want to be here long enough to understand their way of life. I just want them dead."

She clutched the Glock tightly, her knuckles turning white. "Then what are we waiting for?"

CHAPTER 9

Hayden cleaned up the mess in the kitchen he'd made earlier in the day, the congealed blood staining the floor and countertops in wicked spatters. He washed the knives and sharpened them with a carving stone. After the work of sanitation was complete, his stomach growled; he was famished. He opened the freezer to pursue his hunger. The woman's head he'd cut off earlier that night watched him, stealing his attention through the plastic bag. Her eyes were frozen over, but her mouth tried to shape words, the blood that had oozed from her neck now ice.

Moving on from the female corpse, he removed a forearm from a plastic bag a shelf below; it belonged to the burly man he'd killed two weeks ago. He looked to be from prison, especially from the tattoo on his back of two lesbians sitting Indian-style across from each other, fingering one another between the legs.

He carried the forearm to the stovetop and grabbed a skillet from the hanging rack above him. "I think I'll eat it blackened and fried this time."

It's better if it's baked, Hayden.

"I'm in the mood for junk food," Hayden countered Richard's advice. "I've earned it."

He layered the skillet with olive oil and added sea salt and bay leaves to the mix. It was a subtle blend, but enough to remove the off-taste of expired meat.

Work with what you got; it takes innovation to pull it off, Hayden. We'll never be rich men, not with what takes up our spare time. We have to live low-to-the ground to enjoy the kind of lives we do.

He brought down a hammer to the forearm and a chunk of frozen meat shattered into pebbles. He collected a handful, defrosted them in the microwave, and turned up the gas burner on the oven. A small jet of flames shot up from the gas head. He slapped the meat onto the skillet and mixed it together, the olive oil soaking and sizzling into the meat. The aroma of sea salt, a breeze from the

Maine coast, sauntered into his nose. He finished blackening the meat and let it cool.

The aroma drew the same question every night. The meat he procured was from decaying bodies that modified themselves from newer tissue. How come he wasn't suffering from bouts of botulism and diarrhea?

"I'm not camping out on the toilet," Hayden announced to no one. "And until I do, I don't have to stop. So why question it?"

And suppose I do get sick, I can't say with certainty that I would quit.

It's just too damn good.

Hayden gathered a plate and utensils, and when he sat down to enjoy his food in the dining area with Venus as his company, there was a clatter from the back kitchen.

Someone was forcing open the door.

* * *

It was a set-up from the beginning, and when Edwin Mendez figured it out, it was far too late to fight back. Edwin clung to the last remnants of his life in the basement of 102 South End, one of the many residential homes inside the perimeter—whatever this enclosure was called. He was chased from the outer gates and the rotting fiends didn't let up their pursuit until he was running to the end of a cul-de-sac. No choice, Edwin stormed through the front door of the closest house and took cover in the basement.

He had survived for two days.

And this was the third night.

He dared to venture up the stairs once again, wondering if he could leave. *Where are they*, he wondered after each shifting of foundation and whistle of wind through the cracked windows. There were dozens of them scouring the streets for him when he'd first arrived, and now there were none.

Did I lose them? Do they know I'm here?

Upstairs, he hunted through the cabinets and refrigerator for food. He survived on cans of baked beans, fruit cocktail, and Vienna sausages. He ended up in this mess, he recalled, after hacking information from the state's databases: account information, credit card numbers, social security numbers, and addresses of hundreds of officers including where their direct deposit pay checks were sent. He created a private account and stole hundreds of thousands of dollars from law enforcement agencies. Edwin could've stolen a hundred dollars a week and avoided being caught, but retirement flashed in his mind, and it drove him to steal more and more until the FBI smashed in his door, woke him and his wife, and he was arrested.

But instead of hand cuffs, a burlap bag was wrapped over his head and his arms and legs were bound with plastic twine. He was hog-tied in the back of a large vehicle; the rumble of the engine and his back against a vinyl seat was all that he recalled. And then he woke on the sidewalk inside the perimeter without an explanation or reason.

He ambled to the opposite end of the house, curious and satisfied no one was outside, and discovered pictures of a family hanging on the walls, namely a man dressed in military clothing with a wife, a boy and girl.

He does Uncle Sam proud. What a crock of shit.

The bedrooms matched the family in the pictures. Dinosaurs covered the walls of the boy's room, and the girl's room was pink. Barbie figurines were strewn about the carpet, their bodies surrounding an Easy-Bake Oven. In the owner's bedroom, the sheets were sodden in old blood. Torn undergarments were spread in rivulets on the carpet.

No bodies.

A strike and splinter of wood from the living room alerted him.

Oh, shit!

The things were boarding up the windows from the outside. They nailed planks across the doors and sealed every exit possible in a reverse barricade. He gathered up food and water and locked himself in the basement. The *thud* of nails and wood continued for hours until the din finally stopped.

Again, he faced the horrible silence.

An hour, maybe two, the garage door opened. The mechanical whir jolted him, and then the back door of the basement was ripped from its hinges in seconds, blunt objects used to batter the barrier into kindling. Six of them charged at him in collaboration, their faces lost in the shadows, ever moving towards him. He tried to dodge them, hide, but he had nowhere else to go, and pinned against the wall, they drove him to the floor. Restraining him with rope, one of the figures loomed closer, clutching a scalpel. The glint of the weapon matched the figure's gleaming marble eyes, cold and calculating all the same.

Edwin was now able to see the dead man up close. He could see through the open nasal cavity to webs of brain tissue housed within the darkened nook of its skull. Its scalp was bald and sliding from the white dome, the consistency of butter. Its ears were stitched on and hanging by threads. The jaw looked to be stuck in place by metal staples. The figure discarded the strings and leftovers of its face, peeling them bare, everything coming off in a mudslide of flesh, until Edwin stared at a red-faced skull.

The figure raised the scalpel, the hands holding him down gripping tighter. A slit in the back of his neck and around the circumference of his scalp was made, and slashing more, slashing deeper, Edwin's skin became a carving canvas. The pain didn't creep up until the figure with the blade gripped the back of his neck with two hands and jerked upwards on Edwin's skin. The tear was audible as each grain of fascia was broken. Edwin's face turned warm and wet with bullets of blood.

The living corpse raised Edwin's face, a mask complete with hair, and its furrowed, pained expression to its own gaping visage. The dead man fit it snug over its barren features, and for a moment before slipping into deadly unconsciousness, Edwin believed he was staring at himself.

CHAPTER 10

"No...he didn't mean for it to happen!"

"You're going to have to leave, ma'am; your husband's being tended to by the medics. Please stay calm. I know you've been through a terrible ordeal..."

"But Boyd was trying to apprehend him. It was an accident. Why is that officer saying he's going to be arrested?"

"Nobody said that."

"I heard it!"

"Get her back; get her away from my crime scene right now!"

"Both the cars were barreling down the street, and they smashed into each other. I've never seen such a thing happen before. He just flew out of the driver's side. He wasn't wearing his seat belt."

"Don't look at the body, sir, we've got your statement, now move on. You don't have to tell me again what happened."

Boyd listened to the words and conversations, and they were meaningless in conjunction to the ringing in his head, the taste of bitter blood crawling down his throat, and how his neck and skull whirred with a painful migraine. He'd been jostled hard and could be suffering from whiplash or a concussion or both. He kept closing his eyes, and then opening them, and then drifting asleep, waking, drifting, waking, and then he was lifted by three men onto a stretcher. A tiny orange light was flashed in his eyes. The snapping of fingers. They kept snapping, and he couldn't speak to tell them to stop it, he was trying to sleep and stop shining that damn light in his eyes.

"Officer Broman, can you hear me? Boyd, hey Boyd, can you hear me?"

"Iuh..Iuham...Iuham...Iuh..."

"He's not with it."

"They both sped right through a red light. They were lucky it's late enough that there wasn't oncoming traffic."

"Did you see that guy? He's flattened. Jesus Christ. Forget the ambulance, call someone to hose this shit off the pavement."

A screaming, shrill female called out hysterical, "Boyd, are you okay? Honey, are you all right? Let go of me, that's my husband. That's my husband damn it!"

Red and blue lights spun from six blue squad cars.

A face lowered down to his, a paramedic's. He was now in the ambulance. The doors were closed at his feet. The vehicle wasn't in motion yet.

"You're going to be fine. We're not very far from the hospital. You're going to make it, pal."

Boyd's eyes rolled into the back of his head, and before he went under, he heard his wife calling out to him one last time.

Boyd opened the rear exit to the library, cautiously looking out at the schoolyard two blocks down, the playground empty, the swings in motion from a recent blast of wind. Confident it was clear, he crept out far enough to peer behind the edge of a brick wall to the left. Over the barrier, a parking lot contained the shells of burned-up cars. Nothing they could use.

"How are we crossing over?" Cindy watched the parking lot. "I haven't seen any of those things yet."

"We won't be out in the open." He studied the gutter on the other side of the library. "We'll go underground."

"Then we'll need this." She waved a flashlight. "I wouldn't enter that trap without a light. It was inside the desk in the office."

"That flashlight, it's heavy duty," he encouraged her, thinking it over. "It could crack a few skulls if we needed it to."

Cindy's face locked. She was scared, and he patted her shoulder, making eye contact. "Look, we're alive, and we're smarter than them. We're not piecing ourselves back together, are we? Our bodies are our own. I'm here with you. It's going to be fine. If all else fails, we run like hell."

"Run like hell," she repeated, half-believing the notion. "Yeah, run like hell."

He led her to the opening in the gutter. He crawled down first, trusting his ears over the darkness. He touched down on the metal walkway, the clang of his feet echoing. He listened but no sudden movements or grumbles of pursuit came to him.

Cindy crawled down next, flashing her beam and illuminating the green and filmy orange water below them. Stacks of bones floated in the water, but they were hollowed out, the marrow sucked clean, the femurs snapped in half, the vertebra shattered, the rib bones warped, and the sternums bent and broken, everything sapped of worth.

Discarded remains, Boyd determined.

The bones had a life of their own. It was subtle, like the involuntary flex of muscles, or was it his imagination? Cindy froze the beam on a floating skull, affirming his observation. The eyes stared them down from the sockets, moving with jelly squishes. The mandibles snapped open and closed in reaction.

"What could make them do that?" Boyd asked softly.

"I want to shoot it," Cindy warned him, repulsed by the show. "It keeps looking at us. When you're dead, you're not supposed to be staring people down and murdering them. Let me shoot 'em. I'll put them out of their misery."

"You can't, they'll hear us," he advised, forcing her to lower the handgun. "Hold it together; I know it's horrible to look at but just turn away and move on."

He urged her from the horrid sight by pivoting her shoulders and offering her a soft shove forward. They walked in the direction of the restaurant; it was a straight-shot to the other side of the road. Again, the tunnels were blocked and patched over with mesh wire. This was the work of someone else besides the military; these things had taken over, and this was their place to design and protect.

A burst of methane gas exuded from the back of the sewer and Cindy gasped, audibly distraught. "God that's nasty."

"*Shhh*," he hissed.

It was hard to believe they'd only covered five or six yards. He watched out for a step-ladder or another gutter opening. What he detected by accident was a moving shadow. A hand reached up from the water, followed by the body it was connected to. It crawled up and writhed onto the walkway. It was draped in a cape of algae. Its skull was completely black, its legs and midsection dressed in torn-up clothing: jeans and an old polo shirt. It raised a broken arm in one hand, the tip sharpened to a point. Cindy raised the Glock to fire, but Boyd waved the gun down again.

"I'll take care of it," he said.

Cindy approached the thing. "No, forget it, *I've got this one.*"

She raised the blunt end of the flashlight up to the creature's head. Before the thing could close in on her, she leveled it onto its skull.

Crack!

The skull-cap broke, and the thing flopped back into the water. Cindy trained the flashlight's beam on it. The vestiges floated with its brains spreading along the surface of the water, dissolving. The dead man reached to gather the bits, but its arms couldn't perform the task. After a time of failure, the thing scavenged through piles of nearby bones and searched through them with soft porcelain crashes.

"It's still able to function even with its brains oozing out of its head," Cindy said, startled at the revelation. "How can we kill these things?"

Boyd recalled the outside of the restaurant and the charred corpses propped up at the tables. "Hayden has figured it out. He's been burning them. I guess that's a good solution, just not timely."

Ahead, Boyd closed in on a shaft of light. It was another gutter. He hoisted Cindy up first, and then he handed her his weapons and followed her. They were on the opposite sidewalk now, and together they rushed to the alley of Mariatelli's. None of the corpses were anywhere to be seen.

Cindy waited for him at the back door, anxious to take cover inside the restaurant. Boyd met up with her, using the butt of the M-16 as a bludgeon on the padlock; the lock came undone with a rusty collapse after only two blows. Boyd stood confused, staring at the broken remains at his feet. "This is too easy. Why haven't those things broken inside yet?"

She shrugged, eyeing the area around them nervously. "Maybe they've given up. Who cares? Let's get the hell inside before they show up."

After rushing through the door and closing it behind them, Boyd stacked crates against the door as a makeshift barricade.

Secure enough, they faced an industrial-sized dishwasher in a fully-stocked kitchen, and encountered the rank smell of cooking flesh.

"Be careful," Boyd whispered to her. "He's in here somewhere."

He walked to the stove and happened upon an empty skillet. The stink of flesh lingered strong, freshly prepared.

He's never stopped being a cannibal, even here.

Cindy opened the freezer, curious.

"Hey, what're you doing?" he asked.

"There could be real food in here," she argued, determined despite the human waft in the air. "I've been eating out of a can for the past eight days. I'm dying for real food."

Boyd watched every doorway and opening for Hayden. Nobody was coming so far. There was a front area for seating, a back room, and restrooms, all of which Hayden could be hiding in.

"Oh my God!" Cindy yelped, calling out to him. "You have to see this."

Boyd ambled to the freezer, anxious and afraid. Entering, he couldn't turn his eyes away from the shelves. Clear plastic bags were stuffed with human remains. Appendages, organs, filleted and flanked strips of human flesh, and bags of blood, were piled high, but the thing that struck him the most awful was a woman's face in a bag. Her eyes were frozen solid, but her lips quivered—and more so now that she detected them.

"This is how he's survived for so long," Boyd said, astonished. "He's eating them, and so far, he's doing just fine. He probably likes it better here than in the real world. No police are after him and his pursuers are all on the menu. How many has he killed here? How many of them were already dead? It doesn't make sense. Wouldn't eating them make him sick?"

Knowing those were questions he couldn't answer, he continued combing the kitchen for Hayden. Surveying every corner and hideaway, he saw the floors were freshly-mopped and a lemon scent downplayed the wretched smell living deeper in the place. The kitchen was clear, and stepping into a back hall, Cindy opened a storage room. They were immediately overwhelmed by what they found. A woman's naked body was roped in place on top of a table. The skin was tinted blue, and she was covered in lacerations along her abdomen and the insides of her thighs. An orange jumpsuit was wadded up in the corner along with a pair of white panties and bra.

She wasn't one of the dead from outside.

She wasn't modified or altered.

Her head was shaved, leaving black buds on the scalp. Lacerations had turned her breasts inside out, the nipples removed, the fatty tissues hollowed out. Boyd recognized her and was surprised she was here and dead on the table. Her name was Brandy Gwinn; she was considered a knowing accomplice in Hayden's crimes. Hayden took her from the streets—broke and panhandling for food and drug money—and fed her human flesh. Hayden called it a social experiment.

"If they don't know it's flesh, will they like it? And when they find out, will they still like it?" Hayden had said.

Brandy enjoyed Hayden's food so much, she did anything to stay with him, including sexual favors and luring new victims to their deaths by soliciting prostitution and then performing back alley throat slashings. Brandy arrived much later in Hayden's murdering career, and it was at that point the horrors were committed hastily.

Boyd noted the slits on her wrists. The wounds were gummed up, a week old easy. There was no blood in the room, so whatever happened to her—murder or suicide—it didn't occur here.

"Her name's Brandy," he explained to Cindy. "She was an accomplice in Hayden's crimes, and who knows how many people she helped kill. Brandy was sentenced to six life terms without parole, but I guess she's like Hayden and was brought here, too."

"*You're right,*" a voice hissed.

Boyd whipped around, but it was too late. Hayden wedged his arm around Cindy's neck, a flank knife aimed to puncture her throat. The man was different than the last time Boyd had seen him. He'd gained weight; Hayden was at least two-hundred and fifty pounds now. His sandy-colored beard had turned gray, and it was in need of a good trimming, as it completely covered his lips and half his throat.

His black eyes, deep in the sockets, were oil glints shifting in shadow pools, shifty, mean and cunning. Boyd aimed the M-16, but as an ex-cop, this had already become a hostage situation. Boyd would have to proceed with negotiations, not gunfire.

Hayden seethed hatred, offended by their presence. Near tears, he barked, "This place is mine, these people are all mine! What the fuck are you doing here, Broman?"

Boyd didn't have any fancy lies; he couldn't create them in a situation like this; nobody could. Cindy cried, her face turning deep scarlet. Her nose wrinkled, the smell of raw meat exuding strong and pungent from Hayden's body, a 'Hamburger Helper' aroma. "Investigators have found more of your bodies, several in Missouri, in fact. They want to know who else you've killed, and where you put them," Boyd said.

Boyd distinguished Hayden's fat fish belly lips through the cover of his patchy beard turn up into a lecherous grin. "Ah, but you're one of us now, aren't you? This cop's a murderer, yes, oh yes he is." He turned his head to the side, weighing Boyd's reaction, pleased to make him squirm. "Did Samuel Tyson rape your wife, or no, did he rape your kids instead—or both? Why not both, right? I was watching the news from jail. It's hard to watch what you want with a room full of tattooed brutes, but they sure watch the news a lot. I have to ask, did you enjoy hearing Samuel's bones snap under your tires? Did the crack of his spine sound just like your axle breaking? Could you smell shit? Did Samuel shit himself like a fucking baby? Did you enjoy the smell, Broman? Did you hear his final words, or was he killed instantly? Ahhh, I hate it when that happens; no pleasure in that; I hope you at least got to see the life leave his eyes. That's the best part; the way they look, so desperate, so scared, so overwhelmed, it makes you believe there really is something on the other side of death."

Boyd's innermost demon begged him to pull the trigger, but he paused, then nodded at the corpse on the table, changing subjects. "Why did you kill Brandy?"

Hayden considered the question. "She came to me for protection, and I gave it to her, but I couldn't keep her from herself. Brandy drank too damn much from the bar and made all kinds of noise. They brought her here like they did me in some kind of armored car. Why, I have no idea. We were here together and that's all I know. So we made the best of things, I suppose. Made love, enjoyed free booze and food, but after a while, Brandy felt boxed-in. Cabin fever they call it. I found her in the bathroom with her wrists slit, slumped on the toilet."

Boyd doubted the explanation. "And you felt the need to cut her up, huh?"

"I started to eat her," Hayden admitted, recounting it in his own mind. "But I couldn't work fast enough with those things out there always trying to get in. Pieces of her I managed to save; the heart and a lot of skin, mostly. The heart is one of the best pieces. It's the blood-making vessel. The life-giver." A forming smile. "The juiciest."

Boyd grew impatient hearing the explanation. Cindy trembled and her eyes begged him to make a decision.

"Did Richard tell you the heart's the life-giver of the body?" Boyd asked.

Hayden's face turned sour. "You go to hell. Don't ever talk about Richard. You don't understand. Stay away from me. I'll open her throat and the both of us can watch her die. Then I can play Samuel tonight. We can have a reenactment!"

"No, *you won't do that!*" Boyd growled.

"Put down the gun," Hayden ordered as he pressed the knife into Cindy's throat and drew a bead-sized circle of blood. "I can do anything here. There're no rules; it's the law of nature. Every man has the right to everything he wants, and whoever's the strongest can reach out and take what they wish. Now put your gun down, now."

Boyd followed the directions and propped it against the wall.

"I'm going to take this lovely lady with me, and you won't follow me." Hayden lifted the knife from her throat and seized it by the handle to throw it at him. "Still a cop even in this place, huh? They put you in here, too, so why help them? They've left us for dead...*with them!*"

Boyd couldn't refrain from action any longer. Sucking in a breath, emboldening himself, he lunged forward, springing at Hayden and tearing Cindy from his grip. He lodged an upper-cut punch into Hayden's stomach and the man belched, Hayden shrinking to his haunches about to vomit, gagging on bile. Boyd picked up the knife in that moment, and Cindy removed the Glock from her belt Hayden never knew she had and trained it on the fallen man.

"Keep him covered," Boyd said, happy to have the upper hand again. He considered himself lucky after taking the risk that it hadn't gotten Cindy killed. He was confident Hayden would want to keep Cindy alive to torture her instead of a quick death. "This bastard deserves a lesson, and I'm about to give it to him."

Boyd hoisted Hayden up by the collar and rammed him against the wall face first. Hayden's shoulder broke through the plaster, his forehead plowing all the way through the thin wall. Hayden slinked to the ground moaning, disoriented. A line of blood streamed from his scalp and split his face. He mewled, talking dreamily and hateful at the same time. "First, it was from my apartment you chased me out of, and then it was prison, and now you want to take away this restaurant. Where do I go next? I'd love to see what you come up with, Broman. What's your plan now?"

"Enough," Boyd insisted, swinging his fist into Hayden's nose straight-on and inspiring a cringe-inducing crack. "No more talking!"

Blood funneled out of both of Hayden's nostrils in a torrent, his eyes half-open and on the verge of unconsciousness.

"You're coming with us, and no more resisting. I'm taking you back where you came from, and I don't care who's doing this shit or why. You're our only way out of here."

Hayden wheezed, trying to clean the blood from his face and only smearing it more. "So they made a deal with you, whoever owns this place? A trade, me for you?"

"I want you to take a walk out that door to the back of the kitchen," Boyd instructed, ignoring his questions. "You'll follow my orders. I'm taking you out of here."

"Whatever you say," Hayden whimpered, struggling to stand up straight but still woozy. "You better keep your eye on me, though. Your girlfriend's turning me on. Brandy didn't particularly do much for me in the south department, if you know what I mean, especially after she died. I still tried though. It was like poking a warm sack when she was alive, and it was poking wet concrete when she was dead—but you, lady, you're *untried meat*."

"Bastard!" Cindy growled, driving the handle of her gun into his temple with a hard crunch. "I'll bite it off before you stick it in me, you sick son-of-a-bitch!"

"He'd like that," Boyd warned, turning his head down in repugnance at Hayden. "I wouldn't respond to his ideas even if it's to negate them."

Without warning, every door and window was suddenly shattered and broken throughout the restaurant. Dust rained from the ceiling, broken panels breaking and striking the floor, a mock caving in of the roof. The florescent lights were smashed, raining down in a glittering electrical performance. Before it went dark, Boyd caught arms and legs dangling and lowering down from the ceiling.

And Hayden had fled into the kitchen.

"He's getting away!" Cindy shouted, pointing at Hayden's receding form. "We have to go after him!"

Boyd stared in awe at the dozens of figures stumbling towards them in the gloom. "We have to reach the back door!" Boyd yelled, taking in the threat. "Follow me, forget him. He's not worth dying for. Hayden can't hide forever, we'll find him later."

As Boyd picked up the M-16, many of the figures poured inside to dismantle Brandy's body. The crackle and pop and snapping of dry bones and tearing of sinews ushered them out of the room quickly. He and Cindy ducked into the kitchen, buying time to muster a plan.

A knife dinged against the metal freezer door beside Boyd's right arm.

Another one of the dead had tried to assassinate him.

"Get down!" Boyd forced Cindy to duck. "It's time we use gunfire as they know we're here. The back door's a straight shot. I'm going to fire at them, and when I do, you run. Anything approaches, you shoot them without hesitation." He skipped the countdown. *"Now!"*

He swung the muzzle of the M-16 from left to right in a fuselage of bullets, mowing the dead down as patches of flesh and starbursts of blood flung onto the kitchen implements and walls.

Another knife was hurled his way, this time striking his left deltoid. He yanked it free with a spurt of blood, shouting in horror. *"Shit!"*

Cindy stood vigil at the back door when she was tackled and dragged outside by mummified hands. Boyd was half-way to rescue her, moving fast, when a mangled woman fell from the ceiling, a set of wooden rafters crashing down and knocking over a cabinet of pots and pans with a deafening crash. The woman bit into Boyd's collarbone, breaking skin and tissue. An abrupt sucking followed the bite and he realized the woman was drinking his blood!

Boyd tugged back her filthy red hair and tore it from its roots. The hair slid off easily, the scalp the texture of seaweed. He drove the woman face-first into the floor then tossed her at the wall, the flaring pain in his clavicle driving his retaliation. She staggered backwards and went limp, falling back to the floor. Boyd stamped his foot onto her blood-caked face repeatedly and knocked her teeth loose, one row coming undone at once, the rest crumbling in brittle pieces. He kept kicking in her face, and soon, the entire head caved in, becoming a turned-in bowl of blood.

Cindy's insistent screams drew him through the door. He saw Cindy scissor-kicking a corpse that grappled her shoulders, the body flailing backwards and bumping into Boyd. He pushed it up against the stone wall lining the back of the restaurant and jammed the muzzle of the M-16 underneath its chin, unceremoniously firing. The skull cap exploded, bursting open, the gray matter spitting out a confetti stream three feet high.

Still, the creature wouldn't die. It crawled to escape with each limb pulling the body in different directions, a stuttering of mixed brain impulses.

Cindy raised her gun. "What the hell are going to do? We don't have Hayden, and we're stuck out here."

The restaurant was consumed by moving shadows and Boyd now saw they inhabited the entire block. The things would kill them if they didn't get moving.

"Boyd, you're bleeding." Cindy was horrified at the amount of blood oozing from his collarbone. "Are you still able to move?"

He removed his prison shirt, the t-shirt under it sodden in red. He wrapped the orange shirt around the wound in a tourniquet. "I'm fine," he replied, masking his condition with confidence. "We'll cut through the woods. We better get moving before too many of them reach us."

They began running, moving down a short slope beyond the road that led into an expanse of dense trees. He turned around and watched the dead board up the windows of the restaurant. Hayden was still inside. Were they trying to box him in? There was no way to be sure, and Boyd was growing dizzier by the second.

"What is it?" Cindy asked, anxious to escape. "Do you see something?"

Boyd nodded and pointed at the restaurant. "They're boarding the place from the outside. I didn't see where Hayden went, but I think he's still in there. And he's our only way out of here."

"The way out is useless if you get yourself killed doing it," Cindy countered, using his previous logic. "And I watched him leave, Boyd. He escaped. The bastard knew where he was going. He's not dead and he's not in there."

"I hope you're right," he said. The darkness obscured the ability to perceive any dangers ahead. "Do you still have your flashlight?"

"No, I lost it," Cindy frowned.

Boyd paused for a moment, and it didn't take long to make his final decision.

"It doesn't matter, let's keep moving."

CHAPTER 11

Hayden pushed through the tables and booths to the entrance of the restaurant. Chains and a padlock rattled from the outside; the double doors wouldn't budge each time he tried to force them open. The windows were boarded up, the pounding of hammers filling his ears, unending doldrums. There was still one window at the west end of the dining area untouched, the glass still solid. Hayden heaved a chair into it, the shatter carrying above the collective chant of the dead, stealing their attention. He sucked in air to collect the wind that was punched out of him thanks to Boyd's beating; he consoled himself by remembering how he'd received worse beatings in prison. Maybe the flesh was too good for any living human being to indulge, he wondered, but he vowed to fight for it and keep fighting.

He climbed through the window, bracing himself for what could be outside. The beings congested the streets. Eyes in the gutters became hands, and then the hands advanced into crawling bodies. Doors in abandoned buildings swung open, spilling the dead forth, but most of them arrived from the perimeter of the streets in droves. The bodies were at work hammering and nailing—dismantling local stores for lumber—to seal up the restaurant.

This was planned. They were waiting for their chance to drive him out, or were they just playing with him all along? Could they have done this the entire time? They were unpredictable, and Hayden was startled at how little he understood them. They could've murdered him, but they chose to keep him alive. Again, there was no answer as to why. If he couldn't master the dead, he would dominate the woman and Broman, he decided. He masticated at the idea of eating live and warm flesh again.

Straight from the bone this time, Hayden, Richard's voice beckoned him, rekindling his wanton lust. *Roast them on a homemade spit. The organs will marinate themselves inside the thoracic cavity.*

He circled to the back of the restaurant after catching Broman and the woman both retreating. They'd fled into the woods adjacent from the residential housing; he barely caught them disappear between a set of trees. He lunged down the hill in pursuit, splashed across a shallow creek, and slowed to a creep. He was yards from the only other living people in the facility.

The woman aroused him; she was untried flesh. All that it required to have her was killing Broman. Hand-to-hand, Hayden would lose, but with a weapon and the element of surprise, his adversary could be slain.

Hayden placed his fingers to his nose, playing into the possibilities of his desires, sniffing the same fingers that had clutched the woman's neck. It smelled of sweat and skin. No perfumes or soap, it was flesh unkempt, the way it would be in nature.

The human body is organic. It decomposes very quickly, Hayden. Disposal shouldn't be a problem. You leave them in a warm and humid place with plenty of air to breathe, and in a week, the flesh will flense itself without effort—a knife through a stick of butter. The bones are different. You can bury those, but they can be found. It's easiest to grind them up. This must be done by hand, sliver by sliver.

He stared through the dark slots between the trees and trained his hearing to catch their footsteps. Thanks to a crunch of leaves and the occasional snap of a twig, it was easy to follow them. He kept up with the two even when the corpses began to pursue him.

CHAPTER 12

Beth Gaines tramped through a muddy creek. The things canvassed the woods again after hours of absence, interested again in killing her. She'd been in the perimeter less than a day.

One night she was sleeping in her bunk in the Santa Monica Correctional Facility, and the next, she woke up in the woods without an explanation. A band-aid with a cotton ball was stuck on her forearm; they'd injected her with a sedative to knock her out.

"Now, Beth, they're considering a transfer, and you won't be in a cell this time," the warden advised her. "You've strangled two inmates, stabbed another with a fork in the throat, and you drowned your last victim in the toilet. You're making this difficult on yourself. We talked about the consequences of your actions. I'm afraid I can't help you beyond this point. That's why I've been hearing talks of sending you to a special place. And you don't want to go there."

Beth cupped her shoulder blade where the crazed lunatic had stabbed her twice with a garden trowel. She'd smashed the creature's face in with a rock, and it had crawled away, mewling in agony. It left behind shards of skull and brain matter, yet it survived.

Heightening her senses, she heard figures skulk about behind trees, close enough she could distinguish them in the darkness.

Beth continued to bound southwards, ratcheting up her speed. They were corralling her, coming at all corners to box her in. She was a rat lured into a trap and any moment the metal bar would snap down and break her neck. Showers with naked women who'd hidden razor blades in bars of soap were easier to combat next to the strange people in the woods she couldn't seem to kill.

She weaved through trees to escape the encroaching sounds, but she turned her ankle underneath a loose rock. She didn't stop to inspect it, for heads bobbed in the darkness, coming closer.

The moment the trap would snap was soon.

She yipped when one leapt overhead from a tree branch.

It was a woman, her dress split in two down the middle to reveal a line of stitches vertically down her belly; she stumbled after Beth. Her face hung loose from the bones, the visage bound to come off any moment. In her haste to reach Beth, the skin flopped onto the ground like a rubber mask. Infuriated by the loss, the woman pounded her fists against the back of Beth's head, knocking her down.

Two more attackers anchored Beth down, twisting her arms behind her back. Beth gagged at the stink of pungent flesh, so rotten, as pieces of them stuck onto her back like rubber glue. The shadows of many dominated her. The faces she caught in her peripheral were pieced and fastened by staples, nails, stitches, screws, all of it a piece of crude handiwork. They were scarier than corpses, maniacal in any light.

The rattle of shifting metal closed in. Two forms barreled towards her with fence wire. Beth thrashed to save herself to no success. The fence was unrolled, and she was placed on top of it and wrapped within the wire.

She was trapped!

In the distance, she could make out what looked like a porch light.

"Someone help me!" she screamed.

A knife was jammed into her stomach to the hilt. The blade exited her back and punctured the ground beneath her. A razor sliced her forehead next. The blade traced the outline of her face. The cutter was the same woman, her face a black skeleton. The cutting edge worked through the fence grates to uproot the skin from her cheeks. Her prison smock was torn open. A pair of scissors snipped her bra off, her breasts exposed. A K-Bar knife sawed the circumference of her breasts and uprooted them from her chest, reaping the fatty rewards. Two scalpels lobbed out her eyes, as her tongue was yanked free by gangrene hands.

They severed her wrists, sawing through them with box cutters. Her dismantling continued until she was blind and helpless to it. The brief second before her final breath, Beth's midsection was torn open and sorted out among the takers.

CHAPTER 13

"*I*nvoluntary manslaughter? I was trying to apprehend him.*"*

"And you crushed him. Samuel Tyson was in two pieces. We had four witnesses at the scene, and one of them has a seat on the city council. She was horrified."

"So what if she saw it happen, it still wasn't manslaughter."

Boyd had been checked into the hospital, kept for a day for observation, and now Detective Gary Finley was escorting him out of the room in cuffs. "Did you see my wife, my kids? He was going to murder us. We've been looking for this bastard for months. He's killed nine people, maybe more. I couldn't just let him go."

"It's bullshit, I know, but it's the law, and it's my job, Boyd."

"Is it 'cause a city councilman's upset."

"No, Boyd, it's the law."

"It wasn't murder or manslaughter. I'm not a bad man. I arrest these assholes. I'm not one of them."

Detective Finley nodded, itching his brow with one finger, routinely engaged with his perp. "I know, I know, but you're under arrest regardless. Emotions and morality aside, Samuel Tyson's dead. You have to account for your actions, Boyd. He had a family. He had a life too, and now he's dead."

Boyd stood with the cuffs on, confused. The man spoke as if reading from a note card. He'd known the detective for four years, and the man was a jokester, and a professional when it counted, but never unnatural or stiff like he was now.

"I guess I have to call a lawyer," Boyd whispered, shaking his head in disbelief. "Imagine what this will put my wife and kids through. My friends. I'm never going to live this down. I thought I was doing the right thing. I wanted to save lives. I didn't mean to run over him, I swear."

The detective stopped before the door where two other officers waited. "There's media crawling out there. Let's put this blanket over you, hide your face, and we'll get you in the squad car. The *vultures are swooping down for their story. You know how it goes."*

"No, I don't know how it goes. God, none of this has gone the way it was supposed to. I wanted him arrested, not dead. I'm not a criminal."

Finley regarded him as a stranger. "Well, the media think you are, as does the DA."

Bypassing a terrible memory and facing a harsher predicament, Boyd thought now to Hayden and the attackers and how they couldn't be seen in the darkness if they decided to follow, and they would follow, he was certain. Cindy kept Boyd standing by holding him like a wounded soldier, the bites to his collarbone keeping him at a stagger.

"I can't keep going much longer," Boyd said without breath. "I'm bleeding too much."

Cindy paused, unable to decide what to do. "How did it bite you?"

"Dug their fucking teeth inside and bit my clavicle." He went to his knees and leaned against a tree. "Listen, you should leave me. I'm only going to get you killed."

She wasn't convinced. "I'm not going to be alone in this. We can find something to bandage you up. I'm sure there's an end to these woods. We can't turn back. They'll be waiting for us."

The mental image of them crawling through the trees and crouching in the dark sparked a new energy. His muscles were exhausted and his mind weary, but a new force took over. Instinct or sheer impulse, he trudged forward again. It was better than being picked and sorted to death or having the blood sucked from his body.

"I know they'll be after us soon," he finally responded to her concerns. "And Hayden, if he's not fighting those things, he'll be right behind us. He wants you, Cindy. He's got a thing for women, but he's never raped them before. I guess he is now. He's starting to do things he never imagined before; this place is a lunacy playground. And those corpses are smarter than we think. Whatever's on their minds, they're extremely capable of anything they want to do."

Boyd struggled to keep pace, his second wind a short-lived burst. There wasn't much left in his body to give and it felt like he'd been without rest for days.

Cindy pointed ahead of them, deeper into the woods. "Hey, look at that!"

Ahead through the collection of trees, a house materialized. Behind it, a lake formed the color of an oil slick, no starlight to make it glimmer. A white picket fence was half-uprooted and sections were missing, resembling a mouth of broken teeth. Boyd imagined the dead things using them as bludgeons. There was no car in the front drive or the opened garage door. The windows weren't broken and the doors were closed. The next question was: Would the place be locked up and was anyone inside?

Together, they hurried up the steps and tried the front door. It opened easily, and what was inside was a surprise to him. The house didn't look like a regular house, the design leading a visitor to think it was a law enforcement building, but it wasn't full of offices and desks, but instead, shambles of what used to be a functioning establishment. No pictures hung in the living room. There was only basic furniture and appliances. The television in the living room picked up no reception. Boyd eyed the floor for blood and found none. He inspected the kitchen and the two bedrooms but didn't come upon evidence of who lived here.

It was no one's house.

"I'll check the bathroom for a first-aid kit or anything else we can use," Cindy said, hurrying down the hallway. "At least I can wash the wound clean with water, if nothing else."

Boyd parted the curtains of a window. He was scared to flip on the porch light, but what was worse; being attacked in the dark or seeing your enemy before they arrived? The door adjacent to him led back out to the woods. How many miles would it take before they arrived at more of the town, or at worst, a concrete wall? He decided to shed illumination around them despite the risk. After he flipped on the inside lights, the woods were visible from what light spilled out through the windows. Nothing moved or approached in the nearby trees.

He rested his M-16 against the wall. The room bothered him, the emptiness a bad omen. Something awful had happened within the house, he could sense it.

He stepped into the kitchen and discovered empty cupboards, the fridge cleaned out.

"The place is ready for condemning," Cindy said, stepping into the room. "Sorry, I didn't find anything in the bathroom. It's empty and there's no plumbing."

"I'm starting to feel a little better," he said, fighting back against the bleak news. "The bleeding's slowed; it didn't help to have my heart rate shooting through the roof earlier."

He peered outside into the backyard. Stacks of chopped wood lined the outside wall, but there wasn't a fireplace in the living room. Three, orange-colored steel barrels were positioned outside next to a compost bin.

"I don't think we have much time," he said. "I want to check the basement and then the backyard. Someone lived here; there has to be a sign of the fact somewhere. I want to know who they were."

"Are you sure you want to go into the basement?" Cindy narrowed her eyes to the cellar door. "Maybe we can get going and get a head start. Forget the house."

"I have to understand what's going on," Boyd insisted. "This place wasn't cleaned out for nothing. Why would it be here if it didn't mean anything?"

He approached the basement door. "You can check the windows for anything heading this way; I won't be long. Just call out at the first sign they're coming."

Cindy handed him her Glock. "Take this, I'll guard the window with your rifle. And be careful, I don't want to be left alone too long. You die, and I might as well consider myself the same."

He opened the door to see a set of wooden stairs leading down into the darkness. There was no light switch, so he walked down the steps and listened hard. Nothing moved, but it wasn't sound that caused his body to lock. The tang of bleach alerted him. Finally, his feet thumped onto the concrete floor. A silver glint attracted him to the center of the room. He reached up and pulled the chain of the overhead light bulb.

INSIDE THE PERIMETER

The contents of the room were painted in a harsh amber hue, cutting his vision down to a quarter of what it used to be. A startle erupted from his throat; the room wasn't empty. Shackles were driven into the walls and floor; he counted two dozen sets. The drain in the center of the room was rusted over. A garden hose lay coiled in the corner. Bleach, a mop and bucket were stored at the foot of the stairs. The strangest items waited on the far wall. He counted eight of them.

Orange barrels.

They were hermetically sealed. A crowbar rested against the wall beside them.

He had to know what was inside the barrels. Three of them were kept in the backyard, and there were more in the basement. Cindy didn't raise alarm, so he assumed it was safe to investigate. Boyd picked up the crowbar next to the barrels and pried the lid from the closest one. "Open, you bastard!"

The *pop* signaled what he immediately regretted. Putrescence emanated from the opening in heavy doses. He couldn't breathe, the malodorous stench burning his sinuses, the ammonia-strong and inducing tears. The barrel shifted when he bumped it, sloshing liquid; the contents were alive, pockets of air bursting and burping with each twist and turn from what lived inside. He listened to steps, like clopping in deep mud, from within the barrel. He began to back away, but before he could, the barrel had tipped itself over.

"*What in the hell...?*"

The floor was coated in a brackish-fluid, an incoming tide rushing in at him. There was an assortment of dismembered limbs and blood: hands clawing at the air, tongues writhing, trying to speak, necks spurting blood, legs thrashing, eyes rolling along the ground like marbles—two of the red-dyed orbs glared up at him—and a torso flopping and unloosing the organs from within the cavity's rotten opening.

The blood drained from his face, and Boyd leaned against the wall to collect his bearings. Then, he rushed upstairs, fleeing from the heinous sight.

Cindy arrived at the edge of the hall, concerned. She recoiled, her face aghast. "It reeks. What the hell's down there?"

Boyd guided her from the cellar door, wishing to have nothing to do with the house anymore. "Don't worry about it. You don't want to know, trust me."

The command was simple, and she understood not to prod, but she still wanted to know the source of the awful smell. "Then at least tell me what's down there."

He checked that she carried the M-16, and he forced her outside through the back door. "First, let's leave. I can't take that smell anymore. We're finding a way out of this nightmare. These dead things are aware and living like we are. They deserve to be put to rest. Whatever life they used to have, it's now desecrated."

"Tell me what that means? I really want to know what was down there."

Boyd stepped down from the back porch and onto the grass, and together, their feet crunched over bits of bones, many of which were blackened and near ash. A barrel was positioned at the end of the cement porch, and Cindy looked inside of it.

"There's a human skeleton inside. Jesus, it's smoldered. It's like a homemade crematorium," she said.

The light from the windows shed enough illumination that Boyd spotted the outline of three figures creeping into the house. "Now we have no choice but to keep going."

They picked up their pace to a jog, Boyd unable to run full-speed. Each impact of his foot jostled his collarbone, adding new levels of pain. They hid deeper into the woods, the shape of the lake and the house growing dimmer. They crossed a wooden fence barrier and faced an onslaught of what could be one or many miles of dense woodland; it was impossible to tell how far they'd have to go to reach the end.

He collapsed out-of-breath. Cindy took the opportunity to find an answer to her previous question. "So, tell me now, what was in the basement?"

Boyd glared at her, stabbed by the question. He shook his head and sighed, digging inside himself to deliver the explanation. "You want to know, *fine*. I'll tell you. There were more of those barrels down there. Inside were severed human pieces. They moved and flailed as if trying to put themselves back together. A pair of eyes stared back at me, Cindy. How's that fucking possible? Doesn't it take the brain to send nerve impulses to limbs for them to move?"

Cindy tightened her grip over the M-16. "This isn't a reality I could ever imagine, but it's what we've got, Boyd. Our minds aren't at fault. This is really happening, and it can kill us. We have to keep moving."

"I know that," he snapped, frustrated by his condition. "I can't run fast, but I'll go."

"Then let's go," she insisted, looking around for signs of pursuit. "I don't see any of them behind us. Maybe we lost them." She frowned, needing a dose of encouragement. "Let's talk about something else to get our minds off of this, something cheerful."

He smiled at her. "Like what?"

"How did you meet your wife?"

Boyd unclenched his body. He turned around and double-checked that none of the figures had caught up with them. He did his best to shake the previous moment of watching the moving pieces come to life within the barrel.

"I went to the police academy in Pittsburgh, and two blocks from the academy was St. Mary's Community College. Karen was studying business there, but later gave it up and became a dental assistant. She got sick of all the fake people, I suppose, you know, people with greasy handshakes and two faces." He wiped his brow and let out a breath.

"We met under interesting circumstances. The first-year cadets at the police academy are forced to pull a prank; you can call it an initiation into law enforcement. The prank was to pose as officers and raise mischief. It's usually performed on people that go to the Catholic school. Anything from giving out fake speeding tickets to the girls or sneaking into their apartments and planting fake evidence; one friend dripped fake blood on an axe and hid it in a girl's closet and later came to the door with a warrant to search the house. My friend had this nineteen year old girl in cuffs accusing her of murder, and then before he took her outside, he finally told her it was all a prank." He smiled at the memory.

"We were ruthless, but nobody ever got in trouble. Greg Eaton, my apartment room mate, told me about Karen and thought I'd like her. So Greg decided for my initiation that I'd type up a fake warrant and search her house. Greg hid in her bathroom, and I posed the concern that I'd been chasing a murderer throughout the campus—'The Keg Killer,' I called him, a man who only murdered girls at keg parties—and he was spotted entering her house. Greg set me up to be a hero, and I rummaged through her rooms in search of the killer. In the bathroom, I was ready to find Greg who held a pony keg and extended it to Karen when he jumped out and shouted, 'Keg Killer!' and it scared the daylights out of her. I got a good slap on the face, but afterwards, she forgave me, and we went on a date, and another and another until I finished the academy. It sounds weird, but not everybody meets like that, so I guess it's special."

Cindy snickered. "God, if the story was coming from someone else, I'd call you a creep."

"A creep with good intentions," he corrected. "I miss her so much, Cindy. She never lost faith in me. She's a good mother. She's doing it all by herself. Her sister's moved in with her for the time being, but she's the full-time mom. I only had a small part in raising them. Their first day of preschool, adding training wheels to bikes, playing Barbie with them. I actually found myself putting on a darn good Oscar winning performance as 'Rock Out' Ken. I built a three story tall mansion from scrap wood; it had a real pool and running track and the whole nine yards. I made the girls keep it in the garage, though. They wanted it in the living room, but I said no."

He sighed. "They were two months into Girl Scouts before I got arrested. Karen's probably selling Girl Scout cookies right now, acting as if everything's okay for their benefit, and next she'll be teaching them about periods and condoms and not to have sex with boys, and then the prom, and then college, and then marriage...*and I could miss it all.*"

Something broke in him, and he clammed up. He lowered his head and allowed the tears to fall. He expected Cindy to freeze up, but she came to him and hugged him.

"You won't miss it. You're too determined. You'll die trying, right? And I'd be locked up in the library alone if you didn't come along. You're a good man in a bad place. I'm glad you're here."

Cindy's words came as a relief, and he asked while wiping the tears from his eyes, "How was your life before you woke up here? Any fond memories?"

"I made good money working at the DA's office. Hell, I dated a lot, too, even before Brett Anderson. They weren't exactly dates; they were more like one-night-get-to-know you-forget-you-tomorrow dates. I let guys buy me drinks and pick my brain. I partied at the Zebra Club on 80's night with my girlfriends. I love bands like *Wham* and *Boy George*. Other memories before this place, well, there's not much to tell. I had two guinea pigs; I'm like you, I built a special enclosure for them; it's a bookshelf with Plexiglas in the front and holes cut in the shelves so that each row is a new level. Francis and Ranu loved it. Other than that, my life wasn't very complicated, and I liked it that way."

"And now it's very complicated," he said. He was comfortable at the pace they were moving, a determined walk. "I'm sure the guinea pigs miss you a lot."

"Jenna, my roommate, is probably looking after them, but I wonder what she thinks about me disappearing."

"The world thinks I'm a dead man, I wonder what story they drummed up about you?"

Cindy smiled. "I was coked out and found in a tub of lard at a cheap motel with a thousand dollars on the bathroom fixture and a line of guys waiting for a piece of the action. Or I accidentally lit myself on fire while cooking homemade chicken. 'Crisco is dangerous,' the coroner would've said, 'and Cindy was a shit cook.' God, it doesn't matter anymore. If we escape, we can expose what's going on in here, and then we'll find a warm beach to hide out on and grow old and drunk. Karen would go with you, I'm sure of it. The fact you're alive would prove someone was lying and you were telling the truth."

"I'm not so sure. The government controls everything. Maybe a small-time news group can cover it, but they'd be shut down. Our story would be lost."

"But with the internet, you can certainly bring heat into this place—really attract attention. There are nuts that eat up the conspiracy theory crap. Boyd, there's masses of paranoid people out there, and this proves they have good reason to look over their shoulders at Big Brother—even if Big Brother consists of piles of rotting corpses. It might take time and work, but our story needs to be told."

"They've convicted me, you're forgetting. It'll be words from a murderer's mouth. They've slandered my name. I'd be worthless."

"But for a ghost to come back from the dead, that's noteworthy, can't you see that? If we escape, it'll be the beginning of the end for those people."

If we get out to tell anyone, Boyd thought.

The conversation boosted Cindy's spirits; vindication served better than self-doubt or fear. It also helped that they hadn't been attacked nor had to fend off the dead beings for a span of time.

Ahead, the woods cleared. They doubled their pace up a hill, and when they reached the top; neither of them could believe their eyes.

CHAPTER 14

Hayden watched Boyd and Cindy exit the abandoned house, their faces plagued by a horrible sight. When they were gone, he stepped up to the circle of rocks with orange barrels placed in the center, located in the backyard. The burned remains of bones were heaped inside the barrels, four bodies in one and another on the ground among hills of ashes and clothing.

"Somebody had a bonfire, but where are the people who did this?" he whispered.

He rushed inside the house, compelled by the question and was quickly disappointed that it was empty. He scanned the refrigerator for food and the cupboards for booze.

"Not a goddamn thing here."

A smell drew him into a hallway and down the cellar steps. At the bottom, a light glowed, begging him to check into the reason why Boyd and Cindy had left the house so abruptly. He worked his way down, pausing on the fifth stair to spy a hand crawling up the steps tier-by-tier, finger-by-finger. The image of the woman he'd cut into pieces earlier that day formed in his mind, the way her eyes glared at him through the plastic-wrap in the freezer. Even without the body, the limbs still harbored life, a will to survive. The determination was astounding, but it was a waste of time to watch for too long, though fascinating. He kicked the hand aside, and it flopped down onto the concrete floor with a splat.

Completing the stairs, blood pooled on the floor centimeters thick. A spittle-ripe laugh exited his mouth to what he found next.

Coming down to meet the sight full-on, he squashed an eyeball underfoot. Taking more steps and shaking off the mess on his shoe, he stared at many pairs of arms and legs intermingled in one corner, rubbing against each other socket-to-socket to no avail. A midsection wedged itself into the corner of the wall as if blocking the opening of its abdomen. Intestines and innards were loose on the ground, a tell-tale trail of pink meat leading to the torso.

He checked underneath the stairs and discovered a row of seven barrels, the contents of the eighth now upended and left strewn on the floor, empty.

"So that's where you came from, huh?" he said to the body parts.

He rushed to the barrels, urged by a burning need to open them. He picked up the crimson-stained crowbar and wedged the coverings from each of the barrels. Hermetic pops followed the masses of blood and body parts flowing; the thick, syrupy mess was near ankle high by the time he was finished. His stomach grumbled in revulsion at the sight; pieces from at least twenty bodies pulsated in the sludge-like ooze. Hands and feet attempted to connect themselves by grinding at the stumps.

The way the parts were severed interested him; the cuts were clean, perfectly executed. Someone had taken the time to dismember the bodies and store them in barrels, but who?

The *clop, thunk, clop, thunk* from upstairs drew alarm as gathering shadows played at the top of the stairs. The front door opened and closed, opened and closed with a wild clatter. Windows were rolled up or smashed through as more figures trespassed. Hayden had wasted time down here, and now they would soon be upon him.

You're too confident, Hayden. Brandy warped your judgment; sex and meat don't mix. You didn't shave the bones like I told you; you jammed them down a garbage disposal at your brother's restaurant. That's how you got caught. And now you're trapped alone with these things in a basement. That wasn't smart, Hayden. The only person you should blame is yourself.

"No, it wasn't smart, Richard!" he barked at no one. "Not at all. *I know—I know—I know! I fucking goddamn know!*"

Hayden had nowhere to escape, the walls spinning and closing in on him, the basement a living trap. The cellar stairs were the only exit, and he'd have to face the attackers head-on.

He crouched underneath the stairs, out-of-time. Figures trudged down the steps, their legs visible through the slits in the wood. He clutched onto the crowbar, ready to fight. The basement filled with bodies, and they stumbled about the room, bending down and sorting through the body parts like customers at a yard sale. Energetic, many of them pushed and shoved through each other for a better look at the selection. A woman unsheathed a knife, the blade tucked in the flesh of her hip in a makeshift carry-case. She sawed her wrist off and then picked up a different hand—one bigger and stronger—a man's. The woman held it fast to her severed arm and began weaving it with a spool of thread taken from her breast pocket.

The cellar stairs were now empty; this was Hayden's chance to escape. He crawled up between two steps and began to climb.

He shut the door and threw the bolt, locking it. Sharp thuds immediately followed, their feet climbing the stairs and then fists pounding the door in answer to his getaway. The small bolt wouldn't stand up against their efforts for long and he wouldn't make the same mistake twice. He stomped down the hallway, and when he thundered into the kitchen, he was struck on the back of the head.

Hayden collapsed against the filthy tiles, clutching his skull as his vision danced before his eyes. A towering man with his skin intact except his face—it had holes in it, like insects had bored through the flesh—stared him down, clutching a broken tree branch. The animated corpse threw the limb down, planning to execute a new directive. It happened too fast to prevent, and Hayden was helpless until it ended. A scalpel slashed his cheek just after Hayden's head was pinned down by a boot. A square hunk of flesh was uprooted and peeled back carefully. Hayden watched in awe, shouting in pain as the man fastened the square bit of skin to his face by using staples taken from his pocket.

"Son-of-a-bitch!" Hayden barked, rising up and kicking the dead man's chest, sending the assailant flailing backwards into the living room. "I take your flesh, you don't take mine!"

Without a weapon, his words were nothing but wasted air. The basement door crashed open, the frame smacking the floor, wood splinters flying in all directions. Hayden retreated through the back door, reeling in terror.

Looking about past the lake, he'd watched Broman and the woman disappear past it only moments ago, and he now followed them in the general direction.

His face bled profusely, and he yanked back the sleeve of his shirt and pressed it against his wounded cheek. It wasn't deep enough to remove muscle tissue, but the contours of his teeth were traceable through the wound.

Hayden challenged the night. "This isn't over!"

He was hungry now.

You eat too much, Hayden. Alfred Packer was obese. He killed miners and enjoyed their flesh so much that he killed the entire group he led. A fat man leading an expedition to find his party's remains, can you imagine what people were thinking? Alfred was guilty as sin and yet he didn't serve much prison time. I guess you didn't either, Hayden. Something will always get in the way of your happiness, though, but you can have your good thing again. Take it back. Kill Broman and the girl; show them you're the strongest. Find a new place to reside, and then start anew. This is the greatest place for you to be and don't let anyone take that away. This place is precious and worth dying for.

Richard's voice incited confidence.

Hayden stalked the woods at full-speed.

It wasn't long before he came upon his prey once again.

CHAPTER 15

*B*oyd stood side-by-side with Karen's father, Jack Fuller, who was swinging an axe, chopping up a fresh batch of firewood for their cabin. He'd driven out to New Haven, Colorado, for the week with Karen, the second time meeting her parents, but now that he'd dated Karen for almost three years and wanted to propose to her, he decided this was the best time to ask permission. He wasn't sure how Catholics viewed permission, but he thought it was a kind gesture he should commit to for the sake of a good start. Family support was key, he'd read in some self-help book a long time ago.

Jack was a retired firefighter, barrel-chested with the belly of a lineman. He wore his black thermal coat and hood, adamant about splitting the logs into smaller pieces. Another swing, another whoosh of air, another crack and splinter and break, the man was on his way to accomplishing his goal. They'd been standing in the backyard for fifteen minutes, Boyd unable to ask the man permission, so he stared out into the woods, the trees nothing but black shells without leaves, everything cased in three feet of snow. That's why he was grateful when the man read into his vexed expression.

"Something seems to be on your mind, Boyd. What's wrong?"

Jack was a kind man, but this being his second visit, it was a far cry from knowing if he was accepted into the family or not. Sucking in a breath and only getting frigid cold air, he got it over with, and asked, "I want to marry your daughter, sir, and I'm asking you for permission."

I hope I did that right. Shit, he thought.

Jack placed the axe on a tree stump, and he stared off into the distance. He said nothing. Agonizing minutes crept by without a sound, and then Boyd turned to make eye contact. He went stiff, noticing tears fall down the man's eyes. Jack stifled a sob with his gloved hand to his mouth, then Jack gave him a hug from the side, the classic one-arm embrace.

"Boyd, I barely know you, but Karen has told me so much about you. Enough to know you make her happy. You're of fine stock, too. Cops and doctors, I like them. And don't forget the firefighters. All of them are in good with me. Of course you have my blessing, Boyd, welcome to the family." Jack was welling up with tears, but he worked through it, and said, "My daughter's growing up." He patted Boyd hard on the back. "She's found herself a great catch."

The man shook Boyd's hand heartily, and then he made an announcement, looking back out into the empty forest, delivering the prolific words to the empty miles of snow. "We're going to have the biggest Catholic wedding in the history of Catholicism."

Boyd felt a pang in his chest, and he spoke softly, "I, uhm, I'm not Catholic, but hey, I'm game for anything."

A parking lot greeted Boyd and Cindy at the top of the small hill. There were no vehicles, but instead patches of broken glass, random oil spots, mufflers, and parts of vehicles were spread out, resembling a raided salvage yard. The chaos didn't make sense, but for the moment, it didn't matter. Safety and shelter was top priority. Boyd studied the three-story tower less than a quarter mile away. It was a hospital.

"You think any of them are inside?" Cindy was skeptical of the haven, though studying his wound, the decision was made. "At least we should be able to find something to bandage you up with in there."

"It better not be like the house. This town hasn't been lived in by anyone recently. The set-up of this place keeps confusing me. How could you hide an entire town and get away with it?" he asked.

"No telling. It's locked up government property, and perhaps this is also a no-fly zone. So, are we going inside? I don't see any other choice," she said.

They cleared the distance from the parking lot to the hospital by jogging in nine yard spans, Boyd resting when he needed to. The windows weren't covered, and the entrances weren't blockaded.

INSIDE THE PERIMETER

"Keep your eyes open," he reminded Cindy.

The entrance was a revolving door with every glass pane broken. They stepped through and edged their way into the entrance of an emergency room, crunching on the broken glass at their feet. The waiting area was reduced to upturned tables and chairs.

They slowed as they crossed the MRI wing. The end of the hall was a square floor plan of rooms, the center a nurse's station which was nothing but wreckage. Dried blood specked the wall in jets and spatters. Again, there were no bodies. In Room 4, they came upon a gowned torso on a stretcher. Underneath the tatters, the bones were picked clean. Cindy sorted through a metal cart on wheels and removed a roll of gauze and a bottle of peroxide.

"Come here," she ordered him. "I always wanted to be a nurse. My parents were in the medical field. My mom delivered babies, and my dad slaved away in the emergency room dealing with car accidents, food poisoning, and God knows what else. That's the only field of work you're truly respected in. For those that can save lives, what job can top that? But my parents said hospitals were now more about making money, and it wasn't fun anymore; the CEO fat cats were ruining the caregiver role and turning healthcare into one big collection agency. Well, then maybe people like Mother Theresa are more respectable; I guess kindness to the sick goes a long way, maybe even greater than the medicine itself."

"Save your kindness, painkillers are better, something I'd kill for right now," he said.

"I'm sure there's a pharmacy wing in this place."

Boyd propped a chair upright and rested on it, then braced himself for the peroxide. Cindy uncovered the make-shift bandage and winced at the sight of the wound. He turned, and the bite marks were inches deep, the exposed muscle tissue underneath pulsing.

"That maniac sure took a chunk out of you." Cindy held the bottle up to him. "Get ready, I'm sorry."

Boyd clutched the bottom of the chair. "Just do it."

Pouring it over the wound, the sizzle began to burn as it cleaned it, red foam rising up around the edges. Gritting his teeth, he managed to grunt, "I'm not sure if it's good to use peroxide on such a deep wound, but in our case, it's better than nothing."

Cindy wrapped the wound in gauze. "Now how about finding you—us—some drugs?"

"Right on," he concurred. "Pills please, lots of 'em."

They exited the emergency room and cleared a pair of back hallways through Radiology and the ICU. The rooms were in the same condition: beds upturned, respirators broken, and IV's strewn on the floor. Blood covered the wall tiles in every room. The elevators worked, and Boyd was surprised. "I've taken it for granted that the power's been on everywhere." He turned over the idea. "If the town's dead and these corpses are hanging around, then why give them juice?"

"Another question without an answer." She hit the third floor button and immediately regretted it. "What if those things are in the elevator?"

They aimed their guns at the silver door.

Ding.

The elevator was on the floor above them and it now returned to the floor at Cindy's press of the button. Whoever last used it, they were on the floor above them. He pushed Cindy back when the door parted, and gratefully, it was empty.

"This is all too much," Cindy said. "I've aged ten years since being in this place. Is my hair white yet?"

"It can't be any worse than spending forty hours a week behind a desk, can it?"

She chuckled a little. "I don't know about that. Or wait, I do. I really do!"

They entered the elevator, the doors closed, and it lifted, a strange floating sensation filling Boyd's stomach. In seconds, the door opened and the moment was over.

The front desk was stained in blood. Three monitors were shattered, each belonging to sonogram machines. The concave mirror mounted, on the wall near the ceiling at the corner was cracked in spider-web lines from a bullet hole; other bullet holes riddled the walls in countless zigzagging lines. Shell casings slid under his feet. The blinds were up in the newborn observation room, the plastic incubators empty inside.

"This hasn't been used as a real hospital for a while," Boyd mused. He ran his finger down a baby respirator. "It's covered in dust. This used to be a normal hospital, but most of the gowns and clothing are military colored."

"Then what's the point of this place? Why would the government take over a hospital?"

Boyd shook his head. "I have no idea."

A room at the end of the hall flagged his attention. It was wide open unlike the others that were closed and locked. He hurried to it, the muzzle of the M-16 raised. "Hello, anyone in there?"

Cindy was behind him. "What are you doing?"

"The elevator was on this floor. Someone has to be up here. Maybe they know something."

"Or they're like us and don't know a damn thing."

He directed his attention to a janitor's closet. Blood slicked the floor, but it wasn't congealed.

"This is fresh," he noted. "Maybe a few hours old."

Cindy crouched, plucking an orange prison uniform from the tiles, the material sodden and dripping in red. "This is like yours, Boyd. Other people *are* being thrown into this place. Jesus, this is like an operation, and someone's allowing it to thrive."

"And criminals are up on the chopping block. The government thinks they deserve to be killed in this place, maybe."

She leaned against the wall, flustered and out of answers. "We should keep searching then. If someone's here, they'll hear us. Living or dead, we'll have to deal with it. Either way, we need antibiotics for your arm and food supplies."

"I guess it's our only option," Boyd agreed.

Cindy hit the elevator button again. "Why not start with the bottom floors and work our way back up?"

Boyd stepped inside when the doors opened, but then stopped as a phone rang inside a nearby room. They both looked at each other, and he rushed to pick it up. "Hello? This is Broman, hello?"

"Yes, it's me, hello, Mr. Broman."

Boyd recognized the gruff voice from before at the police station. "How do you know I'm here? How come there are no outgoing lines?"

"Isn't that obvious?" the speaker replied, giving him a wry laugh. "I can't have you phoning someone and revealing our secret.

It's no one's business what we're doing here." Pausing, "Have you apprehended Hayden Grubaugh yet?"

"We were attacked by more of those people, and we got separated, but he's alive, and if we don't find him first, he'll be after us soon."

"The offer still stands, Mr. Broman." The voice was smooth and consoling. "You want out of there and your old life back then you bring Hayden to the front perimeter gate where we dropped you off."

"What about my friend?"

"Yes," he lowered his voice, trailing off for a moment. "We've seen her with you. She doesn't matter."

That made Boyd think. *Seen her with me?* Then they must have cameras set up or satellite surveillance.

Displeased, Boyd growled into the phone, "You can't keep this a secret forever."

"Oh, but we have and for a damn good reason. You know what trouble this would cause if we didn't have the perimeter set up around the town. Countless people would be dead."

"That doesn't give you the right to throw innocent people in here, criminals or not, and send them to their deaths."

The man ignored his concerns. "You do as you're told, and you'll be rewarded."

The phone went dead.

"Who was it, Boyd? Who were you talking to?"

He placed the phone back onto the receiver. "I don't know, but it's the man who told me to capture Hayden earlier. He must be in charge of this place. He didn't answer any of my questions except that he'd said he'd seen us together. That means they're watching us somehow. I still say we use Hayden as leverage, and maybe we can work out a deal or use him as a hostage, for leverage."

"Won't those things follow us wherever we go?"

"Yeah, but that could work to our advantage."

Boyd recalled the drive to the facility. The barbed wire, the watchtowers, the multiple fences to cross, it would be impossible to ford. Hayden was their only leverage, and with him, they could make progress.

INSIDE THE PERIMETER

"They won't let us leave," Cindy sighed, turning it over in her head. "Hundreds are dead in this place, how do you expect anyone else to care about two more people? I've seen those concrete barriers surrounding this place, and that means security is everywhere."

"Yeah, I've seen it myself. Barbed wire fences and watchtowers, mostly, don't know if they're manned or automatic with sensors. Hayden is our weapon against them, though. They need him, and we'll have him."

He stepped away from the phone; he knew the man wasn't calling back. "Let's go search the basement. That phone call sure as hell didn't turn up anything new."

Cindy checked the magazine for the M-16. "Not many bullets left."

"The Glock has three rounds, and I have a grenade."

"Are you planning on using it in here?" Cindy laughed, denying the notion. "You'll get us both killed."

"Not if I throw it far enough," Boyd countered, joking, "and we duck."

They stopped talking after entering the elevator, and a few moments later, they arrived on the basement level.

CHAPTER 16

Hayden sprang from the house, the corpses pouring from every direction, hundreds of feet crunching through brush and leaves in pursuit of him. The dead carried their re-pieced and reworked bodies in determination. He raced up the hill that marked the end of the woods, evading them, though only yards separated him from his aggressors. Broman and the woman were held up in the hospital, the tower in the near distance; there was no sign that labeled the facility, but he noticed the rows of wrecked ambulances with their engines, tires, and doors removed. Blood speckled the parking lot mingled with glass, car doors, bumpers, and government-issue license plates.

The hospital was the only clear place to seek shelter.

He cleared the revolving door entrance easily, the glass of the doors missing and strewn on the floor, but one of the corpses latched onto his foot to yank him back outside. He seized his attacker by the shoulders and dragged it inside with him.

Hayden studied the room for a weapon, and settling for what he could find, he heaved a chair at the horrid face over and over again until it caved in with a hollow squish. Black and red muck oozed from the figure's nose and eyes, caramel-thick, and the eyes spit out of their sockets to unleash a noxious tide of cranial matter.

The rest of them would be inside soon, but Hayden came up with a wildcard plan. Searching the dead man's pockets, he found a box cutter. The corpse twitched, its mouth clinking together as its broken teeth slithered from the gums and broke apart on the floor. Hayden dragged the confused corpse down the hall and into a nearby bathroom. Thinking fast to humor a wicked notion, he dragged the box cutter's blade up and down the edges of the man's face, tearing and excising the ends, until a mask-layer could be peeled from the skull.

Hayden continued the extraction, slicing through the scalp and tracing around the back of the head to remove the man's hair, which was a mane of long black tufts of greasy and matted strands.

When he was finished, he carried the pieces to the mirror over the sink. He fashioned the new face onto his own like it was a Halloween mask, the wad of hair glued onto his head by blood and sticky tissue, becoming a messy toupee. Gaining new motivation to stalk without fear, he returned to the corpse, excising strips and flanks of skin from the dead man's arms and then slapping them over his own to complete the metamorphosis.

You've become one of them, Hayden.

"Yes," Hayden rasped with vindication. "I *am* one of them."

Hayden snuck into the hall and spotted the first of the animated corpses rampaging through the revolving doors. They averted their attention from him immediately, seeing one of their own, and Hayden trudged down the emergency room hallway, wondering if he should run or stay put. They lurked towards him, but this time, it wasn't in pursuit.

You are their leader. Guide them to Broman and the girl. Feast among your brethren. This place is yours to thrive.

The elevator dinged. Someone was heading to the basement; it had to be Broman and the woman. Hayden stormed the stairs, using them two at a time. The dead followed him, the door not closing as they kept filing through in a continuous line.

Despite your overzealous nature, you're smart, Hayden. Not everyone's born with that intuition, and not everyone can learn it. You can get away with anything, my boy, as long as you think before you act, Richard's voice praised him.

The stairs winded down to a door, and when he opened it, he came upon two options. One direction would take him to a room filled with industrial-sized washers and dryers, the other a straight shot to the boiler room. The bodies piled up at his back, studying the area with their eyes. Some were already skulking ahead of him, taking an initiative of their own, their hunkered forms tromping towards the boiler room.

A red blinking light caught his eye further down the dim hall. Hayden slipped into the laundry room and waited for them to pass. He might be cunning, he reasoned, but he was also smart enough not to take any unnecessary risks.

And the blinking red light topped his concerns.

A security office to his right, the door kicked in, had been broken into with every monitor shattered and the main console splattered in blood.

No victim inside.

The blinking red light changed to green; it was the lock mechanism of a doorway. He edged closer to the door. He read the biohazard sign, and then he dove behind a trash can when he caught Broman and the woman appear at the doorway. The door in front of them had opened on its own and now the corpses had returned from their search of the boiler room and were closing in.

Hayden waited for the two to cross the threshold.

And then he followed.

CHAPTER 17

Boyd and Cindy faced a hallway with two directions to take. Each darkened side could be occupied by anything. He turned to look at her; Cindy's face had lost its hue and her eyes gleamed in terror. Her mouth trembled, and she bit her lip to steady it. "I...I think we're fresh out of time to sightsee."

"Hold on, we're not found yet," Boyd said as he surveyed the hall ahead of them. "Let me run down it and I'll tell you what I find."

"Make it quick," she begged him. "I hate being alone."

Boyd sprinted to his destination, and he had two doors to choose from, so he picked the one to his left. It was a large storage closet with mop heads, bleach, and other cleaning supplies. The other door revealed a boiler room still operating. It roared and gasped with jets of steam exiting rusted pipes. He traced the area for an exit and failed to locate one. Making a decision, he fell back and returned to Cindy, who was relieved to see him again.

"I hear them coming, Boyd. What're we going to do?"

There was only one other direction to go, and he prayed it was a way out. He clutched Cindy's wrist, and she gasped at how hard he pulled her along. They crossed a security office, but the monitors didn't work, the screens shattered and the console slathered in blood. Next, they crossed a biohazard room, the inside of the small storage unit filled with red barrels to store dirty needles, blood, and contaminated linens. A flashing light drew Boyd's attention to the end of the recess, one he hadn't noticed before. The light was coming from a keypad next to a security door. He ran to it, trying the door, and just as he thought, it was locked. A security camera was mounted above the door, the red light blinking at them.

"Who do you think is behind that door?" Cindy asked.

He shook his head. "There's no way of knowing from here."

Cindy looked up at the camera and called out, "Help! I can hear them coming. Show some compassion. This place is full of them; *let us in!*"

Boyd patted her shoulder, trying to reconcile her anger. "They won't listen. There's probably no one back there; the rest of this place is empty. No one's alive. We have to turn back and find a place to hide."

To the left of them, another hallway waited unchecked with a bright exit sign at the end.

Suddenly, the door to the emergency fire stairs was thrown open and mass of bodies poured forth.

"Get on your knees and crouch down." Boyd kept his eyes glued to them. The corpses paused, unsure of which way to go. One of them took the lead down the corridor into the boiler room, and many of them soon followed.

How long would it be until they decided to check this way, also, he wasn't sure, but it bought them time, if only a few moments. "Watch them. Maybe we can lock them in a room or something."

Boyd realized the ridiculousness of the notion as soon as he said it. They'd break through or crawl out of the ceiling to the other side like at the restaurant. Dozens already occupied the boiler room and more kept adding to the numbers with each passing second.

"I'm leaving," Cindy insisted, her body pointed in the direction of the exit. "What're we waiting for?"

"I don't know. I had hopes for this place. We didn't find any supplies or more living people."

Then the door clicked and the red light turned to green.

Boyd opened the door on impulse, not a decision. He lunged inside with Cindy following at his back.

Hayden watched Boyd and Cindy open the door and go through it, and he saw that the green light was still on.

The dead beings noticed the two enter as well. They were halfway to Hayden, clamoring for the escaping couple, when Hayden lunged to the entrance and beat them there, hoping he'd cross the threshold in time. Reaching out and leaping in a final dash, he snagged the door handle and pushed it back open, forcing his way inside. The moment the door closed, the light turned back to red, trapping the dead on the other side.

CHAPTER 18

It wasn't another corridor behind the security door, but instead, a short landing punctuated by a new set of long stairs. Boyd and Cindy clacked down the two flights and cleared enough distance that they slowed to a walking pace, tired.

Boyd smiled at her. "We're safe now, I suppose. This has to mean something. Somebody unlocked that door. Somebody's here helping us."

"Yeah," Cindy agreed, "but are they friendly or one of the bastards who put us in here?"

Boyd considered the question, but in their position, there wasn't much they could do about it. "We're closer to an answer, and that's about all we can expect for now," he said. "Just keep your eyes open. We've survived so far. You and I make a great team."

"Yeah, scared and terrified, we're a great duo." She listened to the pounding of footsteps from the floor above them. "I wonder what they're doing up there now? Are they waiting for us outside or are they plotting for a way to pick the lock?"

Boyd weakened at the thought. "We need to relax. Those bastards are really taking their toll on us. Every break we can get, we better take it."

"You must've been a good cop," Cindy said, smiling at him. "You're sensible under pressure."

"And you must've been an awesome secretary the way you hold that Glock; I wonder how you handled your stationary."

This time she laughed. "God, you're ridiculous."

They ascended another set of stairs, the din above them fading. The end of the stairs brought them to a new security door. A camera was poised above them like a beacon. The red light blinked at them, indicating no access.

Boyd looked at Cindy. "What do you think?"

"Someone's behind that door," she said and looked up at the camera. "Why aren't you letting us in? Face us, huh?" She stamped her foot. "God, what a jerk."

The door lock clicked, as if in response to her words.

The green light blinked, and they opened the door and shot through to the other side, slamming the door behind them. A long hall marked with white tiles and sky-blue painted walls was on both sides. There were also more rooms. There were no office numbers or signs marking each one, however. Boyd considered them private chambers, and the faint, dead smell hovering in the air confirmed that whatever those things were behind them, they'd been here, too.

"Finally, we're getting somewhere," he said.

"It smells like bleach...*and them*," Cindy said, sneering at the corridor. "I hope none of them are hiding down here."

"You think they're able to scheme that well?" Boyd shook his head. "Lure us down here and have more of them waiting for us, is that what they might be doing?"

"That's what they did at the restaurant." She turned her eyes up to the ceiling. "Dropped from the paneling, listening for the right moment to attack, yeah, I think they're smart enough to do it."

Halfway down the hall, they came upon a restroom and a break room with two vending machines. Inside, there was a hot plate on a table and a set of pans drying on a towel next to the sink. A pot of coffee brewed on the counter hotplate, not more than a few hours old.

Boyd's suspicions were confirmed. "Someone's definitely living down here."

Back in the main hallway, they found a room with double doors and tinted windows. The doors were secure, but Boyd kept trying them anyway. "Everything's locked tight."

"And it's locked up for a reason," a voice called out from the end of the hallway. They both turned and glared at the man. He walked forward, his lab coat flapping behind him. "I'll ask you to step away from that door, please. No entry means no entry."

The man had the look of a mad scientist. He was balding with a gray comb-over poorly disguising his scalp. Dandruff speckled his hair. His lips were chapped. His silver-rimmed glasses hung from a

INSIDE THE PERIMETER

chain over his chest like a necklace. He blinked every two seconds, a nervous tick. "You two need to follow me immediately."

Boyd caught the bulge from the doctor's hip, a holster housing a gun. He glanced at Cindy and agreed. "Yeah, under the circumstances, that sounds fine."

Three rooms down, the doctor opened a door and ushered them inside. He locked it behind them, bolting it secure. Boyd was taken back by the large control room, the row of six television screens and ten smaller monitors lined across the bottom.

The doctor sat in front of a keyboard, issuing a grunt. "One of them followed you inside. But that's okay; it's better than the whole mess of 'em. Now keep your eye on the center screen, please."

The camera's eye zoomed in on a figure skulking down the hallway and sneaking into the break room. The doctor pressed a console button, and the door shut. The thing pounded its fist against the door, caught off-guard.

"Ha, trapped him!"

Boyd was puzzled at the dead man who kept trying to batter down the door to no avail. "That man, he's not moving like the other dead people."

"I've been watching you two throughout the entire building," the doctor said, his eyes not leaving the screen. "You've handled yourselves well. Many people make it this far, and then they die. It's too easy to get trapped, but you two kept your heads together. This man has been following you the entire time."

The doctor typed on the console and flipped a switch. The camera focused harder, and it wasn't until Boyd studied the dead skin mask and the flesh plastered onto its arms and neck that he realized it wasn't one of the dead attackers... it was Hayden.

"We have him where we want him now," the doctor added, whooping once. "We're saved!"

Cindy's eyes didn't leave the monitors. She breathed faster at the sight of hundreds of the dead pounding on the door upstairs. "Are they ever going to give up and leave?"

"Oh, sure," the doctor reassured her. "It might be a week or two, but it'll happen. Someone else comes along and distracts them sooner or later."

Boyd couldn't remove his eyes from the screens. "Can you explain this mess? How are these people still alive?"

"I'll explain that in a little bit," the doctor said, turning to look at them face-to-face. "My name's Henry Glover, Dr. Glover. I'm a surgeon and biochemist."

"My name's Boyd, and this is…"

"…Cindy, I know. I'm notified every time someone is thrown into this dreadful place. You're our special case, Officer Broman, but I'm afraid your usefulness is about over."

"My use for who?" Boyd's body tensed, and he closed in on Dr. Glover. "What do you know?"

Dr. Glover closed his eyes and sucked in a weary breath. "I'm on your side, Boyd. This project should've been shut down years ago, even during its initial conception. I'm the only researcher that has survived, and I'm the only one who's still here."

"You're all alone?" Cindy asked, concerned the man couldn't help them. "How come?"

"It's been that way for more than ten years now." The doctor crossed his arms. "Three of us were left to find a solution to this problem, a way to stop those fiends you've been fighting and running from. Now, mind you, when I say 'stop,' I mean 'control them'. Master them. Use them. They rot out, but it's a self-perpetuating cycle; the new ones use the old as scrap like we use transplants and transfusions to renew our bodies. My colleagues, Dr. Kurt Jamison and Gloria Nichols, both died in that room I told you is off limits. I won't tell you how they died, I don't want to alarm you, but I took care of it before it grew out of control. The root of our problems is in that damn room, and I'll reiterate, don't ever go inside it. Not if you want to stay alive."

"What's in there, Pandora's Box?" Boyd could only imagine what the doctor was withholding from them. "We're here, and according to those bastards knocking on our door, it's going to be a while before we escape. Hayden's locked up tight and we're safe for the moment. It's okay to tell us. So speak up, please, Dr. Glover."

"You won't be safe for long." He couldn't look them in the eye. He cursed in a whisper, his frustration obvious. "It's not about me. Please take care to remember that when I tell you what's going on, but first, let's have a drink. You two have been through hell."

CHAPTER 19

Hayden cleared the door at the bottom of the stairs before it closed again, but his shirt was snagged, and he ripped a sizeable piece from the fabric before fully entering, the door clapping shut behind him. He followed Boyd and Cindy and remained undetected. From above, he could hear the dead rampaging; they knew he was down here. *They want to follow their leader. They'll follow you anywhere.*

Every entry had been locked down the hall...so far. Bleach and embalming fluid saturated the air. Hayden's uncle, Ned, had worked as a funeral embalmer, and Hayden was given a tour of the place when he was ten years old. Uncle Ned babysat him whenever his father traveled on business, selling vacation homes, as Hayden was too young to be left alone. He learned how a trocar catheter sucked blood and fluids from the organs by a puncture through the midsection, and he witnessed how the jugular and femoral arteries could let out the blood. The rest of the work was cleaning the body with antibacterial soap and applying make-up. He'd viewed three dozen naked cadavers pre-funeral before he was eleven years old.

"*They're skin and bones like us,*" Uncle Ned would say as he thrust the needle to insert embalming fluid through the femoral artery. "*Death is the great equalizer. Rich or poor, when you're dead, we're finally all in the same boat.*"

The flesh adhering to his skin itched. He wondered if anyone living caught him down here would mistake him for one of those things. Concerned he would be shot on sight, he was about to peel the flesh off when he noticed a door was ajar. It was a break room. He stepped inside without hesitation, and after taking three steps, the door snapped shut behind him.

"What the hell?"

He didn't detect anyone in the hallway. So who could've closed the door? He tried the doorknob and it was locked. He pounded on the door and eventually gave up. He studied the room, seeing it was occupied by two vending machines, a hot plate, and cookware.

Curious, he rummaged through the cupboards. Canned goods stocked the shelves, and he opened a large freezer filled with beef and chicken.

The refrigerator was full of cans of beer and bottles of wine. He opened a bottle of Pinot Noir and slugged three gulps. He continued drinking until half of the bottle was finished, then plopped down into a chair with his head buzzing. That's when he observed the camera stationed above the door.

"You like watching me?"

He unzipped his pants and pissed on the floor, making a show of it, but he immediately regretted it.

The tang of urine in the open air was potent.

Inspire fear, Hayden, and you're immortal. You tore a man's throat out with your teeth in prison, now you're pissing on the floor. Nobody will go near you. You're masked in dead skin; you're one of them, now. Keep it up, Richard's voice said.

He missed his friend, an influence that had bettered his life. Richard disappeared one night, and Hayden never found out what happened to him. He'd been nineteen at the time, two months from turning twenty. Richard's last words to him were, *"I'm going to Hooker Boulevard; I'll bring back food."*

Richard didn't return. Hayden waited inside his apartment, and by two o'clock the next afternoon, he knocked on the man's door to no answer. He used the key given to him and searched Richard's quarters. He sorted through the man's bed, rolled in his sheets and enjoyed the smell of him—cologne and shaving cream; a fatherly smell—and counted the plastic bags in the man's freezer, the flesh he'd saved up over the years. *"When the police smarten up and I have to stop, I won't be out of a meal,"* Richard had explained about the meat supply.

The next morning, he woke alone. He lingered about Richard's apartment for two more days, and even then, he cased the neighborhoods and Hooker Boulevard for his mentor, and to this day, Richard remained missing.

Hayden balled up his fists to the camera, horrified at the remembrance, pissed off at his entrapment, he unleashed a pleading caterwaul. *"Let me out, you bastards!"*

His demand rang throughout the room with a metallic echo, the words reaching no one. He raced to the trashcan, clutching it in both hands to throw it. "I'll break your fucking camera, how 'bout that?"

He was too drunk to maintain a solid grip on the trashcan, though, and when he flung it, it veered awkwardly into the wall, missing its target. The plaster broke and formed a divot in the shape of a **V**.

Hayden traced the break with his index finger along the crack, seeing the thin lining of wood that separated him from another room.

With a smile on his lips, he picked up the trash can once again.

CHAPTER 20

Dr. Glover invited Boyd and Cindy to a recreational area comprising of a ping-pong table, pool table, dart board, pinball machine, and Pac-Man arcade game. A treadmill was folded up on the far wall alongside a set of free weights and a bench press. There was a counter, and behind it, a tall standing shelf full of hard liquor. He removed a bottle of Southern Comfort and three highball glasses, and poured each of them a strong drink.

"Here you go," he said with a smile.

Boyd slugged a burning mouthful, but his focus remained on the doctor. "So you're on our side, huh? Then what is all of this about, Dr. Glover?"

Cindy finished the entire glass in one gulp. "Fill 'er up again. My nerves are shot. By the end of this, if there's an end, I'll need a nerve transplant."

Dr. Glover eyed her tenderly. He hadn't had human contact for a long time, and Cindy was an attractive woman. The doctor's eyes couldn't leave her face. "You're doing fine, my dear. You two are troopers. It's a shame they want to kill you."

"Who wants to kill us? Those things out there?" Cindy's relief vanished.

Dr. Glover reassured them quickly, realizing his error. "I shouldn't have put it that way. I'll start by with telling you this. Chris Stapleton, a former member of homeland security, ex-CIA operative, and current commander of the Green's End Project—what surrounds you, this town—is the man who's been calling you on the phone, Boyd. He's in charge of keeping the facility locked down. The military guards this place for miles, and we're twenty-five miles from any civilian towns in all directions. Commander Stapleton wants Hayden for questioning, as more of his bodies have been found—something you've been told, I assume. It'll be a private interrogation, and I imagine the tactics will be brash. No one cares for the rights of a dead man."

"I'm a dead man," Boyd countered, staring him down sharply. "Does anyone care about my rights?"

"I do," Dr. Glover insisted, honest in his answer. "You're my way out of here."

Boyd was confused. "What do you mean 'I'm your way out'?"

Dr. Glover stole a nip from his glass, and his tired eyes glowed with a flicker of hope. He removed a necklace from under his shirt and showed them a red plastic card on the end. "This door unlocks the front gate. I stole it from one of Stapleton's idiots, his 'body shields' I like to call them. Stapleton's a coward, and that's why he's not stepping into the complex or has yet to for the entire ten years we've kept this operation running. The perimeter is rigged with cameras. He's going to send his 'body shields' into this facility to pick up Hayden once he was captured. They're on their way now that we have him locked up. It means there's no more use for you, Boyd. But it buys us some time."

"You're getting ahead of everything," Boyd complained, demanding the doctor slow down. "Why do those things out there even exist? How do they exist?"

Dr. Glover braced himself to give a detailed explanation. "Do you remember Chernobyl and the nuclear leak? They sent people inside to shovel out the pieces of wreckage protected with nothing but a thin body suit and a paper face mask. I guess this was before people understood the true nature of radiation. Holding your breath with a paper mask isn't enough to protect you from cancer and the long-term affects of exposure. And imagine the United States and Russia during the Cold War with chemical weapons poised at each other with the readiness of a trigger-pull. China and Japan have always boasted their nuclear capability, and why shouldn't the Japs feel the pressing need to after Nagasaki and Hiroshima? Harry Truman didn't know what the hell he was doing; he just signed a paper and up went villages and cities into human vapor. And don't even start me on the Middle East; we're talking terrorists with massive weapons, chemical weapons, *and* worse intentions." He took another sip of his drink.

"Okay, here's the point to my arms rant," he continued. "The military decided when dealing with chemicals, radiation, and atomic weapons, we needed to approach the crisis without losing human lives. So then the government begins to think 'what if' we can avoid losing human life altogether in war-time situations. No causalities whatsoever, no condolence letters sent to the victims' families, imagine how wonderful that would be. Imagine a full-scale war without a single American life lost? It sounded good on paper, in theory." He rubbed at his eyes, trying to remove the fatigue sown deep and failing. "The best way to explain this entire operation is that they built humans wholesale. From scratch, *sort of...*"

Boyd listened enthralled, but the last detail didn't make sense. "'Building humans wholesale?' Explain, please, so a normal guy like me can understand this fucked-up shit."

Dr. Glover wiped his forehead which was now drenched in sweat. His face was flushed; he was ashamed. "It wasn't my idea, remember that. We've had the ability to clone human beings for quite some time, but this wasn't about making duplicates of people. And to clone a functional human being for war requires investments of time and money. Imagine it. You'd have to raise the kids, essentially. That's eighteen years wasted. You'd be paying for their food, health care, education, and living expenses, and then what would we do with them after their use in the military was over? You can't release human beings into the world without revealing that they were cloned. Humanitarians and legislation and human rights would squelch that immediately. No, it's too messy, or rather, it would make scientists and government officials resort to humane purposes and that requires money and long-term commitment.

"What I'm talking about is a way to build human beings, construct them like robots, to serve a specific purpose without that long-term commitment. Teach them to hold a gun, teach them to walk into a minefield, teach them to fly a jet like a kamikaze, teach them to activate or de-activate a car bomb, teach them to enter nuclear-infected areas and have them handle nuclear weapons, and all-the-while, our normal soldiers come away unscathed. This idea was long-in-the-running, and we were only halfway done before we began to experience problems," he cleared his throat, "and things happened that we didn't expect."

Cindy hadn't taken another drink during the entire speech. "You created drones to do our dirty work? I think Boyd's with me on this one; how the hell can you 'build' a human being? Who are you, a modern day Dr. Frankenstein?"

Dr. Glover ignored the literary quip, and continued. "I can say this, the original people on the project built these people by hand. There weren't that many prototypes, perhaps a dozen at first. The process is similar to cloning, but instead of growth, the parts were already created, and it was simply a puzzle for the scientists to piece together. Organs and body parts were built wholesale, like an assembly line—cost effective and the supply plentiful. There's an actual reason why those things out there are the way they are. The government wanted these 'soldiers' to be fearless. Walk into fire. Capture extremists. Take a dozen bullets and keep coming. Step on landmines and be okay with it. The ones who built them added certain chemical elements to the bodies. Adrenalin mostly, but they also replicated the instinct to hunt, to survive, the will for self-preservation personified and magnified and embellished. Imagine the toughest son-of-a-bitch alive and multiply him by thirty." He took a drink, finished his glass, then refilled it.

"By then, they were out-of-control, coming alive without being built, pieces coming to life independently, putting themselves together to form bodies, and attacking the scientists and then using them for scrap material. Once the pieces had been soaked in the chemical solution, they had to be taken down a notch. Body parts would fight to the death in the labs. My job entailed dissecting the pieces and finding ways to shut them down. Drowning it in harsh chemicals such as acid, tearing up the muscles, the core nerves, it didn't make a difference, they couldn't be stopped. I learned that burning the pieces would terminate every function, but it wasn't a satisfactory solution. People like Stapleton wanted their subjects to be kept alive, controlled. A lot of money was poured into their research and work. But they can't be controlled no matter what I tried." He sighed, thinking back to his days of trial and error. "There's no off switch."

Cindy broke into the explanation, craving something sensible. "You built these people from scraps, arms and legs, heads and necks, bones and flesh? How, surgically?"

"I didn't build them. Let's clear that up right now." Dr. Glover's face darkened at the idea. "No, if I knew what this project meant, I never would've stepped foot in here. This place used to be a small town called Green's End. A sewage leak in the late 90's caused the place to be unlivable, and the government bought it for private research and cleaned up the leak. The town turned into a research facility and military housing; that's why there are houses and businesses and a full-scale hospital here. There are training grounds too, places that were meant to train these built individuals to do the military's bidding, but they didn't get that far." He looked at Cindy. "And yes, to answer your question, Cindy, bones were shipped from one end of the country, muscle-tissue from the other, blood from somewhere else, and limbs and everything else came from government facilities, what we've called 'flesh factories'. I hear the bones were crafted from corpses taken from their graves. That's just speculation among many other speculations, though. One speculation I put more stock into is that the government has stored and saved up skin and organs and have kept them on ice. None of the parts were built or manufactured, but instead, dug up and saved over the course of many decades. My best guess is that they're stealing them from the soldiers murdered in the past thirty or so years during our other wars and the bodies that lay unused in the cemeteries. Again, I could be wrong. I've explored this dilemma again and again. I can't imagine a factory spitting out human bodies from scratch. It's ridiculous; it's all ridiculous." The doctor looked at nothing, trying to imagine a different time and place. "I'm the last researcher to survive. The others were killed in the process of dissecting these people and trying to effectively shut them down. The parts would pretend they're dead, and then a hand would suddenly choke a throat. Intestines would come alive and wrap around a neck and snap it or strangle the person to death. Mouths would open and start biting. Since my fellow workers have been killed off, I'm simply a watchdog, and I'm damn sick of being locked up in here. I'm not staying even if it means risking my life. I'm no one's secret anymore. That's what you need to believe, the both of you."

"I'm with you on that notion," Boyd chimed in, sensing the walls grow smaller and their chances of survival following the same route. "This project shouldn't be kept a secret."

"No, it should remain a secret," Dr. Glover argued, raising a finger to make his point, "and immediately be destroyed. Nobody can know about this. Other countries would try and replicate it—improve it. We'd never see the end of war. The dead would reign over us. As long as we're alive, they'd have pieces and parts to replace their own with. It'd be global extinction."

Dr. Glover removed the gun strapped to his side, a .28 Dellinger, and he cradled it like it was a lover's hand. "I haven't seen my wife in ten years. I don't know if she's still alive or dead, or if she thinks I'm dead, and knowing your story, Boyd, I bet I'm a war casualty. I was in the army as a med tech; it was a fake mission they gave me, that's how they tricked me into coming here. Barbara probably has the remains of some other poor solider in an urn over her mantle. I was K.I.A., that's what they probably told my wife. But I have to know what she's doing; I have to see if she's forgotten me or not, and remind her that I love her, and then try to start over."

Boyd's stomach sank listening to the man lament to them. The doctor's entrapment had spanned over a decade. Karen and the kids played on his mind. Would they forget him? He was dead in the literal sense to them. He was a headstone to be mourned, a marker to place flowers on and visit once a year.

Dr. Glover's eyes didn't leave Boyd, sensing his personal anguish. "Do you want to know how we're getting out of here?" he asked.

"You have a plan?" Cindy brightened, relieved to be done with the original conversation. "You know a way out of here?"

"It's not safe, and we'll be outside again, but it's the only way." Dr. Glover clutched his Dellinger. "I have a small supply of arms. My plan is not to use any of them; it's safer to avoid confrontation. We're outnumbered. Noise draws them in." He placed the red plastic keycard on the counter. "This unlocks the front gate. I know a back way out of here, and all we have to do is circle around the perimeter and make our way to the front entrance. I was hesitant to go it alone, but now that you're both here, I have heads looking over my shoulder, so to speak."

"What about Hayden?" Boyd remembered the only leverage in the situation. "What'll happen to him?"

"Stapleton will send his men up here to take him into custody and have him questioned. They watch us through surveillance throughout the facility, and they know Hayden's already here and trapped, so they're coming soon. They've kept close watch on you, Boyd. If we get enough of a head start, they can't catch us. There are miles of woods outside this facility, we can run for it."

Boyd wasn't sure about the idea of entering the woods, but the fact the man had a key that unlocked the front gate was promising. The next endeavor would be to escape the military outside the walls, but he would encounter that dilemma when it occurred.

Cindy followed his line of thinking. "Are you confident we can find an escape route once we're out of here?"

Dr. Glover nodded. "I was given a tour of the facility before I came to be in the position I'm in now, and there's a sewer channel that leads back into the city. I know of it because my colleagues mentioned it, but we didn't have the courage to go through with the plan because we didn't have a key to the front entrance. Now that I do and you're here, my confidence in escaping," he clutched his gun, "is pretty high. They have this place under surveillance, but once on the outside of the perimeter, there are few cameras between the woods and the final barriers."

Boyd turned to Cindy, weighing her reaction. "Sounds like a better plan than hanging around and waiting and talking, right?"

"Hell, yeah," Cindy agreed.

Boyd had no choice but to trust the doctor, and the bite on his shoulder reminded him that the best reasoning would be the one that led them straight out of the facility.

CHAPTER 21

Hayden pummeled the wall with the trashcan, and when it was too beat up to use, he drove the steel legs of a chair into the damaged surface, gouging through the wood and plaster. The panels were solid, but slowly began to splinter with each new blow; it was only a matter of time and effort before he would break through to the other side.

The buzz from the wine earlier had worn off, now replaced by a stream of energy. He lifted up his hand, the gray dead flesh coating it dangling from his arm in strings.

"You sick bastard," he whispered, and then he bent to his side in laughter. *"You sick bastard! You're a dead man, a dead man!"*

He drove a different chair into the wall, pumped up, ready to reach the other side. The wooden beams bent inwards, creating a hole almost large enough to crawl through. Tired and determined, he launched the chair like a spear, the leg becoming stuck between two boards. He struggled to dislodge it, and yanking back to reclaim the tool, a huge block of wood clunked to the floor upon its retrieval. The action splintered four other panels, and he was easily able to clear them aside, breaking them with more blows. Now the opening formed was large enough for him to crawl through, and he peered into the next room, checking for safety.

The smell of Uncle Ned's funeral home sprang to his nostrils. Enticed by the unknown, he kicked and plundered through the wall, finding new purchase, until he could squeeze through the narrow opening, worming through. Bent over, his hands slapped onto bare tiles. His foot clunked against a metal shelf; it was bolted to the floor. He scanned the shelves and the items, ambling like a blind man, and his hands touched upon many sealed cardboard boxes, some feeling as large as television boxes or as small as shoe boxes.

He located the light switch, and flicking it on, lights came on overhead, the florescent bulbs projecting ample light. Looking in every direction, he took stock of the numerous bookshelves in what appeared to be a small library. The room was the size of a basketball court. Three-fourths of the area was boxes upon boxes, resembling the back of a postal office during Christmas, but in the backmost section was a hidden, open space.

Twin gurneys stood side-by-side on the bare concrete floor with a drain installed in the center. Leather straps hung loose at both ends of the gurneys, worn down by use. A hose lay coiled up in the corner alongside containers of bleach, a mop and bucket. On the left side of him, eclipsed by the shelf's shadow, a laboratory was full with vials, beakers, oxygen tanks, Bunsen burners, five gallon jugs of embalming fluid, scalpels, forceps, pinch clamps, jars of cotton balls, sterilizing solution, suture tape, electric bone saw, stethoscope, heart monitor, EKG machines, respirators and dialysis machines, and a variety of other medical tools he couldn't identify. Hayden studied a patch on the wall that was blackened, the floor ash-colored. The fire extinguisher had been removed from its wall mount and now sat on the floor beside the discoloration.

Someone's been busy, he thought.

Curios as to what it was all for, Hayden tore through a box on a nearby shelf and paused at what he found, astonished: a human liver vacuum-sealed in plastic and soaking in an unknown fluid. He tore it open, the fluid splashing at his feet, and he smelled it. It was the color of gasoline and reeked of dead fish, cod oil and embalming fluid.

He dropped the liver and the box after the rattle of a chain alerted him that there was someone else deeper in the laboratory.

A form moved ahead of him, splitting up the shadows where it hid. Hayden took slow strides to reach the source, also finding a long work table with a notebook and a set of keys on the surface. He flicked on the desk lamp, but he removed his attention from the notebook when the source of the movement was clearly illuminated.

A man was naked and chained to the wall by both wrists. The man was sheet-white, his body emaciated and defined by prominent bones. His darkened eyes fell upon Hayden, and the stranger removed any signs of fear from his face. He turned his face up to Hayden, interested.

Hayden was confused until he remembered he looked just like the dead things out there.

You can walk among them with confidence, Hayden. They're yours to lead.

Who the man was, Hayden didn't know. The body inspired other questions: why were there stitches along every point an extremity connected to the torso? How the man still lived, gaunt and sickly—like the many outside—he couldn't know. The liver in the box, sealed and preserved with embalming fluid, could be a clue, he decided.

Hayden hurried back to the shelves, inspired by the question and ripped more boxes open. Arms and legs vacuum sealed stocked one box, but the next one brought more cause for alarm: the head of a woman. Her eyes opened when the light struck them; they were green with bubbles in the corners of each eye. Her nose twitched. She spat out the fluid, gargling to scream as her head thrashed to be free. He dropped the sealed head to the floor, and the head's attempt to break free continued, the bag twisting and vibrating on the floor. She was biting at the plastic, gnashing and gurgling and mouthing venomous nonsense.

He fled from the shelf and returned to the man huddled in the corner. The man waited with a confident demeanor. Expectant. The man struck the chains together wrist to wrist, a signal. He opened his mouth, a globule of spit draining out both ends of his lips in a glittery rope.

Hayden, seeing the keys on the table, connected the dots.

He grabbed the large set of keys and trudged closer to the shackled man.

Before he tried the first key, a box slipped from the shelf behind him. Seconds passed, and another crashed, and then another, and another, and another until there was a cacophony of collapsing containers, the shelves rattling and clanging with activity. Tape tore from boxes, cardboard ripped asunder, the boxes themselves reduced to ribbons. Fluids spread out, ranging from small leaks to gallons splashing onto the tiles.

The first key to the dead man's chains didn't fit.

Another shelf tipped over, banging onto the floor.

Hayden worked the next key to no avail.

Skin slapped the gurney behind him, scaring him with a spine-straightening start. Falling into a new state of shock, he blinked to ensure his vision wasn't deceiving him. A pair of hands cut off smoothly at the wrists climbed up the gurney, their fingers acting as legs, both extremities somehow able to carry pinch clamps and thread with them; he finally caught sight of the wooden board propped up to the gurney, creating a makeshift staircase. Next, a torso was lifted onto the plastic surface with the aid of more hands, swarms of them working together like a colony of ants. Hayden witnessed in morbid astonishment as two arms were sewn into the torso's bare sockets, fingers threading and weaving to secure the appendages. A head was secured onto the stump of the neck by staples, each *ca-chunk* rendering blood and creating u-shaped gouges into the flesh. Random sheets, squares and rivulets of see-thru tissue was draped over the abdomen, also pinned down by staples, the hands crafting the surgery trigger-happy and swift in execution. Breasts were planted over the chest, pert and new, sewn in by hairpin nails, what was once sexual to behold was now jagged and repulsive. Next, bones clinked into place at their points of connection, muscle tissue grafted and sewn together by threading until every limb was sutured into place. Upon completion, the body was awake in moments, compelled by an unknown force.

The woman with the green eyes, the head in a bag, rose up, standing at a loose swagger, her head about to slip from the neck, bobbing loose. Hayden couldn't help but gasp at the sight. The woman didn't care about him, ignoring him, skulking about the floor as she collected human pieces and tore and punched through the cardboard boxes.

She carried what she'd gathered and placed it onto the table. It was a man, started from a head, and then completed the rest of the way with parts taken from the boxes. She worked to piece him together, meticulous in her goal. Hands severed at the wrist continued to cart appendages to the table, a carnal assembly line. Soon, the second body awoke and worked with his cohort, a monster version of Adam and Eve.

Hayden returned to his effort of unlocking the pale, probably dead, man shackled in the corner, unable to stare at the show any longer, finally understanding he was in no danger.

INSIDE THE PERIMETER

Six keys later, he unlocked the living corpse. The dead man tossed down his shackles and joined in the effort of re-building the parts. Hayden counted twenty bodies created in a half hour's time. He was so mesmerized by watching that he joined in the effort, and began piecing together the room's stock, limb by limb.

CHAPTER 22

Dr. Glover allowed Boyd and Cindy time alone in the recreation room to talk and rest. At the moment, Cindy was taking a nap on the couch, and Boyd sat across from her with his feet on the coffee table with a dated issue of *Mud Magazine* and an old issue of *Time*, the front caption criticizing President George Bush's handling of Desert Storm. He nursed his glass of liquor, unable to take in a buzz thanks to his thoughts rushing in at him, a result of sizing up how to escape the perimeter.

Cindy stirred as she woke up, asking him a question that matched what kept circulating through his head. "What do you think about Dr. Glover's explanation?"

Boyd offered a wry laugh. "It doesn't matter because those people, those living *dead* bodies are out there; that's truth enough for me. The evidence is clear and we have only one option to take."

"Do you think Dr. Glover can save us?"

"We'll save ourselves. He's just pointing the way out."

"What do you think will happen to Hayden?"

"When the 'body shields' come to pick him up, I bet they'll interrogate him to an inch of his life. Lots of torture. The world thinks he's dead, so what's to hold them back from tormenting the shit out of him until he gives them the answers they want. Being a detective, I have a few tricks up my sleeve, too."

Cindy sat up and moved closer, craving more personal talk. "What's the first thing you're going to do when we escape?"

"Clean myself up and take these damn prison clothes off and burn them, and then I'll visit my wife. Thank her for everything she's done for me. For believing in me when my story turned into a tabloid frenzy. My mug shot was on the TV for weeks, even after the trial. She's a strong-willed woman for putting up with the world's reaction. Damn them anyway. They'll believe anything you tell them as long as it's on TV."

"You think she'll be ready to see you?" She rephrased the question, sensing his apprehension. "I mean, you're a dead man, in theory. Maybe she'll think you're a ghost or a hoax? I'd be scared. I wouldn't trust myself if I saw a dead loved one just one day up and come back to visit me."

Boyd would have to handle the home visit with care. How did you drop in on someone who thought you were dead?

"Karen wasn't much of a spiritualist to believe in ghosts, though she grew up Catholic, I think the church thing got away from her later on. And I'm more of an agnostic. At this point, with those bodies coming to life on their own, I believe now that we must have a maker of some kind beyond men and women."

"I'm with you on that one," Cindy agreed. "If you really break down religion, it comes down to one question, is there life after death? A Heaven and a Hell? I'm closer to believing in the afterlife now. There's obviously life after death. But if you hadn't died to begin with, if you were created from surplus materials, did you ever die in the first place? It's like some of them haven't lived or died, they just *are*."

Boyd stopped the philosophical talk by changing the subject, "Well, what will you do when you're out of here?"

"Mexico sounds good to me," she laughed aloud, catching onto what he was doing. "I saved enough money, I have a small nest egg, but I don't know if I can get to it if I'm dead on paper. My brother, Allan, was my beneficiary, so I can pay him a visit and see what he's done with his life. Allan was looking for a job in software engineering, but before I was taken away, he was burnt out and reconsidering his career. Yeah, he'd go to Mexico with me. Margaritas and sun await me beyond that perimeter fence."

Dr. Glover entered the room and Cindy sat up exhausted, matching Boyd's condition.

"I have a question," Boyd spoke first. "Cindy and I cut through the woods and we found a house surrounded with barrels full of ashes. In the basement, there were barrels packed with moving appendages, heads, arms, torsos, you name it. Care to explain that, Doctor?"

Dr. Glover frowned, knowing exactly what Boyd was referring to. "That was from a group of military officers that banded together to have the project destroyed after the first scientists on the project were killed. The government allowed further research and more bodies to be built, and it led to more deaths, and later, more of the resurrected bodies running rampant in the facility. Over a hundred, by a colleague's calculations, were dead and moving about and killing. You can call these military officers a small militia. They gathered and stole as many of the bodies as they could and cut them to pieces and began burning them in barrels. They did it at that house you found." He walked into the room and leaned against the closest wall, crossing his arms over his chest.

"Green's End was first turned into temporary housing and a training base for the dead once they were up and moving. But after the bodies initially came alive, so many of the researchers were killed, the military disbanded any recruits from staying on the premises, but like I said, a group of them found out what was going on and set out to slaughter the newly created constructs. Higher ranking officials came in and had to execute the group. There was no hearing or trial. That goes to show you how determined the government is to keep this operation functioning. They don't want to lose out on their investment; they still believe I'll come up with a solution to their problem on how to control them." He sighed, believing the upcoming explanation more. "Or there are others working on it that I don't know about."

Cindy's voice cracked in exasperation. "Then what are we doing here? I worked for the DA's office, and Boyd was incarcerated and thrown into prison. Why the hell would they force people inside if they were keeping it quiet? Why let anyone else in on this secret?"

Boyd sensed Cindy's anger, and it transferred to him. "These government assholes weren't thinking this through, were they? Like always, they throw something at the wall, see what sticks, and if people get killed, it's collateral damage; throw some money at the widows and widowers, then call it a day. With this as a secret, I can only imagine what else they do that we don't know about. Sure, okay, I was placed in here to capture Hayden, but Cindy, her reason to be here isn't so clear. If she found out things she wasn't supposed to know from her district attorney boyfriend, why not kill her on the spot? Sorry to speak like that in front of you, Cindy."

Dr. Glover looked down, reluctant to reply. "As you noticed, those things out there are rotting."

"Obviously," Boyd spat out with impatience.

Grim faced, the doctor shared the truth. "You're here to keep their pet project alive, Boyd, both of you. Without new bodies, the strongest of them can't survive. They might have a different research team somewhere else trying to find a way to control them, but from my standpoint, I don't know. You're here to assure that enough of their creations live on so they can be studied if need be, even used again if they find a way to use them as planned."

Cindy struggled to speak, flabbergasted, raising her fists in the air. "So we're keeping them going, my body for theirs, huh? They've ruined my life, and they went to great lengths to fake Boyd's death in prison to bring him here. I've had enough of this. I don't know how, but I'm going to see to it that this place is firebombed and incinerated."

"First, let's worry about escaping," Dr. Glover interrupted, appreciating her determination. "We're not out of here yet."

Boyd clutched his wound, living the truth of the doctor's words. "One of those things out there bit me, sucked my blood. What the hell is that about?"

"Yes, they like blood. It's what they use to sustain themselves, I suppose. They don't eat anything else, I've learned, and they don't have a strong enough digestive system to handle meat or real food, so blood's the best they can do. They suck it from your skin, your organs, your muscles, but they never eat anything solid. Everything else they use to upgrade their bodies."

The explanation furthered his dismay, and Cindy suffered the same doubts. Filling in the dramatic silence, Dr. Glover continued, "And I've noticed Hayden has taken a liking to eating our friends out there. A real gourmet psycho that man is. He's butchered so many I've lost count. I can only see so much from the video surveillance. I've often wondered how he can eat them without falling ill. And then I thought about the chemicals we've used; it's a preservative in a way, but also a disinfectant. It must not be poisonous enough to kill a human being. Hell, knowing the components of it, it's probably chemically addictive. He can't get enough."

Cindy's face went slack, and Boyd sensed she was going to be sick when the color drained from her face. "It's okay, don't think about it, Cindy. I don't think eating the dead will come into fashion anytime soon." He fake checked his wrist for the time. "Isn't it time we got moving, Doctor?"

"They'll be here soon to pick up Hayden, so yes, I would have to agree."

Cindy was up first, trying to ward off the sick feeling suffusing her body at the thought of Hayden eating the dead. "You told us you had weapons. What exactly do you have?" she asked.

"It's nothing worthy of fighting a war with, but it's good enough for three people to use. Follow me."

Dr. Glover directed them to an adjacent room. He unlocked the door and flipped a switch. The room was about as large as two bathroom stalls. There was a locker against the far wall, padlocked. Dr. Glover spun the combination, and it opened.

"We've got a Remington Sharpshooter rifle, two Desert Eagle pistols, and at the bottom," he hoisted up a large jet pack looking item with a grunt, "a blow torch. This will be the most effective weapon against them. Guns will slow them down. Shots to the head keep them on the ground, but they can still scramble to put themselves back together. Most of their bodies were packed with embalming fluid when shipped, and that means the chemical is in their skin, and they'll ignite if exposed to a prolonged flame."

Boyd was disappointed at the weapons, but he felt the bulge in his back pocket, the grenade reminding him of what it could do if he just pulled the pin. He held it up for them to see, like it was an item during show-and-tell in elementary school. "I have this, and we've got our two guns, but they're nearly out of ammunition. It'd be a waste to lug an M-16 around with five rounds, not if we're doing a lot of running."

"The blow torch looks heavy," Cindy said, concern creeping into her voice, afraid they couldn't use it. "Who's willing to carry that?"

Dr. Glover strapped it on, volunteering. "I am, my dear. This is the best weapon, and no offense, but it's mine."

Boyd shrugged his shoulders. "Fine by me. I'm not lugging that heavy thing around."

He hoisted the Remington Sharpshooter and strapped it over his good shoulder. Cindy picked up the two Desert Eagles and clutched them like a cowboy and then eyed them like she was clutching something sticky. "Are they ready to fire? There's something I have to do first, right? God, I don't know what I'm doing."

Boyd turned off the safeties. "Now you're good, kiddo. Pull the trigger and *bang, bang*."

Dr. Glover stepped into the hallway, expecting them to follow his lead. The doctor faced the door at the end of the hall, an emergency exit, his eyes filling with a weary determination.

"This eventually takes us to the sublevel exit into the parking lot," Dr. Glover said. "It's a large access the military also used to transfer the body parts without being seen by the military recruits in training. I haven't been down there since I arrived; I was too scared to go alone. I'm not sure if it's changed or how safe it is to go through there now."

A crash resounded at the opposite end of the corridor, startling each of them. The sound of pounding against the double doors followed a series of shrieks, screams and unidentifiable garbles, a mob of savages popping up in seconds. The hinges on the door were coming loose, dozens of bodies banging against it at once, the insistency to break through auditory as it was sensory, the barrier throbbing.

"How many are in there?" Boyd studied the doctor's face, hoping to force an explanation from him. "Now would be a good time to tell us. Spill your guts, man. We're running low on time to chit-chat. Those things came from that room, didn't they?"

Dr. Glover stammered, horrified, beguiled to speak, but then finally spitting it out, "I...it's our storage room of h...human parts. They were in boxes, sealed in chemicals. They were dead and going to stay that way. Someone's let them out; someone woke them up. I...I...I have a whole specimen in there chained up for research, but h...he couldn't have escaped. No, it's not just one alive behind that door, not anymore."

Boyd rushed to the break room, unlocked the door, and discovered a gaping hole in the far wall. Hayden had escaped, torn through the wall to the other side. It was too dark to make sense of what was going on from his standpoint, but he sensed the movement of many bodies through the edges of the breach.

Heads peeked through the opening, sensing him. Gobs of saliva foamed down sneering, seething mouths, tongues licking the froth from their lips in mastication and anticipation. Teeth clattered as the response grew widespread, enraged eyes adjusting and turning to catch a better view of the humans within close range, using their fingers and hands to fight their way through the wall, peeling and tearing new slivers of wood to widen the gap. Slamming the door shut, sped up by ensuing screeches, Boyd reeled back into the hallway, mortified.

"They want our bodies," Dr. Glover warned, passing Cindy who stood vigil at the emergency exit, yelling above them to be heard. "Hayden must've done something to them. Woke them up. All he had to do was open one box, and they'd come awake. The darkness of the boxes and the dim room made them believe they were dead, like in a coffin, trapped in the afterlife, whatever you believe in, but if he opened one, they all sensed it once the light hit their eyes, their skin. I had it under control, and that son-of-a-bitch *ruined it*. He ruined it!"

"We have to leave," Cindy insisted, shaking Dr. Glover's arm to the point she almost knocked him to the floor. "It doesn't matter, they can be destroyed later. Right now we need to save ourselves!"

"They may never be destroyed!" Dr. Glover shouted, lost in doom-laden thoughts. "Don't you see, I was going to burn that room when we left, and now it's too late. I can't do it with them alive. *I can't, I can't, I can't!*"

Boyd urged them through the emergency exit, shoving the doctor extra hard to knock some sense into him. Behind him, he could hear slivers of wood and paneling break and clatter with a hollow ring against the tiles so loud he believed they'd dismantled the entire wall. The slap of their feet filled the inside of the break room. Only one barrier left between them and the living dead.

Cindy was the first to open the exit. The moment the horizontal bar across the middle of the door was pressed down, a red siren blared, the halls going dark except for the blaring lights. The double doors of the break room were forced open, the dead forcing their way forward, stomping and fighting each other's zealous nature to reach the three humans first. Faces strangely untouched by experience, pale, unblemished except for the evil and alien lust scrawled into their features, corralled themselves forward, hell-bent to desecrate the three humans' bodies.

Dr. Glover locked the emergency exit door, hands visibly trembling, and the moment the door was secure, though moans and unholy hollering matched the thud of fists against steel from the other side.

"It won't hold them for long," Dr. Glover gasped, shaking his head, horrified, disappointed, and almost falling down, his knees wanting to buckle at the rising din contained by a single barrier. "Down the steps, hurry! No time, there's no time left!"

They descended the first set of stairs, Boyd staying in the rear, his legs pumping fast, though he couldn't feel the effort. Every part of him was shaking like the doctor, his senses on high alert, adrenalin speeding up his processes to the point he thought his heart would explode and his thoughts would tangle and he'd fail to decide his next move.

They hit another door.

Dr. Glover threw back the passage immediately, lunging through without reserve. "This is the access to the tunnel; it leads to a parking lot and to the outside. I think we're going to make it without them catching us."

The door above them crashed open, the door itself rattling down the steps and thundering into the wall below, discrediting the doctor's statement. Boyd saw Cindy jump, spasming in terror. He wanted to comfort her, but there was no time. One wasted word, one second spent on indecision or poor planning, and they'd be overtaken and rendered to scrap for the dead.

Dr. Glover led them down a long hallway and secured the entrance behind them, buying them more time, precious time. In seconds, the dead had reached the final barrier, shaking the door with their ramming bodies. The three humans sprinted to the end of the hall, a lengthy stretch that left them coughing and struggling for breath. The infernal noises kept them compelled to race forward, pushing their bodies well past their breaking points.

Dr. Glover tried the last door, the final barrier between them and the outside. Opening it, a gust of frigid air blasted them, their sweating bodies grateful for the fresh air until the cold chill settled into their bones. Looking on, Boyd spotted a station wagon parked a few feet from the entrance, the door barely able to swing open, the vehicle impeding the way. The car itself was embedded in barbed-wire mesh, layers and layers of it, transforming the car into a piece of post-modern art.

"Wrap your hands in your shirt," Boyd advised, studying Cindy and the doctor who didn't have the slightest idea of how to deal with the fork in the road, "and tuck them inside so they won't get cut. We have to climb over it. No choice, right, so let's get to it. Barbs or teeth, which do you prefer?"

"Neither," Cindy gasped; she held her breath for a time. "So much for good options!"

"I'm with her," the doctor added, jaw clenched and staring in horror at the door behind them, seeing the moving shadows over the square plate of glass set in the door. Grease and blood obscured the glass, the skin peeled back on the dead's fingertips, revealing crimson-tipped bones.

Soon, they would break through.

Boyd opened the car door, parting barbs to do so, cutting his hands while wincing and cursing. Inside the car, the seats were loose, as if someone had been trying to take them out for some unknown reason.

"Wedge out the car seats, they're already loose, we can light them on fire; set a barrier between them and us! Hurry, help me."

The doctor joined in the effort, snapped out of his moment and ready to fight off their impending assault. Boyd bent down, removing the front car seat, and then rolled it back down the hallway like an awkward bowling ball. Without having to signal him, Dr. Glover blasted a jet of flames, the plume far-reaching, resembling a fire-breathing dragon's breath. The cone of incendiary heat rendered the seat into a burning pyre, up in flames instantly.

Cindy waited by the car, deciding on whether to scale it or wait another moment for them to follow. Boyd shouted back to her, waving his hand for her to move on. "Get a head start and run, but watch your ass. We're right behind you. Go!"

"I'm not going without you, Boyd."

Boyd's throat ached as he delivered the harsh command, "Move your ass, Cindy, you hear me? I can't always be Velcro'd to your ass. Do what I tell you and beat your feet!"

After he ripped out the passenger car seat, she took the cue, climbing over the car's hood, careful not to cut her hands.

Boyd tossed the car seat into the hall, and Dr. Glover again cased it in flames, the material blossoming into flames.

Boyd looked to the doctor, then pointed at Cindy who had just scaled the car and was on the other side. "Cover Cindy, Doc, I'm right behind you. Keep your eyes wide open for them!"

The doctor climbed over the car without hesitation, struggling to get up, lugging the heavy flame thrower with him. Boyd turned the other way, checking the hallway. He assumed his law enforcement role, and in this case, he had two citizens to protect, and he put their lives before his.

"Are you coming, Boyd?" Cindy shouted in the distance, her voice wavering. "Boyd, answer me!"

The door crashed open before he could summon a reply, the hinges undone, wrenched from the door, the door itself clapping down, breaking the tiles. Naked forms, orange in the firelight, tribal in movement, advanced unaffected by the flames until one of them crossed the burning car seats, unknowing of its impending harm. As the body began burning, it ran into others of its kind, their bodies then igniting in a single *whoosh*, as blue and white chemical flames engulfed them, snaking up each limb and eating into the core, the heads burning like torches. It was disturbing how their faces didn't reflect pain, their eyes drawn to Boyd to study him.

More rushed through the fiery barrier, their flesh curling, puckering, and smoldering, giving way to boiling muscle that shrank into black, overcooked bacon. Boyd fired random shots at them, hoping they'd be slowed, and then finally retreated.

Leaping over the station wagon, convinced he was out of time, he'd forgotten about the barbed wire mesh in his haste, snagging his thumb.

"*Shit!*" he cursed.

He leaped from the station wagon, dealing with his wound, and landed on the other side. He reached Cindy and Dr. Glover as they climbed over a military jeep ahead of him. Following them, he sliced his shoulder and cheek as he maneuvered over a green and black spray-painted van. After the van, a stretch of ankle-high barbed wire obscured the path. He raised and lifted his legs to clear the hindrance. His shoes were torn in the process; the skin up to his knees cut and nicked, a death of a thousand cuts. He couldn't take much more, his heart chugging, his nerves battling to function in the dire situation. Fire-lit shapes landed behind him, crash landing off the vehicles, wrapped up in barbed wire, the living pyres tangled and fighting, many breaking limbs or chewing them off to slip free from their impediments.

Clear of the tripwire, Boyd ducked behind a concrete roadblock. Dr. Glover and Cindy waited behind a nearby stack of tires and were happy he was the first to reach them. Overhearing the crash of a vehicle, tipped over in all likelihood, and the pursuing of the hundred strong horde. "You two take cover, he snapped. "I'm throwing the grenade. Hide behind something!" Boyd served up the command without having to consider it for too long,

"One Mississippi," he counted, drilling it loud enough from his lungs so he could hear himself over the attacking dead, recalling his days as the quarterback for his high school, the Gilmore Heights Eagles; he was number 32, the number later taken by Chad Wisenthal, the asshole who broke all of his records the year immediately following his senior year. "Two Mississippi—Hike!"

He hurled the grenade, praying the dead didn't know how to count. "Three seconds before it explodes!" Boyd yelled and ducked, his hands over his head, the explosion deafening.

The vehicles ahead of him detonated, the gas tanks rupturing and adding fuel to the explosions. The concussion reverberated underfoot, as shrapnel and barbs flung across the way, audibly slicing and cutting through bodies.

A ball of blue and white flames arched high during the new explosion that pounded the air and spread like a vibrant mushroom cloud. Fires danced behind Boyd in burner jet fashion, the dead slowed by the frenzy of heat, some dodging it, others slapping their bodies to fend off what they didn't understand.

This was Boyd's final chance to escape, so he lunged over a set of tires, battling onward. He sensed his friends' efforts ahead of him, though vaguely through the veil of smoke. He surged ahead, catching patches of the night sky. When he caught up with Dr. Glover, the victory was cut short. The flame thrower spat gobs of fire into a group of dead awaiting them on the other side.

They were surrounded, and Cindy was missing.

CHAPTER 23

Hayden cleared a stack of tires by hurdling them, and upon landing on the other side, he navigated to an opening in the parking complex. Pitch black, he assumed it was two or three in the morning. He charged in the right direction to meet the three escaping humans. He had battled through the hallways, pretending to be one of the dead, even dodging the fire-filled hallway and burning bodies to reach the parking lot. And now here he was, successfully tracking his prey.

A loud explosion turned the night into day and he looked behind him to see vehicles on fire, some lifting off the ground, tires, fenders and glass raining down and shooting in all directions, everything encased in blue and white flames. Silhouettes of bodies were thrown everywhere, a few slamming into the ground to break apart, while others were blown in half.

Hayden tromped out of the parking garage and caught Cindy stumbling from the exit of the building. She slipped and hit the pavement on all fours. The woman couldn't make it to her feet, disoriented and weak, choking on smoke.

He noticed movement from the nearby road. More of the dead materialized, roused from other hideaways in the perimeter. Fifty or more were approaching from out the darkness, while fire-lit beings added to the surmounting total. Hayden watched the man in the lab coat utilize a flame thrower, wielding it successfully.

Cindy still didn't get up. Hayden closed in on her, careful to stay out of eyeshot of the man with the flame thrower. Looking down at the woman, he saw that a gash bled from her forehead, her face slick with blood. She breathed softly, her sweater ripped and torn, cuts and barbed-wire lacerations covering her from head to toe. Hayden lifted her up, and he heard the man in the lab coat shout, "Put her down, you bastard!"

Carrying her in his arms, Hayden sprinted through a crowd with the payload, charging down a nearby hill, slashing through a creek, and clearing a quarter of a mile before slowing down. The man didn't follow—couldn't follow. Bursts of orange flickered and died, flickered and died, the fight unending and growing. The woman was heavy in his arms, but the warmth of her body, the smell of her blood—the smell of meat—coaxed him further into the large expanse of an open field.

Hayden questioned his choice of direction. The woods were too far away; perhaps a mile to the right of him, but forward and to the left was darkness. It encompassed everywhere, the destination ahead mysterious.

She spoke dreamily, half-submerged in unconsciousness, "What's...what's going on?"

Hayden dressed up his voice to be soothing, craftily mimicking Boyd's. "It's okay, we're safe. I'll keep you safe, I promise. You took a mean knock to the head, but I'll find a place to hide. Close your eyes and rest. It's all behind us, it's almost over."

The words were effective, her body giving her permission to put down her guard and sleep. Crossing yet another creek, Hayden turned his ankle on a series of loose rocks while treading uphill. His shins were wet with mud, each step a waterlogged clop, until he stepped upon land again.

Racing into the darkness, fearing he was going nowhere or about to hit a perimeter wall, he was reassured by the sight of a flag waving on top of a pole in the distance. Pavement thumped underfoot instead of earth. A large facility with a tin roof formed through lifting shadows, and when he approached the front access door, he looked through a window into a mess hall. Tables and chairs were stacked inside with no one inside; the facility was dark, no lights.

Hayden placed the woman on the front steps and opened the door to inspect inside. She was asleep or unconscious. She'd lost so much blood, he couldn't be sure, but he couldn't leave her unattended for long. He imagined the dead getting hold of her and having their way with her, and he was displeased at the sinking feeling in his guts upon considering the potential loss of good clean female meat. He dragged her by the arms through the door, procuring his load. Picking her up again in his arms, he weaved through dozens of dining tables, trying to figure out where to go next. Nothing had been used in the large room for a long time, everything covered in a thick layer of dust, cobwebs in the corners and between table legs, the tables clear of utensils, plates, even salt shakers and napkin holders.

He came upon the kitchen area, the door unlocked. He opened it and rested the woman on the counter top closet to the stove. He searched the place for rope, rifling through shelves and drawers, failing to locate anything to bind her extremities. Instead, he removed the woman's stockings and tied her arms together. She was helpless, at his whim like the hookers he'd drugged into unconsciousness before being thrown into inside the perimeter.

He wasn't a torturer, but he gave into his morbid urge to play with his victims on rare occasions, talking them up as if he would have mercy on them or that he'd let them go, or perhaps promising that he'd just take one bite, and yes, he believed them when they said they wouldn't tell the cops about them, and yes, they could go free.

Other desires popped into his head, his appetite for depraved desires whetted. How far could the knife enter flesh before they screamed in mortal terror? What emotions could he drudge up if he ate that woman's meat in front of her? Could he get her to eat her own skin, and would she take pleasure in it? Could he convince her to take pleasure in it like Brandy had enjoyed it?

Desiring to act upon his wishes, though predicting the hard work to obtain those desires, he selected a five inch blade and a boning knife from a drawer. He noticed a first-aid kit hanging on the wall. Inside, he removed a small bottle of peroxide and a roll of gauze. The woman's legs were bared without stockings, the wounds cut in the shape of fish hooks, inflicted by the steel barbs, the severed skin glistening like ripe cherries.

He placed a towel wet with peroxide on her wounds, staunching them, and the woman stirred, annoyed and mumbling, still under the spell of weakness. "No, Boyd...it *hurts*."

"It's okay," Hayden cooed, once again mimicking Boyd's voice. "We can't have your wounds infected." Under his breath he said, *"It will spoil the meat."*

Hayden was more interested in eating skin than sex, but he didn't avert his eyes when he peered up her skirt to her blue silk panties. They were dirty, sweat stained, along with the rest of her clothing. She needed to be cleaned, but first, he decided to search the entire building and the surrounding grounds. The mess hall was one place to remain safe, but there were more offices and rooms, better places to hide, and he decided not to trust the darkness of night so easily to keep him hidden.

He cleaned the wound across her forehead next, the gash tracing across her hairline. The woman's clothes stank of smoke and chemicals. He didn't want his olfactory senses getting in the way of his pallet when he finally carved a juicy piece from her body and tasted it.

Taking a moment for himself, he splashed his face in the sink and cleared his mind, plotting his next move. He would take the woman with him to survey the rest of what was around him, what he assumed was a military encampment of some kind.

Carrying Cindy out in his arms, and whisking her deeper into the building, Hayden looked forward to what he might find.

CHAPTER 24

Boyd was thrown to the ground from behind as fingers plunged into his clavicle wound, fresh blood seeping from the opening, teeth pressing down on the exposed meat, and bringing giant conflagrations of pain.

Fighting through the raw sensations, he yelled, driving his elbow into his attacker's pale visage, the sharp crack of bone forcing out cold fluids to drip out of its face and onto Boyd's neck. After kicking the corpse in the chest, the dead man tumbled into four more of his brethren charging Boyd's way, knocking them down upon the connection.

"Get down!" Dr. Glover shouted from five yards out, raising the nozzle of the flame thrower. "I'll blast 'em!"

A ball of orange enshrouded the figures seconds after the warning was issued, their skin immediately parting to muscle tissue, the dermis sizzling into a blackened crisp. Boyd sent a round of gunfire at the incoming horde, most of the dead battling to escape the parking garage, caged in by flames, flailing and thrashing to be free before they were too damaged to live on.

"They're coming from everywhere!" Boyd cried out, looking on at the surrounding streets and houses where the dead continued to creep closer. "How many of these damn things are there?"

"It's impossible to say," Dr. Glover shouted in reply, equally as horrified at the human-to-dead ratio. "More of them were being stored throughout this facility as the years went by. I never knew the exact number. Perhaps hundreds. I pray not a thousand."

Boyd's mind returned to Cindy, instantly concerned. "Did you see where Cindy went? Tell me, man, did you see anything?"

"I'm not sure, I couldn't see much." Dr. Glover pointed behind him, to the west. "But I'm afraid to say that Hayden took her beyond the creek. Go after her, Boyd, I'll distract them for as long as I can. I'll follow you eventually."

Boyd didn't hesitate to act. Cindy was in danger, his only real friend right now. He didn't know where he was going, though he raced forward anyway, plunging ahead into the blackness. Most of the creatures were attacking Dr. Glover who stood his ground, the effectiveness of the flame thrower slowly growing weaker and weaker as it ran out of fuel.

Boyd sprinted through an open field, the area devoid of anything, the din of the dead fading behind him. He was out of breath after a quarter of a mile, his shoulder oozing blood.

But they're out here somewhere, and there's not a goddamn thing you can do about it.

Thinking about Hayden, Boyd knew the man had continued to slip into insanity. The cannibal was now draping dead skin over his body to walk among the dead safely. Boyd understood that Hayden was a murdering cannibal, but he was also cunning and clever. "A psycho with an organizer," many of psychoanalysis's had dubbed him. This was the kind of situation a man like him would thrive in, and it was best to assume Hayden could do just about anything to Cindy.

Boyd's gut tightened thinking of another issue. Dr. Glover kept the plastic card key, the only way out of the facility. If something happened to the doctor, then Boyd would be trapped, but then again, Cindy was alone and in trouble. What would it mean to escape if she were dead? Despite the level head he fought to maintain, he knew he couldn't accomplish this alone.

He sucked in a series of breaths, his ribcage aching, mustering the courage to battle on. Boyd treaded through a creek, the water ice cold. He completed a sprint up a hill, then back down the other side, then crossed yet another creek. Tramping through the mud on the far side, he cleared the mess and came upon land, to find he was running on cracked pavement.

A green-painted building formed in the distance; the sign he read across the top of the main door read **MESS HALL**. He sharpened his eyes on the background and distinguished a series of cabins and enclosures, all featureless boxes with no indication of their purpose. Military quarters, he figured, but why did the place appear to be abandoned if they were running operations here?

If the military couldn't escape, what makes you think you can?

"I'm not giving up yet," he muttered, eying the scene with new energy. "The system's already killed me once, what will a second time hurt?"

Boyd rushed into the mess hall, the inside comprised of chairs stacked on wooden tables. Down the center aisle, he aimed the rifle. Anything could happen at any moment; the beings could burst through any of the entrances or exits or through the ceiling after him. They were scheming bastards, and they were more than predators hunting for human remains and blood; they could think, rationalize and outsmart him.

The trail of blood stopped at the entrance to the kitchen. Boyd forced open the door, and lifting the rifle again, finger arched over the trigger, he sucked in a deep breath after finding that the kitchen was empty. Dirty footprints smeared with blood surrounded the counter, proving recent occupation. A first-aid kit was left open; a balled up cloth colored in red lying on top of the counter.

"*Hayden.*" It was said as a curse.

The back door wasn't closed entirely, and he assumed Hayden had used it. He exited the building, walking down a short set of steps, the cold night air inspiring a shiver. The din of guttural cries and the movement of a large group of the dead carried over the hill. Dim flashes of yellow and orange repeated to tell Boyd that Dr. Glover was still fighting the dead.

Boyd doubled his pace and studied the first nearby cabin he came to. He couldn't see inside, the windows dirty from age and neglect. Giving up, he checked the next couple of cabins, receiving the same results. Shifting right, ducking low to remain unseen, he ran up to a series of cinder block walls without a roof, a structure of some kind.

He turned to the right, hearing footsteps, and without hesitation, he ran in that direction, stopping at the end of one of the walls.

Edging closer after hearing the patter of footsteps against concrete, this time followed by a spray of water, he pursued the noises.

CHAPTER 25

Hayden carried Cindy over his shoulder, struggling to support her weight. His mouth had coated over in saliva to the point he had to spit, his thoughts roaming to the woman's body.

Mastication is a sure sign of hunger, Hayden. It's deep-rooted. The body can acclimate itself to ingest more, whether for survival or for pleasure. The stomach will stretch itself and make itself bigger, if you train it over time. And I've been thinking, when you digest another person's body, how does your body break it down? You're sustaining yourself on the human body's components, and you're getting exactly what you need to survive. It's a beautiful thing, Hayden. More people should take serious thought into eating human flesh.

The smell of Cindy and the warmth of her body against his own, drove him to consider two things. Nobody knew he was here. The dead corpses at the hospital said that Broman could be dead by now. That meant this place was his again and he now had a woman at his disposal. Brandy was an easy fuck and her meat suffered for it. He tasted himself in her: sweat, the grime from his hands, and his semen—the infernal tang of snake venom. It ruined his appetite. He wouldn't make the same mistake with Cindy.

The mess hall was behind him as he darted inside a concrete brick structure without a roof, and once inside, he discovered a series of toilets, and along the other side, a dozen shower heads.

He should clean her, he decided, knowing the moment to flense her skin and play games was coming soon. He grabbed a series of towels in an overhead compartment above a long bench. Then, he placed her on the wall under a showerhead. Hayden tugged down her skirt and panties, the darkness concealing her nakedness though he did try to see her body in the gloom. Next, her sweater went up over her head, and he unhooked her bra. Her breasts were full and voluptuous; so generous, the kind you couldn't clasp with only one hand. He tossed the clothes aside and started the shower, watching the water trail down her body, her hair a tangled mess, greasy and spread thin. There was no shampoo, but he gathered handfuls of soap from a dispenser inside the bathroom and rubbed her hair and body down, the suds smelling of lavender. The cold water stirred her fully awake, and she opened her eyes, gawking at him in horror and repulsion.

Hayden grabbed his knife from his belt loop once she screamed louder, the yell high-pitched. He aimed the blade at her navel, twisting the blade into her stomach, but not pressing it into her flesh. "You run, I'll plunge this into you. Do you know anybody nearby that can stop your bleeding? Internal bleeding is especially hard to stop without a surgeon."

"W...what do you want?" She covered her breasts with one arm, the other hand concealing her pubic region, every inch of her shivering, denying the predicament. "P...please don't hurt me, okay? I...I don't know what you want."

"Tell me your name," Hayden demanded, cutting her pleas short by squeezing her larynx. "Everyone else is dead. Your friends, Broman, and the other asshole, they're gone. So you're here with me. Like I said, tell me your name."

"It's Cindy," she spat, refusing to completely go along with the Q&A session willingly. "And I know who you are...Hayden."

He ignored her last statement, focusing on her body. "First, dry yourself off before you catch a cold, I want you healthy. Your clothes are on that bench."

Cindy didn't take her eyes off of him as she toweled dry and slipped her clothes back on. "What now?" she asked.

"We're going to find a cozy place to hide," he said, keeping the blade aimed at her belly. "We'll let things blow over. Calm down some. My nerves are worked up, and I'm sure yours are too."

"You're going to kill me," Cindy guessed, her eyes wide, knowing the truth. "I might as well run back out there with those things, huh? Like I said, I know who you are, Hayden Grubaugh. You're not going to lure me into a dark hole and have your way with me. Are you going to kill and eat me? If so, then you're going to have to do it now, whatever it is you plan to do. I won't cooperate."

Hayden balked at her defiance. "Do you appreciate your life, Cindy?" He moved in closer to her, training the blade on her neck, the tip resting on her femoral artery. He whispered angrily, "I'm offering you a chance to hold onto your precious little life. I'll take a piece from you every once in a while, enough to keep me satisfied, but I'll be sparing enough not to kill you. You may never die if you work with me. *If you obey me.*"

"I don't trust lunatics," she growled, though her antagonistic act was obviously a front, her body shrinking in his grasp. "My last boyfriend was the same way; I trusted his word, and I woke up here. Your promises are nothing to me."

Her fists curled. She wanted a fight.

He couldn't figure her out, scared one moment, defiant the next.

"Fine," he sighed, unleashing his disappointment, as if he'd been told something trivial. "Then I'll just kill you now!"

He was about to drag the blade across her trachea, but Cindy elbowed him in the gut, the unexpected blow sending acidic bile into his throat and out his mouth a pink and yellow mix of gruel.

After clearing his head enough to move, Hayden reached her as she was scrambling from out the showers. Crawling to where she had darted, he spotted her shadow disappear behind the corner of another building half a block's distance from him. It was two stories high, the outer walls painted dark green, the same as the mess hall. She didn't go inside, but had ducked around it.

Rising up, he ran full-speed in pursuit of his delectable damsel. He gained on her fast, so fast in fact that it took seconds for him to reach her. He easily leapt forward and tripped her up by kicking out with his foot. They became tangled together and crashed to the dirt, spinning and colliding into each other. Seizing her legs, then losing them, his hands slick with her sweat, he managed to crawl up her legs, catch her skirt with both hands, his fingers raking up her back, to place the knife against her throat once again.

"Don't move or you're dead," he hissed.

Before she could decide if she should try to escape or give in, he struck her head with the hilt of the knife.

She went still, her eyes rolling up into her head, stunned.

"They'll hear us if you keep crying out," Hayden warned, lowering his tone, sensing movement in the distance. "I've been in this place for a long time, and you came along and ruined everything. I had what I wanted, and now it's gone." His voice curdled with lascivious ambition. "You're the beginning of getting everything back, Cindy. If you want to die, I can give you your wish. You saw the corpses in the fridge. I can keep you fresh. All I have to do is get back inside and lock it up. That's your future, leftovers in the freezer."

She was catching her breath, and he could feel her lungs exhale and inhale, an embryonic state.

Maybe she finally understood his threats and they were sinking in.

And then came a metallic click of a gun from behind him.

"Let go of her right now, Hayden."

CHAPTER 26

Hayden tensed as Broman trained the rifle on him. Cindy renewed her efforts to escape, springing awake, but she stopped when Hayden kept the knife under her throat.

"One swipe and she'll be choking on blood," Hayden warned.

"Try it, Hayden," Boyd threatened, both hands on the rifle, ready to send a bullet through his cerebral cortex. "You do it and your brains go out the back of your head. And you know I'm good on my promises."

"And you'll be a murderer once again." Hayden scrutinized Boyd's crime anew, enjoying the damning recital of his words. "Did Samuel Tyson crunch under your wheels? I ran over a cat once, shit and guts came out its ass, and a whole lot of blood came out the mouth. Did Mr. Tyson's body do the same? God, your family must hate you. First, you're a hero for helping to catch me, and then you're thrown into prison with the likes of me." He cocked his head to the side. "How did that make you feel, being loved and then hated so quickly?"

"Don't listen to him, he's desperate," Cindy insisted, frantic to escape his clutches. "I was unconscious, Boyd, and when I woke up, he was washing me. He's crazy."

Hayden moved the knife under her earlobe slightly and drew blood. She winced at the assault.

"Quiet, *you bitch*," he hissed. "I was only cleaning you so I can eat you later. You were filthy." She slackened her limbs.

"You won't do it, Hayden," Boyd countered, witnessing Cindy go weak. "I can hold this gun up all night; I'm a very patient man. I've been through Hell and back again, so push my buttons all you want; I don't feel it anymore."

A sudden commotion drew all of their attention. Bodies by the hundreds clamored to reach them over the horizon. A few were burning, the firelight enough to reveal their staggering numbers. Over five hundred, if not more.

"It's your move, Hayden?" Boyd growled.

Hayden laughed, shrugging off any reason to make a hasty decision. "I look just like them, and I've had no problem slipping past them before. You, on the other hand, are fair game. What's *your* move, Broman?"

"What do you want?" Boyd demanded, the dead close enough they were now in his peripheral. "What do I have to do to make you let her go?"

"Nothing except die!" he shrieked in horrid amusement, belly-laughing. "I'm taking her with me, end of discussion."

Boyd peered at the enclosing bodies, sensing that they'd be too close to fend off very soon. The crowd had bypassed the mess hall, and growing closer with each passing second.

"Not much longer before they get here." Hayden's snake eyes glowed, the man knowing he was the dominant one, that he had the upper hand. "A shame, I'd hoped to eat you, too."

The wall of dead bodies closed in, and Boyd was forced to turn and fire upon them, slowing their advance. Hayden slipped away, cashing in his opportunity to evade Boyd by forcing Cindy into the closest building.

Opening the door of a two-story, steel-walled structure, a box without windows, captor and captive vanished from sight, hidden from the approaching dead, protected; leaving Boyd to battle the horde alone.

CHAPTER 27

Boyd decided it wasn't worth wasting the ammunition, as there were simply too many bodies around him, making it impossible to gain added safety with only one weapon. Running from them, he tried the same door that Hayden had used; it was predictably locked.

No surprise there, he thought.

Boyd speculated that Dr. Glover was dead, overwhelmed by the creatures.

Which meant the key card was lost.

No time for commiserating, the dead beings crowded every corner of the building, and Boyd ran for his life. Upon reaching a tree, he slung the rifle over his shoulder and climbed it, the dead crowd seconds from grappling him. He shuddered with pain, his clavicle wound opening and puckering as he maneuvered. The trunk was thick and tall enough that he could evade their reach.

Bodies crashed into each other on the ground, flailing their hands upwards to reach him, to pull him down and dissect him.

Then one of them began to climb the tree.

His safety had lasted a mere ten seconds.

Boyd worked his way across a branch and balanced himself across two overhanging limbs. The roof of the building was close, his last option.

The trunk grew shakier as he scaled it, drawing further across the thick branch and closer to the building's edge. One wrong step or a slip, and he would drop into the horde. He'd be helpless and dead in moments.

The tree shook as more climbed after him, roaring and yammering nonsense. The edge of the roof was only a jump away, but the branch was too thin at the end to get him nearer. Boyd saved up the strength to push off, bracing himself, closing his eyes for a second, and then gaining the composure and the desperation to do the impossible. He leaped forward, arms outstretched, hands ready to brace against the edge of the building. The branch under his foot snapped the moment he sprang forward, the dismount shaky, the connection against the building awkward and jarring. Both hands caught the edge of the roof, palms now scraped and bleeding. The strange sensations offered up a much needed jolt, a primordial vigor to not let go.

He pulled his body up to his elbows and then hoisted his upper body over the roof, then his left foot. He landed back-first against the tarmac surface, releasing a pent-up breath. The blood rushed to his head and blotted out the night sky. The dead bodies swarmed the tree like raving birds, clutching the branches, many breaking them, their need to reach him fierce. They couldn't clear the gap; the last foothold was the broken branch that he'd snapped off during his daring jump.

He reached for his rifle, but it was gone; he'd dropped it sometime during the climb and preceding jump. He rose to his feet and looked out at the tree and onto the ground at the crowd.

Every shadow-etched face glared up to him, their mouths locked in grim determination, their rotting faces beckoning to him in throaty jargon, a language of nasal grunts and growls. Many in the group were already falling apart. Arms fell from sockets, the meat losing its strength and elasticity. Eyes slid out of their heads and threatened to slither out—select individuals had already lost their eyes, the orbs now bobbing on long strings of orbital tissue—and some had skin worn thin to the point the organs showed through, the rot visible in fungal patches. Many were the weaker beings on the lower rungs of life, desperate for the parts they needed, the parts Boyd owned.

If I stay here long enough, he thought, eying them and their condition, *maybe they'll rot out. Or I'll starve to death first.*

The creatures showed no signs of moving on, however. They wouldn't die, but instead trickle on even if they became heaps of bones, and somehow they'd continue to exist, unlike him.

Boyd trudged to the roof's access door, done with the pointless vigil. The door wasn't completely shut, and he was relieved he wasn't trapped on the roof. The flight of stairs inside winded down until he came upon the door that led to the top floor. It opened easily and he found himself in a wide and expansive room, harboring numerous rectangular tables such as what would be used in autopsies, as well as sinks and drain fixtures, the set-up resembling a high school biology class. An overhead water sprayer equipped each table along with a tray of surgical tools, shelves, jars of embalming fluid, trocar cables, and many steel instruments he didn't recognize were housed in glass displays. Overhead, the ceiling fans were unmoving. The sight that troubled him the most was the empty body bags that littered the floor between the tables and the sinks. Boyd went to them, knelt down, and unzipped a bag carefully to see if there was a clue inside as to what they were used for, though he was fairly certain he knew. The zipper was ice cold to the touch and nothing was inside them. He nudged the others with his foot to check for contents, and again, they were empty.

"What in the hell is this place?"

He checked the labels on the body bags, but there were no names, instead there were locations on the labels. They were from areas spread across the United States, others in Europe and the Middle East. He picked up one of the bags, shook it, and clumps of soil fell out of the opening.

The body bags are from corpses taken from graves.

The room was clean, faded bleach dominating the air. The floors and drains were spotless, the tools and equipment untouched. He imagined military or medical staff like Dr. Glover working on corpses among the tables, dissecting the dead.

But he didn't have time to figure it out; he needed to find Cindy. Hayden could be doing anything to her at this point, and Boyd couldn't let that happen. She was in peril, and he was studying evidence to build a case in a crime, but what jury would hear it? And that's if he escaped, and that chance was quickly becoming a diminishing possibility.

At the opposite end of the room, where the lights were off, was a set of doors, the egress beckoning to him. It was difficult guiding himself through the shadow-filled areas beyond the main room. There was just enough light to supply a depth of detail that he was able to navigate down the stairs safely.

Once on the bottom floor, what he assumed to be the first floor, he found offices. The windows were shattered and glass crunched under his feet.

INSIDE THE PERIMETER

He snuck into the first office, scanning the shelves and filing cabinets that looked as if they had been ransacked, many knocked over with drawers hanging open. Documents of personal information were scattered everywhere: career status, criminal offenses, social security numbers, weight, height, and existing relatives.

He picked up and read a requisition form from a funeral home. It listed the casket numbers, burial locations, and date of ceremony for hundreds of individuals. And many listed were from Arlington Cemetery.

His jaw dropped. *This is beyond just blowing a whistle.*

It didn't matter what the military or government promised him in exchange for bringing in Hayden alive, he wasn't going to stay here and be forgotten or executed. The impulse to escape with or without Hayden flooded his resolve, but first, Cindy had to be found.

Boyd was about to step out of the room when the phone on the closest desk began to ring.

CHAPTER 28

Hayden throttled Cindy to the floor, both hands clenching her neck. He let her go to lock the entrance door, the insistent metallic bang and rattle of fists and bodies quickly growing in volume. He was out of breath, the struggle to carry Cindy and escape to shelter leaving him drained.

Cindy stayed face-first on the ground, eyes closed, gasping for air; she wasn't going anywhere. He scanned the walls for a light switch but didn't see one. The building's purpose wasn't obvious; it was a steel square two stories tall.

Hayden listened for Boyd's cries of agony to come to him from outside and was disappointed not to hear anything close to his desires, only the dead's chaotic chatter. Haunted by their din, scared to be in a room so dark, Hayden continued his search for a light switch. "Awful dark in here, don't you think?" he said to Cindy.

No reply.

The silence was a challenge. He was running the show, and had decisions to make. Her presence brought about nervousness. The hookers, he used alcohol as a social sedative—nothing new in the history of the human race—but the present scenario wasn't a bar, his apartment, or his Honda truck in an alley; this time, it was a closed off facility in a building that had no obvious purpose or identity.

He didn't feel in control of the moment; Cindy was a fighter, a woman with a reason to live, even in this place.

She would be difficult to break.

Richard's voice took over. *Talk her up the best you can, Hayden. Loosen her up and convince her to drop her defenses and let you in. What can you talk about? Try some common ground? What do you share?*

They had no previous history together, but the close calls on their lives were a common thread. Tragedy brought people closer, and he hoped it would for Cindy, too.

"I'm scared," he confessed, his tone neutral, inviting her to identify with him. "Sure, you consider me a monster, and by your understanding, I am. I'm not going to validate myself to you; that's beneath me. We're trapped, my dear, and we're going to have to deal with it together."

She was hard to visualize in the dark. She was curled up into a ball with her back against the wall, arms to her body, face bent down, draped in shadow.

Hayden started to wonder if she really would be that hard to break.

He was distracted by the revelation when a familiar odor swept over him again, reminding him of a funeral home. "Do you smell embalming fluid?"

"No," she whimpered, body cringing, struggling to talk to him. "I wouldn't know."

She believed he was playing mind games with her, and he was, but the last question was harmless.

He continued the search for a light source. "I wonder what's in this place."

"Quit talking to me, you bastard. I'm not interested in anything you have to say."

Fear soaked through her façade and he knew this was the moment to exploit her. "The words we use to insult each other, it means nothing. You can cut someone off on the highway, you can flip people off, cheat on your significant other, and hurl words and lies until your tongue dries out into leather, but it's very base." He paused, gaining impetus in explaining his motives, "I eat flesh because I enjoy it. The taste, the effort of butchering my meat—like hunters who eat the deer they kill—and the chase, it turns me on in many ways."

He smiled slightly. "But it's also my way of cursing humanity. It's a superior insult. I never fit in, at school or society, and this isn't my sob story. Far from it. But I do hate people in great numbers. We lose our personality that way, and I struggled for years trying to find my own character among others. A man named Richard helped me tap into something so great that it cast me out of society and put me into prison, but it was for a greater purpose."

He sighed. "I ended up here, and I've never been happier—that is until those things tore down my home. They were scared of me, Cindy. I burned them outside to show them I mean business, and it worked, but they were toying with me. They broke into the restaurant and watched me, but now that you're here, you've brought out the bloodlust within them. They've never been this active, and their numbers have doubled. They're hidden throughout this place. Compared to the dead and what I've discovered in life, what I've experienced, the way you insulted me just now is pitiful. After surviving this, words like 'bastard' don't affect me in the least."

Cindy was confused at his oration, and letting it slip, she scoffed, "What's the point of telling me all of this?"

"It's crude what you've said, my dear, but it's true, I am a lunatic. I've eaten many people, and I've digested them. What's more lunatic-like than turning someone into fecal matter and flushing them into a sewer among more sewage? When most people die, at least you receive a funeral, a ceremony, a padded casket, but with the way I've discarded people, there's nothing holy about it. Those things out there also insult humanity. They deserve no compassion. They're meat, just like us. We're meat, and eventually, we'll all be eaten or used in some way by others."

"Maybe they don't know what they're doing," Cindy commented, growing more comfortable speaking, perhaps buying time, Hayden believed, before he could cut her up to fit on a plate. "Who says they're thinking individuals? They can't talk, they resort to violence, and they're decomposing. But I don't care what you have to say to me. You're babbling like a fool."

"No, you will care!" he shot back, unwittingly unleashing his rage at her lack of understanding. "In due time, my belief system won't be so far fetched. You haven't lived much outside yourself, have you? You go to work, date, enjoy dinner and a movie, and you fail to notice the world around you; to really scrutinize it."

"It's my life, and I live it the way I chose, you arrogant bastard." Cindy was on her feet now, arms posed to punch and body flexed to fight. "You live by butchering people and shitting them out; I decided to keep my life a bit more normal than that. You think you're exploring yourself and the world, but you're really nothing more than a murderer who can't validate his actions. That's why you went to prison."

"I'm a dead man," Hayden said, trying to explain himself better to her. "It doesn't matter if I went to prison, because I'm free now. No laws apply to me here, so I'd shove those brave words back down your throat if I were you. No one's here to save you. Boyd is dead, and we're alone."

Cindy lowered her eyes and didn't speak. The truth was sinking in, and it was apparent by the sadness demurring her face.

Moving on, Hayden located a row of light switches on the far wall and flicked them on. They were large dome fixtures, high up, like that of an assembly room at a school gymnasium, and it took moments for them to blink on and bathe the room in white light.

What the light uncovered surprised him.

Cindy studied the room with a start.

In the first half of the space, various military vehicles were parked: Jeeps, Pathfinders, a medical unit, and dozens of Land Rovers. The back was too far to make out, mostly hallways and offices that channeled well beyond his vision. Hayden rushed to the closest Jeep, enticed, but there were no keys in the ignition. He threw open the glove compartment and checked the back cab, combing the obvious hiding places but there were no keys.

"Useless," he snapped, feeling a migraine form in his head. "We can't do anything with a car without keys." He turned to her, honestly asking, "Can you hotwire a rig like this?"

Cindy shook her head, staying put. "No, I've never tried it before and I wouldn't know what to do if I wanted to."

Hayden disregarded her attitude, and prevented a violent reaction of slapping her, by thinking what piece of flesh to take from her first. It would have to be a portion where the bleeding could easily be remedied. Flesh from the back was good, but there wasn't as much meat there as the abdomen or the thighs. The triceps was one of the better parts to taste; it was like pork, but it was naturally bland.

The way it was prepared was the true redeemer of any flesh.

The leg region, perhaps. I'll take from the calf or the hamstrings. I hope she's shaved her legs recently. I'll probably have to do it myself. But that'll be fun, too.

"Looks like this building is secure. It's a good place for me to start over. I might like this better than the restaurant," he mused.

Cindy, afraid to initiate an attack, meekly asked, "Start over?"

The crack of her voice drew his smile. The truth was sinking in for her. Boyd wasn't here to protect her, he wouldn't be saving her, and it was just the two of them now.

"Yes, my dear, start over. The restaurant's boarded up thanks to them, but who's to say I won't journey back there to collect the booze I left behind? And I've frozen a lot of their bodies; the pieces are ready to eat. I can move them here easily under the cover of darkness once things quiet down outside."

"That's disgusting," Cindy groveled, imagining him transporting the remains. "It's bad enough you were murdering innocent people, but you cannibalize the dead."

"They're dead, and that's the beauty of it." Hayden stepped over to her, challenging her dissent. "Nobody can call it murder. Broman was put here to return me to the police. They found more of my victims in the city, but those were also Richard's victims. Almost fifty, if I recall right." He came in closer to her. "And you know what the funny thing is, Cindy? I can't say where I put them all. One time, I chucked a human mandible on the interstate. It shattered on impact, and by the time someone realized it was human teeth smacking their windshield instead of gravel, it was too late to identify me. I was *long* gone!"

Cindy's face beaded sweat. "W...why are you telling me this?"

"Because you're going to obey me from now on, no more smartass comments. I'm capable of so much, and you better realize it."

She swallowed hard. "Are you going to kill me now?"

Hayden removed the five-inch kitchen knife from his back pocket and cleaned the blood off with his shirt. "I was planning to keep you alive for a while, but I thought the same about the woman that was with me in the restaurant. Do you remember the body in the storage room? She rotted out too fast, and her insides went bad, *an awful waste.* I'm not letting your body go like hers. And Brandy was a dirty slut, but you, you keep yourself clean. You're quality merchandise."

Her face turned powder white, and she stifled the urge to vomit. She curled up again, her head pressed to the wall, grinding her head against the surface to abate a headache. His shadow draped over her, he was so close. "What is it you're trying to do? If you're really going to vomit, I'll stick my finger down your throat for you, and then we'll see how sick you really are."

He grabbed her neck, but she uncurled, dropped onto her knees, and reaching out to squeeze his crotch. She clenched and twisted his groin until Hayden fell backwards and landed in a fetal position, both hands cradling his manhood, shrieking out, *"Fucking bitch! I'll kill you slowly, and you'll feel every bit of pain when I shred you!"*

A line of spittle dribbled from his mouth, a thick globule. He clamped his eyes shut, the pain accelerating into a blanket of electricity over his entire body. The recoil traveled up his abdomen and created the urge to puke. After minutes of taking the pain, Hayden rose to his knees, and he returned to his feet, careful not to disturb his throbbing groin. The swell in his midsection continued with every step he took, slowing him and he had to pause and rest, his breathing coming in short gasps.

He spotted Cindy's head behind a Jeep.

There you are, he thought.

"I see you!" he hissed.

Hayden tracked the patter of feet, the metal gratings on the floor making it difficult to tread silently. He weaved through a Pathfinder and caught Cindy head-on. She pushed through him and sprinted to the opposite wall, screaming. She struck something on the wall with her hand and a green light flashed; a mechanical groan followed the grinding of metal cables, though the noise was muffled, echoing from under their feet. She spun her head back and forth from him to the metal door, nervous as he came in closer. When the walls opened, revealing an elevator, Cindy lunged inside, pressing the switchboard with her hand. The elevator doors began closing, and Hayden reached out, attempting to gain access.

He was too late.

"Damn it," he growled.

The 'down' arrow was lit and the numbers glowed above the elevator. There were three floors to the building, he saw, and she was heading to the basement.

"You're not getting far, *dead bitch.*"

He pounded the button after the elevator reached its destination. The mechanical churn answered his command, and the doors soon returned to his level and opened. He hit the panel on the inside and waited. The elevator was large enough to fit ten people standing side-by- side, he observed, brushing his foot across a small pile of dirt spread out on the floor.

That's strange, he thought.

As the elevator went lower into the building, the tang of embalming fluid became stronger. The building was more than a military storage facility, he now believed. He had speculated that the hospital was the only source of the dead beings, but after evaluating this building, he wasn't so sure.

His next haven was already ruined before he'd even moved in, he feared. He wanted his life back to how it was yesterday, just him, alone and fed. Now *he* was being stalked, his food more powerful than him, and to make matters worse, his testicles were on fire.

"I'll find you, Cindy," he whispered, determined to enact vengeance in exchange for his pain. "You're trapped down there."

The doors were about to open, and soon, he'd be with her again.

CHAPTER 29

Boyd picked up the phone. "Hello."

"Mr. Broman." The reply was overconfident.

"How do you know I'm here?" He scanned the room's walls and ceiling, looking for a camera, but not locating proof of surveillance. "Are you here in the facility? I thought you were on your way to pick up Hayden at the hospital?"

"The corpses surrounded the place. The windows, entrances, and exits are all boarded up. They're smart. We can't get in, and besides, Hayden is no longer in there. No loss."

"Dr. Glover might be dead, or do you give a shit?" Boyd asked.

"It's better he's gone, Mr. Broman. We can't pull him out and never could. He was doing important work for us. They have to be controlled, you see, but there's nothing you can do about that, so let's move on. The offer's still good if you're interested. Hayden in exchange for your freedom."

Boyd wanted to meet the man he was talking to and really give him a hearty thank you for stowing him in this hellhole by putting a bullet in his head. But it was best the man believed he was counting on them. At least for now. "Okay, I'll still get him for you. But I need more time, I'll capture the bastard."

"Fine, I'll check in with you in an hour then."

"How will you know where I'll be?"

A chuckle. "We keep an eye on our facility, Mr. Broman, believe me. Don't worry about how we keep track of you."

Boyd attempted to coax more information out of the stranger. "So this was a military base, or used to be one, right?"

The man disregarded the question and said, "Hayden happens to be inside the building you're in right now. I'm sure you can apprehend him easily. Inside the desk your standing near, you'll find a set of keys. It will start one of the vehicles parked in the loading dock adjacent to the room you're in. The dock door opens and closes like a garage door. Once you have Hayden, you drive through the crowd outside and reach the police station where we first talked, and I'll have someone pick you up. And then you're a free man."

Free to die is what he means. He makes it sound so damn easy, he thought.

Agreeing, and pouring on the charm, Boyd replied, "Okay, I'll meet you at the police station with Hayden."

"Very good, Mr. Broman." The phone line went dead.

Boyd searched the desk as instructed and discovered the set of keys next to a pack of cigarettes and a plastic Bic lighter. He stowed them in his back pocket, enjoying the thought of indulging later on with a cigarette.

A shrill scream echoed from outside the office, startling him.

He dashed out of the room, down a short hallway and into the loading dock. Turning on the switch on the wall, the overhead fluorescents were soon flickering on and bathing the room in neon-white. Military vehicles occupied the room, and there were so many that he was concerned how long it would take to find a match for the keys in his hand.

His eyes went wide when he spotted Hayden lurching between vehicles, his gait shrunken, a hand cupping his genitals, the other clutching a knife. Then he caught a glimpse of Cindy disappear behind a Land Rover.

Relief flooded through him; she wasn't dead.

Boyd ran after them, but when he came upon Hayden, he paused, ideas popping into his head on how to handle the man. He saw Cindy scramble into an elevator, having successfully escaped Hayden; she was safe, and now it was just between Boyd and the cannibal.

Boyd crept from bumper to bumper, skulking silently. Hayden waited at the elevator, massaging his groin. Boyd assumed he had taken a pounding, and he knew who had delivered the damage.

The elevator doors opened, and when Hayden entered, Boyd sprung to attack before the door could close. With both of them now inside the elevator, Boyd drove his knee into Hayden's pelvis, taking advantage of what Cindy had already started.

"And I bet you thought it was bad enough you were hit in the balls once today!" Boyd yelled.

Hayden's mouth unhinged, moaning in agony as he crumbled to his knees, face clenching, eyes shut tight. Boyd seized the man's greasy hair and drove the palm of his hand into Hayden's nose. The distinct crack inspired blood and Hayden's lips became wet with blood as it dripped down his chin, bright red. Hayden's eyes fluttered closed from the impact, and with a short struggle, his sinuses popping and boiling with crimson, he dropped to the floor, unconscious.

Boyd eyed the prone body and nudged Hayden in the ribs, double-checking if his assailant was down for good. "If you're faking, I'll do worse, Hayden."

The elevator dinged, indicating it had reached the basement level. The doors opened and a breeze blew across Boyd, alarmingly frigid. The wind harbored a fecundity, sickly sweet and organic. Humidity gave a dampness to the air, repulsing him with each intake of breath into his lungs.

Alert, afraid more of the dead lurked in the unknown chambers, he listened but heard nothing. Boyd locked the elevator on the basement floor before moving forward, ensuring a quick getaway. Focusing harder, he couldn't make out anything, it was pitch black. He searched his back pocket for the lighter taken from the desk and flicked it. The lone flame did little to show the way, but the wall beside him displayed a panel of switches. When he reached out to turn them on, something skirted behind him.

He whipped around to face the threat, but a blow to his face knocked him to the floor, disorienting him. His ears rang with sharp piercing whistles, trails of blood flowing down his cheek from a gash on his forehead. He fought through the blinding agony to roll onto his back, arms up, hands ready to challenge the attacker. White filled his eyes, cotton thick, the room a moving blur, a roaring locomotive filling his ears. He was so dizzy, the walls leered down on him, and he couldn't get up; he was helpless.

So when the attacker spoke, he was relieved to know who it was.

"Oh my God, it's you!"

Boyd instantly recognized Cindy's voice, and he complained, letting down his defenses. "Jesus Christ, what the hell did you hit me with?"

"A chair; it was a chair," she apologized frantically.

He blinked, she was two specks floating in front of him, the rest just blotches of reds, purples and yellows.

"I didn't know it was you," she said, lowering her voice. "I thought you were dead. How did you get in here?"

"Let's just say climbing all those trees as a kid paid off." Boyd smiled despite the constant throbbing in his skull. "I jumped onto the roof, and there was an access door into the building. If it weren't for that, I would have had to break it down, but I'd be damned if you were going to stay alone with that murdering son-of-a-bitch a moment longer."

Cindy helped him to his feet, and she gave him a hug. She clung tightly to him, and she wept, grateful to be in his presence again. Tears escaping between words, she whispered, "I'm so glad you're not dead. I waited in that library, and I hated how much of a coward I had become. Thank God for you, Boyd."

He blushed at her words mouthed so close to his ear. It alleviated the ache between his ears for a moment, replacing one harsh emotion with a positive one. "We're getting out of here. I just need to get my bearings." He pointed at the wall panel. "Let's turn on the lights and see what's down here."

Cindy became silent. Startled by the notion.

"We have to know what we're up against," Boyd reassured her as he stepped to the wall. "Don't worry, I'll get you out of here, I promised, right?"

She nodded.

He waited a moment before flicking on the switches. The darkness was banished in pale white light a second later, the source dim, muted a nicotine yellow, the electrical wiring poor. The rotten odor lingering in the air turned into visible evidence. Cindy clutched onto him and cried into his shoulder, aghast. "Christ, what's next in this damn place?"

Rows of funeral caskets were piled tall, hundreds of them, scattered and strewn in disorganized heaps. They occupied half the room. He stepped closer, the floor softened by a layer of black soil half an inch thick. Studying everything, Boyd was attracted to a clipboard hanging on the wall with names and dates that ranged from the early 1980's to less than five years ago.

Disturbed from reading the list, the sight Cindy had gasped at was located in the back of the room. Rows of work tables, scratched and scarred from use, formed a square. In the aisles between the tables, naked corpses hung from hooks driven between their shoulder blades, the bodies themselves suspended from the ceiling rafters. The corpses were nothing but withered skeletons, mummified. Human limbs were scattered on the floor, a sloppy chopping block, many of the pieces flaccid and leathery. A plastic tub of heads rested on top of one of the tables, and another contained a heap of unidentifiable and desiccated organs. Many severed heads were strapped into vices on the worktables, the mouths open, the eyes missing, and many had lobes of their brains removed, the hemispheres decaying to the point that whatever research had been committed was lost. Jars of eyeballs and vials of blood occupied the table tops as well, random in purpose. Boyd then took a mental list of the tools used in the diabolical project: mallets, hammers, chisels, scalpels, surgical scissors, hacksaws, and masking tape.

He regretted turning on the lights now. Cindy was sobbing so hard she was shaking, her body wringing out every ounce of raw emotion possible so she could come to terms with the macabre scene.

He kept canvassing the room and came upon a metal chute—similar to a laundry chute in a residential home—on the far left wall. Bodies were sprawled out by the dozens on the floor, dropped down from the floors above. Cindy gasped, turned away from the grisly sight, and retreated back to the elevator.

"I...I...I have to leave, Boyd. I'm not feeling so good all of a sudden."

"Yeah, I know how you feel," he replied.

He guided her back to the elevator, supporting her. Hayden remained on the elevator floor, unconscious and harmless. Deciding it was best to leave, Boyd hit the button for the first floor, and the elevator doors closed in response. Cindy quivered in his arms. "This isn't right. They stole dead bodies from the graves. Who do they think they are?"

Boyd decided to skip the lamenting and return to the challenge of escaping the perimeter. "We have to work with what we've got,

Cindy. I have Hayden in my custody. We can finally do something to get the hell out of here."

He pulled out the keys in his pocket taken from the desk. "These go to one of the vehicles in the loading dock. We'll drive to the abandoned police station, and they'll come for Hayden. Whatever happens, we'll face them together, and maybe we can escape. I don't know how, but we have to try something." He paused a moment, making sure he believed what he was saying. "I might have an idea, but first," he removed the lighter and the pack of cigarettes from his pocket. "Care for one?"

"Why not?" Cindy smiled, happy to be distracted by something other than terror and death. Tears blotted her eyes, and she wiped them away before he lit a cigarette and handed it to her. She accepted it with an addict's zest, inhaling hard and holding the smoke in. "That's good."

Boyd lit one for himself and relished a pull. "No shit it's good." He thought about their situation and how it had affected their lives. "What doesn't kill you only makes you more pissed off at everybody else, right?"

"I can deal with anything from now on," Cindy laughed at herself, pressing her free hand flat against her sternum. "I'm bawling, and I normally don't. When my parents divorced, I didn't cry. My dad was sleeping with his assistant manager at a video rental store. My mom didn't take his shit and threw his ass out. Her strength, that's why I didn't cry at the time." She dug deeper, remembering another situation, "And when I broke my leg in cheerleading—if you can picture me in a short skirt and waving pom-poms—when I did a triple jump and landed wrong, breaking my right leg, I didn't shed a tear. I guess that's ridiculous compared to this."

"You should be proud," Boyd said, adding weight to her words, filling her up with genuine remarks. "When I spotted Hayden hobbling after you with a knife in one hand and the other holding himself I knew what you'd done to him." He patted her back. "You kicked him in the balls. That was smart thinking. You're one tough woman."

"I didn't kick him, I squeezed them?" She mimicked the action of squishing Hayden's testicles, embracing her prior actions. "He was ranting about how eating a person was the ultimate insult to humanity. And shitting people out afterwards was an offense against humankind."

"Well, he received a double dose of pain," Boyd chimed in, giving her a wink. "I kneed him in the groin, too. Then, I probably broke his nose afterwards." He looked down on the unconscious cannibal. "He's breathing; that's all I care about. The military or whoever they have on Hayden's case will do a lot worse to him in the interrogation room. It will be a ball damaging extravaganza."

The elevator opened on the first floor. Cindy stubbed out her cigarette against the wall, the delicacy spent. "Can I have another one?"

He handed her the pack and the lighter. "Have as many as you want; cancer doesn't exist here, right?"

He dragged Hayden out of the elevator and left him on the floor after making sure the man was still out of it, that he wasn't faking. Then Boyd advanced towards the parked vehicles. He pictured himself on a game show. *You've got five minutes to start the right car. You do so in time, you win fifty grand, and a bonus, you get to leave the perimeter without being cut up into spare parts!*

Cindy kept behind him, fiddling with the Bic lighter and a cigarette at the same time, when they arrived at the first Jeep and he tried the key. It didn't fit into the ignition.

He grumbled under his breath, already trying the next one. "This might take a while unless we get lucky."

The din from outside continued, the walls throbbing and resonating with the impact of determined fists; guttural screams and unintelligible demands adding to the overall mob effect raking against their ears.

Determined to shut the noise out, she finally asked, "So what's really your game plan for escaping?"

Continuing his search, he explained to her, "I got another phone call not too long ago. Back in those offices near the front of the perimeter, it was the same man who called me before, the man who said he'd meet us at the police station if we delivered Hayden. I do believe that someone will be there to take Hayden from me, but they'll probably leave us, maybe kill us. I don't believe him for a minute that he's just going to let us walk free. We know too much about him, this place. I say we negotiate. The dead beings are everywhere, so there won't be time for us to talk much. I say we hide Hayden somewhere, and when they come for him, we make them take us out of the facility first. There's embalming fluid jugs upstairs. We can stuff rags in them and set the place on fire, blaze a trail between them and us, and hopefully buy as much time as we can."

"Dr. Glover had the best plan," Cindy said, knowing the doctor was dead. "He had the card key, we could've walked out the front door, no problem."

The loss of Dr. Glover became real; he had been crucial to their escape, and they had barely known him for more than a few hours.

"There's nothing we can do about him, unfortunately," he said. "I can't be certain if negotiations will work, but we can't let the opportunity slip by without trying. Hayden's the key. And with the embalming fluid jugs, if we're surrounded by those dead people, at least we have a chance at holding up somewhere and staying alive. That's my best plan."

"What if we don't escape?" Cindy's face curved into a frown, uncertain about Boyd's strategy. "We lose Hayden, and then we're stuck here for sure."

Boyd knew the conflicts of any path they chose, and he thought of one other idea. "If that happens, we could find Dr. Glover's body and the card key."

He tried a series of other vehicles, Cindy watching him in anticipation, and finally a Land Rover started up.

Cindy clapped happily. "All right, Boyd, you found the one!"

A plum of smoke coughed out of the exhaust. "All right, we've got a set of wheels," he said.

He picked up Hayden, still limp and unconscious, and lugged him into the back seat, laying him on his side. There were no cuffs or rope to bind him with, so he had to leave him be.

He closed the rear door of the vehicle, hastening his efforts upon remembering the second half of his plan. "Shit, I almost forgot. Let me run upstairs and get the embalming fluid and the scraps of cloth."

"Okay, hurry up," she said.

"I'll be no more than five minutes, I promise," he said as he opened his door, climbed out, and rushed to the elevator.

On his way, he picked up Hayden's knife that had fallen onto the floor. He turned and ran back, offering it to Cindy. "Hold this, and if he wakes up, point it at him, and if he moves to hurt you, stab him."

Cindy clutched the knife, unsure of herself, holding it with two fingers, but when she eyed Hayden's dead skin mask, her mouth bent in determination and she finally held it firmly in her grasp.

CHAPTER 30

Boyd arrived on the top floor, coming upon the same darkened room as before. Wasting no time, he lifted four glass jugs of embalming fluid from a well-stocked shelf and placed them inside the elevator. Taking a lab coat, he returned to the elevator and ripped it into pieces.

Keeping the pieces, he returned to the first floor, rushing back to Cindy, ensuring she was safe before carrying the jugs to the Land Rover by propping them between the driver and passenger seats.

He gave her instructions, seeing her ogle the jugs. "I want you to open a container, douse one of these pieces of cloth in the fluid, and close the lid with a part of the cloth hanging out. We'll light the cloth, throw the jug, and when the glass shatters, the fire will spread. It's simple, and it's our only weapon, and I don't remember guns doing much to those creatures except maybe slowing them down a little. I've shot one of them in the head before, and it still didn't go down for good."

Cindy nodded, understanding. "Whatever those researchers did to build those bodies, it's insane. And with us knowing that," she regarded him with doleful eyes, "the people in charge of this place will never let us out of here, let's be honest."

"Yes, I know; I've known that the entire time, and that's why we have to make our own way out. Even if we have to destroy this place from the inside out, it's going to go up in smoke. Maybe they'll let us out when every one of those dead things is nothing more than a pile of ashes. No project left to maintain, right? That's if our attempt at using Hayden as a pawn fails. You see, we do have a contingency plan."

Cindy smiled slightly, mulling it over. "I want this to be over. But everything's against us."

Boyd urged her close, hugging her from the side. "Our chances aren't great, I know, but we're fighting. That's all we can do. We've been alive for this long, and I'm sure there's a reason for that."

"You're the reason I'm alive." Her eyes glowed bright. She turned so they were facing one another, and she hugged him closer. She whispered in her ear, lustful, needy and honest, digging her nails into his back lightly, enticing him as she said, "I know you're married, but we might not make it. Would you kiss me? Just once?"

He ran his hands through her hair, parting the strands over her eyes. Their lips met in that moment. Her body unclenched, broken from a spell, and her hands wrapped around his back, closing the deal. She wouldn't let him go, her mouth opening to let his tongue inside, their lips pressing harder, absorbing each other's affections. Finally, she broke off the kiss, her face flushed. "You're a good kisser."

"Well, I figured it might be my last one so I did my best."

Moving on from the heartfelt moment, they climbed into the Land Rover. Cindy peered over the backseat at Hayden's body. "You think he's okay back there?" Cindy observed him for another moment before turning her eyes back up front, deciding the question herself. "He's bloody and unconscious; good enough for now, I guess."

"Shit, I forgot something else." Boyd said. He backed up the Land Rover to give him a head start to pick up speed, imagining he'd be ramming through many of the dead once the loading dock door was opened then jumped out and ran to the loading dock door. He had forgotten that someone had to open it manually.

He called out to her, "I'm going to have to open it and run back. Brace yourself, I'll be fast. Just sit tight. Everything's gonna be fine."

Striking the control panel, he opened the barrier between them and the dead waiting outside and dashed back to the waiting vehicle.

CHAPTER 31

Cindy and Boyd believed Hayden was unconscious, and he planned on keeping it that way.

The clang of the glass embalming fluid jugs filled the interior of the Land Rover when it jerked forward, and Hayden opened his eyes slightly at the disturbance. Cindy was in the seat in front of him, his knife now clutched in her hands, a tool of false protection. He could steal it back in a split second, and he imagined doing it many times.

Boyd bolted out of the vehicle, and seconds later, Hayden heard a motor's hum and a metal door opening. Loud voices from outside filtered in, then doubling in volume, raging now that they sensed their prey was coming out of the building.

Boyd leapt into the driver's seat, foot slamming on the gas pedal, and the Land Rover sped through the opening. Like a charging battering ram, the vehicle shattered torsos in a steady musical beat, there were so many to crush. Heads and other body parts bounced off the windshield, leaving a coating of fluids that made seeing difficult, so Boyd turned on the wipers.

Fragments of faces came and went as did the twisting bodies, their parts spring-ejected from their ripe forms, all of it a cyclone of anatomy: a broken foot, an arm, an eyeless face, a gaping mouth, a sloshing tongue smacking the glass, a decapitated head, and a torso that burst open upon impact, shedding visceral coils of red meat. The bodies thumped over the roof and were spit out the back side, flung loosely. The dead tried to open the door handles to no success, though they kept trying, the clawing adding to the overall overwhelming chorus of human bones breaking.

Boyd picked up speed, surging faster, separating the Land Rover from the wall of bodies and then he was traveling on flat, unimpeded territory.

Hayden waited until they cleared more distance before stealing the knife back from Cindy.

Boyd studied the rearview mirror. Many of the dead in the Land Rover's wake were strewn on the ground with their backs bent inwards and broken, their arms and legs flailing and shifting, unable to lift themselves up.

He slowed down; confident he had a moment to think.

"What are you doing?" Cindy cried out, frustrated, scrutinizing the path behind them. "They'll catch up. Keep going, keep going!"

"Light one of those jugs," Boyd demanded while ignoring her pleas. "There's at least two gallons of that stuff in each one. It'll slow them down; it'll be less of them on our tail later."

Cindy struggled to flick the lighter, nervous with jitters. "They're getting closer."

The undamaged bodies were ten yards out, an ever expanding crowd coming in to swallow them up.

He pounded his fist against the steering wheel. "Come on, come on! Light it!"

She lost her grip, and the lighter dropped between her feet. She bent over to retrieve it, cursing. She reached to scoop it up, and once reclaiming it, she flicked it once, twice, three times before the flame was produced. Panicking, she dropped the lighter again, forgetting about immediately as it fell between her feet and slid under her seat.

Opening her door and hanging halfway out, she lit the cloth with a *whoosh*, and she held it high before heaving it in the dead crowd's direction.

The jug spinning through the air, the container struck one figure on the head, shattering into liquid fire and covering its body. Blue and white flames encased the first row of them, their bodies slowed by the torrent; others deterred and frantic to escape the burning heat.

"Good shot!" Boyd yelled.

Cindy leaned back into the vehicle, closed her door, and Boyd drove away, passing the mess hall in a blur as he picked up speed. The property spanned for miles in the distance, a continuation of the military base, but it was a waste to survey it now, whatever it could be; Hayden's delivery was Boyd's number one concern.

"Wow, will you look at that!" Cindy stared in awe, face highlighted in moving yellows and reds. "The hospital's going up in flames."

The structure was bustling with fire from every window and access door, the openings spitting out black smoke. The building was unstable, the roof off-kilter; it would collapse at any moment.

"You see, aren't you confident we can destroy this place if they don't let us out? Maybe someone will notice the flames from outside of the facility?" Boyd reasoned.

"We don't even know where we are. You said so yourself that this place is guarded with all kinds of security, and I don't know about you, but I haven't seen any planes fly over us yet."

Contradicting her, a helicopter soared overhead, revealing itself in the night sky. It swooped down low over the hospital, dropping a thick powder onto the burning building. Furious, Cindy pounded her fists against the dashboard in a fit. "What the hell are they doing? Seriously, stop it. *Stop it!*" She was yelling at the helicopter as if it would hear her and obey.

Boyd bit his lower lip as he gripped the steering wheel with trembling hands. "The bastards are really determined to keep this place going and those things alive. They can't control them. They're dead. Why keep trying? Why don't they just cut their losses, already?"

He drove through a street littered with debris and soot, nearing the town center, back to the places he'd already been.

"We're almost there, Cindy. Not too much longer and maybe we can put this all behind us. If this doesn't work, then we begin project *fuck this place up*."

But the presence of the helicopter broke both their spirits, and Boyd voiced what they both knew was true. "Fine, we can't lie to ourselves, we're screwed, but I'm sure that fire killed many of those things. We'll just have to keep at it. They can't breed. We can eradicate them. That's the plan if trading Hayden fails."

Boyd waited for Cindy to agree, but instead, she screamed.

CHAPTER 32

Hayden glanced up to the sky to see the helicopter angling down to snuff out the flames encompassing the hospital. Two more choppers were right behind it. It was a relief that someone was preserving the facility.

He felt it was designed for him; there were enough secure places to hide and he was confident he could start over again. Knowing this, and choosing the right moment to act, he crawled through the seats, and finally, seeing that Boyd and Cindy were distracted, lunged at Cindy and squeezed her throat—so soft, so breakable.

Take a bite out of her neck. It's the easiest to render. Do it now, Hayden, before she fights back! Richard's voice screamed in his head.

Hayden did as he was told, biting into the nape of her neck, so hard that his teeth severed through the skin and clacked together. Blood squirted into his mouth and spilled down his chin, warm and slick. The morsel of flesh from Cindy's neck rested on his tongue, and he kept it there, letting its heat marinate on his tongue before swallowing it.

The ingestion was abbreviated by an elbow to the face. Thrown back, head whip-lashed, he crashed between the back seats, shaking his head like a wet dog. Cindy was about to deliver the knife into his chest when Hayden dug his fingers around the back of her neck and jammed the tips of them into the open wound.

At the same time he wrenched the knife from her. *"Now you'll listen to what I have to say!"* he growled.

"Boyd, help!" Cindy shouted out, horrified she'd lost the knife.

The Land Rover swerved when Boyd ran over a pile of bones in the road. A tire exploded and shredded, the rim scraping the pavement, and he lost control of the wheel. The vehicle careened headfirst into the brick wall of the abandoned post office.

Hayden braced himself for impact, Cindy jerking forward and her head struck the windshield. She was stunned, face covered in blood. Hayden assumed she'd been stunned but not severely injured, as the glass was still intact.

Dead beings from behind them were catching up over the hill; they would be upon them in moments. The fiery hospital illuminated the horde through the open field, easily a hundred at a glance, blackened faces now burning a phosphorescent red in the dull glow.

Hayden checked the front seat, knowing the time to escape was upon him. Boyd was slumped over the steering wheel, unconscious.

Let the dead assholes disassemble Broman's body. I'll take what's left of him and fry him up in a skillet, Hayden thought.

Cindy stirred, trying to wake up. Hayden hit her on the head with the hilt of the knife until she cried out in pain, to then ultimately black out. He climbed out of the vehicle, picked her up and placed her over his shoulder, then studied the area, reevaluating his next move. In the distance, he saw the beams were warped and walls now crashing in, the hospital coming apart in thundering explosions. The entire structure would topple at any moment.

He began to head out.

Watching every street around him, the roads and businesses, dead bodies crawled and pursued them, limping from the entrance of the bowling alley, the shattered grocery store fronts, hands and faces materializing out of the gutters, crawling like rats escaping a sinking ship, and looming from further off from every residential house to meet them.

There was only one place to hide.

Hayden fled to the post office. The front door was blocked by a military Jeep, so he crawled through the seats and smashed the glass door to reach the entrance. Next, he dragged Cindy through the opening, pulling her through, careful not to cut either of them; he'd do plenty of that to her with better instruments when he could exact clean, precise cuts on her body.

The light from the burning hospital shed visibility into the darkened corners. The lobby was an open space; the rope partitions for a patron line were strewn on the ground, long disregarded. The mail area at the back of the building was empty of mail. Shelves, tables and display cases were knocked onto their sides; the place looked ransacked.

He rolled a long table up to the front entrance and wedged it in place, securing it. He peeked through the cracks of the glass door of the military Jeep and observed the dead beings scavenging the streets, more of them arriving by the second. Soon, they would dominate the area.

Hayden spat, feeling victory pulse through his veins. "I'll see you burn in Hell, Broman," he muttered angrily.

He rushed down a lone hallway, carrying Cindy in his arms. The mail sorting room was unoccupied. He found a row of desks in one of the corners and stopped at a paper cutter. Leaving her on the floor a moment, he unscrewed the cutter from the board with his fingers and carried it like a machete.

Seeing Cindy was unconscious and wouldn't be escaping, he left her for a moment and went to the bathroom, taking a moment to check himself in the mirror. His gray skin mask glistened with blood—his and Cindy's—looking the worse for wear from all the abuse he'd suffered lately.

He noted the, sticky fluid where the mask ended and his skin began; his arms shined with sweat and decaying skin. He proudly looked on at himself, admiring his work, fixing what flesh he could to make himself look more like one of the dead beings.

When he was finished, he returned to where he had left Cindy, and he froze.

She was gone.

Where the hell did she go?

CHAPTER 33

Boyd's forehead throbbed from slamming into the steering wheel, a permanent gong going off in his skull. Crusted blood filled his nostrils, and he snorted it out. He spat out the taste of iron in his mouth, repulsed. Horrified, but awake and weighing his situation, he didn't know how long he had blacked out. He tried to start the Land Rover, but the engine was damaged, only a dull clicking sound emanating from under the hood each time he turned the ignition key. Radiator fluid spread in a growing pool underneath the front end. Behind him, new fires had sprung up, the hospital's flames spreading to the cars in the parking lot as well as embers blowing into anything nearby, everything an increasing inferno. The choppers kept coming and going, attempting to put out the flames.

Boyd wasn't sure if they'd succeed, and he didn't have the time to watch. Cindy was missing, and he called out to her, but there was no answer.

Damn it, what else can happen? he thought.

Human silhouettes shambled in every direction of his peripheral vision; the moving dead bodies were circling, dripping, gargling and pleading for him in prolonged moans, faces of death taunting him, sizing him up, systematically planning how they would use his body parts to their benefit.

Boyd checked up and down the streets for evidence that Cindy or Hayden had been attacked, but there was no fresh blood or screams for mercy. He stepped out of the Land Rover, his head heavy as a cinder block, his body tilting at the extent of his bodily ache.

Hurried by the prospect of delivering violence, the dead bodies were prepared to disembody him. They were armed with unconventional weapons. Handfuls of concrete, palms clutching shards of glass. A few carried street sign poles taken from the road or they'd torn planks of wood from the siding on houses. He even caught them carrying broken femurs as bludgeons.

INSIDE THE PERIMETER

Boyd ducked behind the Land Rover, dodging a flensing knife that bounced tip-first off the hood. "Holy shit," he said staring at the undead horde.

A chorus of sharpened steel implements clinked against the ground, deflected from the hood. Thinking fast, Boyd crawled back into the vehicle to get at the embalming fluid. He checked his pockets, knowing he was missing an important item.

The lighter—Cindy had used it.

And had then dropped it.

Boyd scanned the floorboards for it, sliding his open palms across the carpeting desperate to locate it. He searched desperately, and his hand finally touched it. It was right where Cindy had dropped it, under the passenger seat, but was just out of reach.

A brick shattered through the window of the passenger door, covering him in a layer of safety glass. More knives pinged against the vehicle's fenders like deadly hail. Their numbers grew in mass, and Boyd saw there was nowhere he could go without confronting them; this would be his final stand against the walking, living death of beings.

Boyd stretched his arm, his clavicle wound puckering open and leaking blood, forever an open wound as long as he was trapped inside the perimeter. The Land Rover rocked to the side, a shove by four synchronized sources. The shocks kicked out a rusty squeak, warning him of danger. Another window shattered, this time by a blackened, still smoking skull.

He extended his fingers to claim the lighter from underneath the seat. "Come on, *come on!*"

The back tire deflated, and the car slumped to the right. Another brick broke through the driver's window, the brick itself striking his left calf and causing him to yelp as he bucked forward. And that's what he needed, shoved forward that final inch; he was able to clasp the lighter, dragging it towards him.

Ducking low, he gathered a glass jug, and lighting the cloth tip, he kicked his door open and launched it into the incoming path of the crowd. The glass container shattered on the street, and the embalming fluid splashed up from the surface, catching the circle of figures and setting them aflame. The street pulsated heat, attacking feet, orange flames crawling up legs and eating into torsos. The figures stumbled about, confused and horrified at the arching and bending flames, many instantly blanketed, their advances halted.

Boyd gasped at one who came in too close, much too close; the woman hurled a handful of broken glass at him. He turned around and gave her his back, the bits penetrating the skin along his spine. Every movement was torture, triggering the tiny wounds, and Boyd wished to pay her back the favor. He lit another jug and heaved it into the dead woman's face, literally smashing it down upon her skull. The shatter marked a ball of fire melting down her from top-to-bottom, the tar-black body instantly cooked to a crisp, the skin melting as the air grew thick and noxious with the smell of charred flesh.

Boyd reached to pluck the glass from his back, but he couldn't maneuver without upsetting the small wounds, and there was no time, they were still coming. He spotted movement from within the post office, seeing a shadow pass by one of the windows. Someone was inside, and when he looked closer, aided by the firelight, he knew it had to be Hayden. The man was alive, and that meant there was a good chance Cindy was with him.

But Boyd was cornered, just paces from the post office entrance, and more of the bodies were coming out of the night.

One jug left.

He weighed it in his hand, and then lit the wick, unsure where to heave it. He needed time to enter the post office and track down Cindy and recapture Hayden.

Hayden couldn't be killed; it would render the possibility of negotiation with the people who wanted him impossible, and poor Cindy, he couldn't let her die by the cannibal's hands. It would be useless to throw the jug in any one direction because the dead were everywhere.

The post office was his only escape.

Deciding then what he had to do, he smashed the jug underneath the Land Rover. Flames stewed beneath the undercarriage, and Boyd retreated to the post office, punching and kicking any attackers that came at him. He crawled through the Jeep parked across the main entrance and struggled through the front doors, shoving to throw back a table wedged across the opening. After it collapsed to the floor, Boyd landed palms-first against the tiles. The glass in his back shifted, the unbearable pain delivered anew, and forced from the agonizing moment, something darted from the shadows and swung at him.

Missing by less than an inch, a metal spark flickered up from the tiles with a scraping sound. The weapon was the sharp end of a paper cutter, helmed by a dead man, his flesh hanging loose from his body with blood smeared hastily across his arms and chest.

Boyd locked gazes with the eyes of the dead man and he saw life there and knew his attacker wasn't one of the dead.

It was Hayden.

Boyd distinguished a sneer through the flesh mask, disgusting beyond any living dead face he'd encountered thus far. Spittle was flying out his mouth as he screamed, "I'm going to throw you to those things out there, Broman! I'm going to cripple you so they can dismantle you even faster. Richard said that's the best punishment for you!"

"Oh, really? So does Richard still talk to you, then?" Boyd asked, backing up enough distance so he wouldn't be touched by the weapon without seeing it coming first, Boyd aimed to buy time, using craft over force. He remembered the psych evaluation on Hayden, how the man said Richard talked to him, helped him in what he needed to do.

But nobody had actually found Richard's body or ever seen the man; many of the investigators questioned if Richard actually existed. Hayden's next-door neighbor was really a retired woman in her eighties named Rosa Felter; she was clueless about her neighbor's morbid pastimes. "Richard's body was found, didn't you know that?" He lied, crafty in the spur-of-the-moment. "He was discovered in a sewer channel blocking up a heap of shit and a crew had to dislodge the human cork. The coroner did a full autopsy. Richard was asphyxiated, and his esophagus and throat were expanded. Do you know what he choked on, Hayden? A dildo was shoved down his throat. The coroner also found one shoved up his ass. His genitals were retrieved in his stomach half-digested, too. Richard had worked himself up a fine reputation. I'm sure a pimp or whoever owned these sluts he kept eating kept track of their investments. They finished your hero off in a fitting style."

Hayden clutched the paper cutter, shaking his head in denial. "That's not how he died. He didn't die, he's alive! *How dare you lie about him?*"

"You don't sound so sure of yourself. You should see your eyes, they're brimming with tears. Did you love the man? I think you're obsessed with him. A man that doesn't exit."

"You'd never understand, fuck you for even trying!" Hayden screamed and then lunged at Boyd, the paper cutter missing again, a slash of air sounding out between them. Boyd lowered to his haunches and delivered a fist into Hayden's lower abdomen in a power arc. The cannibal folded to the floor like a sack of concrete, coughing up Cindy's skin in pink vomit.

"One hit, Hayden, and you're already down. You've let yourself go, haven't you? Eating human flesh has softened you up; fattened the little piggy," Boyd said.

"Do you miss your wife?" Hayden challenged, spitting out the remains of Cindy's skin from his mouth. "I'm sure she's missing her murderer of a husband. How about your kids? You've fucked your children up, Boyd. You can beat the hell out of me, but nothing will ever change that. You won't escape this place. They don't want me dead, so they put you here to capture me, but the sad thing is you can't force me out. I'll slit my fucking wrists before you force me back out there. This is where I want to live, and this is where I'll die."

Boyd stared at the man and realized how much power Hayden owned.

"I'm not dying because of you," Boyd hissed. "This is my chance to take back what was stolen from me, you got that? I may not get it back, but I'll do what I can to mess up their plans for this place and to kill as many of those things out there as possible."

He kicked Hayden in the abdomen to ensure the fight was over, Hayden collapsing, clutching his belly and shrinking into a fetal position. Boyd lifted him up by his hair and delivered a fist to his nose once again; blood drained out both nostrils, the fight in the man removed.

"If your nose wasn't broken earlier," Boyd growled, admiring the blood on his knuckles, "it sure as shit is broken now."

Hayden covered his face to stem the red trails leaking out of his nostrils from under his skin mask. He eyed Boyd with pure contempt, an odd display from the decayed mask. And that's when Hayden suddenly launched to his feet with a burst of unexpected strength and fled to the rear of the building. Boyd pursued, but Hayden escaped out the back exit door, too fast to catch.

Then the building rocked on its foundation as the windows were blown in, glass raining down onto him.

The Land Rover had exploded thanks to the fire he'd set beneath it.

Boyd's feet absorbed the concussions. Objects banged and rattled against the outside walls, random debris. The beings outside unleashed a caterwaul, streams of fire and hot shrapnel cannoning in flaming balls in every direction. The acrid scent of gasoline and burning tires invaded Boyd's nostrils.

And then he heard a voice, soft at first, and then quickly gaining volume. "Are you out there, Boyd? Is that you?"

Fists pounded from behind a door in the hallway, ringing out close enough he could establish the location. He jangled the knob of a nearby closet, but it opened from the other side, the interior harboring Cindy.

"Stand back, I'm going to kick it in." He used his right foot, repeatedly kicking the door in its center, and on the third blow it cracked. It wasn't made for security and soon was in pieces from his actions. Cindy huddled within, her eyes filled with fear, but a defiance and strength was there as well.

He studied her body, checking for injuries. "Did he hurt you?"

She shook her head, relief washing over her features. "He left me for some reason, I guess, thinking I was unconscious, and I woke up in the lobby and he was gone. I found this closet and hid from him. Then I heard fighting and talking, and I knew it had to be you, and thank God. We need to get out of here," she said and headed back to the lobby.

"No, not that way. They're out there. I set the Land Rover to explode, so it'll keep them away for a time."

"Is Hayden finally dead? Did you kill him?"

Boyd shook his head and squeezed his hands into fists. "No, I swear, he has more lives than a damn cat. The bastard escaped out the back exit. Don't worry, he's not getting far. There's too many of them out there, and they're everywhere."

Cindy raked her fingers through her hair, horrified. "But we can't just let him go. You said so yourself, he's our only collateral."

"I don't know what to do about that right now," he said and leaned against the wall. He was attacked by pain all over his body, the glass the dead woman had thrown at him shifting beneath his skin. He couldn't focus beyond his inflictions, the prospect of escape a dwindling notion against insurmountable fatigue and raw pain.

"Shit, it hurts all up and down my back. You should've seen it, Cindy. They were throwing knives and all kinds of crazy weapons at me after the crash, and then one of them heaves a handful of glass at me." He felt blood running down his back like a crimson river. "Where do they come up with these weapons?"

Cindy inspected his back, eyes widening in shock. "Look at you. We have to pull those shards out. Those cuts won't stop bleeding as long as the glass is in them."

"We're fresh out of peroxide and bandages, Nurse Cindy," he smiled slightly.

"Step into the bathroom and let me help you," Cindy offered, determined to do what she could to mend him. "It's better than leaving it in your skin. I imagine it's painful to even stand. And you fought off Hayden with your back like that, too.

Entering the men's bathroom, Cindy positioned him in front of the sink. "Okay, I'm going to start pulling them out. I don't know how else to go about this. I can't even take your shirt off, there's so much glass sticking out through it." She took a breath for herself as much as him. "You ready?"

Boyd clasped the sink, clenching every muscle, anticipating the pain to come. "All right, just do it. We don't have a lot of time here."

She plucked the first shard out.

Yellows, blues, and whites filled his eyes, and he felt his jaw and spine crackle with electricity, as his toes bent into the floor, grinding into the tiles to channel what he couldn't release. "*Shit!*"

"I'm sorry," Cindy apologized, nervous at his reaction and hesitating. "Did I pull too hard?"

"It'll hurt no matter what," he barked, digging his fingers into the sink again. *"Finish it."*

The first bloodied piece dropped into the sink. It was an inch in diameter and the shape of a jagged tooth. Boyd sucked in a breath before the next piece was forced out. The onslaught continued for minutes. Cindy grunted to express her frustration as she kept finding new pieces to remove. Boyd counted twenty shards in the sink. He worried how much blood he'd lost, and what he could do to sustain himself.

But it could be worse, he figured, and pictured a group of the dead beings dismembering him piece-by-piece and wearing him like clothing.

"I'm done," Cindy said, stepping back, out-of-breath. "Sorry if I hurt you."

Boyd stepped out of the bathroom, checking the hallway. "We've got other things to worry about now. They'll be coming in soon once those flames die down."

He peered out from the edge of the hall and into the front lobby, where he could see out through one of the shattered windows. "Hey wait, they're leaving."

Cindy joined him, sticking her head out farther than his. "It's like they see something up ahead, like they're attracted to something else."

"It has to be Hayden." Under his breath, "What's he doing now?"

"He's going to get himself killed," Cindy groaned, eyes heavy and staring at Boyd. "What are we going to do if he dies? I know the people outside these walls will betray us, but without him, we have nothing. They put out the hospital fire, so we know that we can't firebomb the place if we get desperate. No one can see what's happening here. I know we've talked about this, but damn it, I don't want to die here."

"Calm down," Boyd said, holding her hand, regarding her with patience and understanding. "Hayden's survived this a lot longer than we have, he'll be fine. He's a sick fuck, but he's strong. Our options aren't used up yet. It'll take time if we're going to do this right."

Cindy's eyes were bloodshot and tired. "I just want to go home."

"I know, I know, Cindy." He sat on a bench in the lobby with her, confident now that the dead weren't going to rampage in and attack them. "We can go back out once they've cleared some distance from us. Hayden isn't going far. And if you haven't noticed, he wants you, Cindy. He has always cannibalized women; he claims they taste the best. I have a feeling he'll come to us even if we don't try and find him again. But we need weapons. We can't battle those things and find Hayden at the same time while unarmed."

Cindy leaned her back against the wall, agreeing. "I guess you're right."

They rested in silence, grateful for a moment without having to fight.

A short time later, their peaceful moment was shattered by the echo of automatic weapons.

CHAPTER 34

Hayden crept around the back of the post office, darting to evade the dead beings. He was slowed by the awful pain of his nose broken; he knew he wouldn't be able to snap it back into place or repair it, it was too badly damaged. It would heal crooked, and he'd look ridiculous. But it didn't matter here, he consoled himself, knowing his features were hidden underneath a mask of dead skin. Nobody's ridicule could reach him beyond the concrete walls ever again.

He ducked behind a blue mailbox for a better view of the dead crowd. The dead beings were gathering at the end of the block. He couldn't tell what it was yet, but there was a large truck at the end of the street. Possibly military. The back cab was draped with a green and beige camouflage tarp. The trap on the rear of the truck was thrown back and a group of men jumped out and aimed M-16's into the crowd.

Hayden counted ten of them, soldiers, agents, or goons, all wearing black vests, their faces vilified by gas masks.

Someone yelled out, "Now!"

The sputter of gunfire broke out into the crowd of figures in the street. Hayden dodged the torrent of gunfire, bending low, the pavement near him pinging and shooting sparks, and he was forced to dive behind the broken shell of a nearby Impala.

He clutched the blade of the paper cutter, ready for an approach of either the men or the dead.

Hayden sprinted up the block, needing a better view of the newcomers, and hid behind an oak tree. He was half a block from the line of gunners. The dead beings were pummeled with bullets, their bodies dancing and twitching, flesh and blood spitting out the exit wounds; but it didn't slow them.

Another man overlooked the shooting gallery, the only person not firing a weapon. His head was shaved, and like the other men, there was no decoration on his uniform, just black fatigues and a bulletproof vest.

"A blow to the head will put them down!" the man shouted through his gas mask, muffled but audible. "Break their skulls in two. They're approaching fast, keep firing! Try and avoid killing too many. They're expensive and worth more than your life."

Hayden nodded to himself. So they were protecting an investment; the firing squad was here for him, Hayden understood instantly. The police must have finally discovered more of his victims' bodies, and they wanted answers. He'd have to teach them a lesson so they'd stay out of this place forever and fear him, tremble at the very thought of his existence. There were ten men, he counted, and he had many places to hide and assault them from. Inspired by the idea of human dismantling, Hayden crawled underneath a fire-damaged car for an even closer view, knowing he was in danger if he stayed out in the open for too long.

One of the gunners cried out, releasing a gut-wrenching howl. Hayden looked left, right, and back left and pinpointed the screaming man.

The man had a knife jammed hilt-deep into his right eye. A dead being had launched it from a few feet away before getting mowed down by bullets. The blade's tip stuck out the back of the man's head, and he dropped to the ground, dead after his vocal spasms.

The row of gunners were becoming nervous, their confident gait diminishing. Canisters of tear gas were shot into the dead crowd, obscuring the air with thick smog. Hayden's eyes became bleary, his throat rejecting the tainted air, and he coughed it up, choking.

"Break up, and we'll meet back here in fifteen minutes. Find Hayden!" the leader of the men yelled, his voice cutting through the din.

Hayden turned and crept away, his eyes tearing from the gas. He wasn't sure where he stumbled to after walking for a time, his eyes watering and half-blind. Eventually he came to a building and by touch alone found the entrance. Once inside, he tripped over a shelf of canned items, falling onto a dust-covered floor; he'd crashed into shelves, mostly empty except for meager leftovers.

He was inside a grocery store.

INSIDE THE PERIMETER

Standing once more, his eyes cleared and he was able to see. He passed the freezer section and burst through a set of double doors, met by a blast of frigid air. It was dark everywhere, but his eyes finally adjusted. A door to his left led to a meat locker, but it was empty except for jangling hooks, absent of meat. He tried another door across from the meat locker and entered a room with meat slicers, a chest-high grinder, and the glass display case for fresh meat cuts, all barren.

"I should've found this place a long time ago," Hayden whispered, astonished at the tool selection. "Now I can grind these bastards down."

A shuffle of feet at the head of the store drew him to duck behind the counter.

"I saw him go in here," an exasperated voice announced into a walkie. "I'll find the sick fuck."

Hayden fled the display area and hid in the meat locker. Crouched behind a stack of crates, he stared at the frost-covered door and waited for it to open. The man's steps outside came closer, a hurried shuffle that slowed. The rays of a flashlight cased the area like a miniature searchlight.

Come on in, he thought as he held his makeshift weapon tighter.

The handle turned.

The door squeaked open.

Yes, yes, just walk on in.

The man wrinkled his face at the hooks, confused; he didn't understand he was in a meat locker. The beam of his flashlight roamed up and down the walls of the small room, and Hayden knew it would soon illuminate his hiding spot. He didn't give the man the chance to locate him.

Hayden clutched a hook and shoved it in the man's direction. It swung forward on a chain, rattling and jangling with momentum, smacking the startled man in the face with a bone breaking *crunch*! The man folded to the floor, sputtering blood from a mouth of broken teeth. He was convulsing, legs dancing, arms stiff at his sides, fists clenching and unclenching.

Hayden dragged the man into the butcher's display area. He stripped the man of his black garb from top to bottom, finishing the undressing by pulling off the man's boots. The man, cop, solider—it didn't matter who he was, he worked for the same villains who planned to extricate him from this facility—was bright white on the floor curled up, pathetic and naked. He was shriveled, even his penis tucked into itself, his body limp despite his muscular frame. He kept shaking, unable to accept the fact he'd been struck with a hook, half the bones in his face shattered. The blow would end his life, ultimately.

The cleaver Hayden selected from the butcher's block could easily sever bone. Leaning down over the man, he hacked the blade in sharp, swinging motions. The man moaned with each strike into him, muscle and bone giving with each new cut as he slowly died.

He removed the arm from the shoulder socket first, peeling the last traces of muscular tissue holding it in place, and dropped the appendage into the meat grinder. The spout spat out lines of meat the size of straws after being revved up, circular in diameter, resembling ground chuck. He sampled a handful, the meat melting on his tongue.

Next, Hayden chose a smaller knife, one designed to flense meat from bones in fine strokes—what a butcher called a 'skinning blade'.

Like a potato peeler, except it's a lot sharper and the cuts can be controlled, Richard once told him.

Hayden sawed the flesh from the man's face, a rough cut of his features. Then he carved down to his neck and continued down the chest and to the navel. From there he circled back up to the face again. It was difficult to peel the layer of skin off without breaking it, but he managed to remove the skin from the man's face and midsection. Hayden then stripped off his old, hanging flesh and tossed it across the room. He dressed himself in the new skin, the warmth quickly turning cold. His body heat would take over in due time.

Hayden clutched the cleaver in one hand and the skinning blade in the other.

Fear is the key, Hayden. It conquers people's ability to fight back against you. Scare them, and you'll win every time.

He picked up the remains of the very dead solider and lugged it to the meat locker. Hayden would have time to work the rest of the meat from the body later, but for now, he had other obligations. There were nine more like the dead bastard outside plus their leader.

Before he left the room, he eyed the M-16 that had fallen onto the floor, dropped by the man when he had been hit in the face with the hook.

"Not painful enough," he sighed, shaking his head, unimpressed with the firearm. "I don't like it. They deserve to be disemboweled and live to see me do it."

Hayden walked to the front meat display counter to check the man's clothing for anymore weapons. He located a grenade and tucked it into his pocket. Trying to decide what to do next, Hayden spotted a fire exit, ran to it, and opened it, leaving the grocery store.

As he stepped outside once more, the din of the dead beings filled the night, their lust for death never-ending. They were everywhere, their voices echoing from every direction.

He smiled, convinced *his side* was winning.

Pleased by the idea, he raised the cleaver to reflect the starlight.

It was time to hunt.

CHAPTER 35

"Who do you think is shooting out there?" Cindy asked while Boyd peered out the window from the women's bathroom stall.

He could see a large military truck was parked at the end of the street, and it was covered with the dead beings. He'd counted nine or ten men dressed in black, each armed with M-16's.

At first the men did fine holding off the dead, but soon, they realized they couldn't win and they began to panic as their dead attackers never stopped coming, no matter how many bullets were pumped into their bodies.

In no time, the dead crowd began to disassemble the vehicle. They'd rendered the backmost tires flat and two of them had opened the hood of the truck and removed pieces of the engine and battery, spark plug wires and mechanical guts jutting out torn and ruined.

"It doesn't matter," Boyd sighed, shaking his head. "They can't escape even if they catch Hayden, not with their vehicle ruined. They look and act like soldiers. They wanted me to draw him into town center, I suppose, but who can say for sure? They didn't trust me to do the job so they came and beat us to the punch."

"You really think so?" Cindy asked, worried that all their work could be for nothing. "Then you're right; that means we're not going anywhere."

"Wouldn't be going anywhere anyway," Boyd laughed, a sincere sentiment. "The stooges didn't know what they were doing. They fired into the group and then dispersed without protecting their transportation. It's totaled now and they're stuck in here just like us."

"But they'll find us," Cindy reasoned, growing scared by the moment. "They'll probably shoot us. They have no reason not to."

"Not if we lay low." Boyd stepped down off the toilet and away from the window. He'd seen all he needed to.

"Yes, they might find us, but maybe not. There's so many of them, this place is infested. They have enough on their plate to worry about two more civilians."

"Then what are we going to do?" she asked again.

Boyd peered back outside again. "That truck is huge. They came from somewhere."

"There has to be another exit?" He considered where the truck could've come from and decided the first place was deeper in the military base. "I wonder how well guarded the rest of the place is? The entrance I came in from was an iron door, but this other place could be a base of operations."

They stepped into the lobby, Boyd taking the lead.

"What do we do next then?" she asked, still wanting an answer. She hated not knowing what was going to happen next.

He expected the question, but there wasn't anything they could do until the dead beings outside cleared out. "We wait."

"For how long?"

"Hours, maybe a day," Boyd sighed, rubbing his eyes, pained by the idea. "There's no telling."

"And Hayden slips away again," Cindy grumbled, throwing up her hands. "I don't want him coming for me again, Boyd. He saw me naked in the showers, the bastard. I can only imagine what he'd do to me if he finds me."

"Chances are he'll be looking for us in good time. Sick bastard should've been given the death penalty."

"Freeze you two," a voice demanded.

Boyd cocked his head at the command, heart chugging instantly, fearing what he knew to be true. One of the men from outside aimed an M-16 at them. Boyd studied the soldier, and the man stared back at Boyd from behind a gas mask, anonymous. The faint scent of tear gas exuded from outside, but it had spread so thin it was harmless.

"Hands in the air," the soldier barked, waving the gun, seconds from pulling the trigger if they failed to obey. "Boyd Broman, we've been looking for you, up against the wall!"

Cindy was frozen, her eyes drawn to Boyd for an answer. He didn't have one. He was still too weak to attack, making hand-to-hand combat out of the question. And he would easily be taken down, plus with a rifle aimed at him, the choices were limited. Boyd had no option but to turn and face the wall.

"Hands at your back!" the soldier snapped.

"Please, we're only trying to make it out of here alive." She was now in tears. "What do you want with us?" Cindy pleaded with him, the sadness creeping into her voice.

"Hayden's no longer in your custody, and we need him. That means you two are useless. Your purpose here is over," the soldier said, his voice muffled behind the gas mask.

"Does that mean I can leave?" Boyd asked, trying to appeal to the man's humanity. "Am I going back to prison, or are you going to shoot me in the back of the head?"

The soldier's silence answered the question.

"You can't do this to us," Cindy bargained, weeping harder, uncontrollably. "W...we didn't do anything to you. Y...you're putting people in here and murdering them. Why are you keeping those things alive?"

Boyd was facing the wall when it happened, and he missed the short-lived battle. From behind the soldier, a shadow appeared holding a heavy piece of wood in its hands like a club. The man with the M-16 was hit over the head to fall to his knees, his rifle dropping from limp hands. "Take your mask off, asshole."

The soldier did as he was told, and removed the mask, showing the face of a man in his forties, the eyes wide in shock and pain at being ambushed.

"Bastards think because you're Uncle Sam's boys that you can knock people around without an explanation! Is that it? Just how you locked me up here for over ten years and forgot I had a life, a family! The government doesn't have the right to do this to innocent people, even to guilty people!"

"Dr. Glover!" Cindy exclaimed, joy lighting up her face. "You're alive!"

Dr. Glover had lost his lab coat, and he was bleeding from both forearms and chest, but his flame thrower was secure at his back, the nozzle now aimed at the fallen man, the club of wood now forgotten.

"They almost got me, but they couldn't kill me. I have to see my wife again, but first, let's have a conversation with this bastard."

"I'm not saying anything to you," the soldier spat, though his face was still locked in concern. "You'll have to kill me."

Dr. Glover shot out a small, controlled burst of fire at the soldier's legs. His boots crackled with orange heat. Forced to kick and flail to put them out, screaming curses in the process, he was convinced. "Okay, okay, stop it! Shit, shit! What do you want to know?"

"Who are you?" Dr. Glover demanded.

"Dale Edwards," the soldier replied, slapping at his legs to put out the flames. "I was in the marines for twenty-five years. I'm too old for combat, but I'm not too old to aid in terrorist situations, and in this case, government research."

Dr. Glover was pleased his scare tactic had worked. "What were your orders, Edwards?"

With the flames out, the soldier relaxed slightly and continued. "We were supposed to find Boyd Broman and apprehend Hayden Grubaugh, but they didn't warn us about what was in here. Commander Stapleton briefed us outside the facility, said a group of criminals were inside trying to wreck the training base, the living quarters, and the research facilities."

Dr. Glover sighed, asking the next question. "Were you sent here to kill Boyd Broman?"

Edwards swallowed hard and looked from Boyd to the doctor. "Yes, shoot to kill; especially anyone in the way of apprehending Hayden."

"So you knew that Hayden wasn't really dead?"

"Of course, and I know a little bit about this place," Edwards admitted, buying time, purchasing his life with information. "Research mostly, and it used to be a training base, but it's been closed for years. Off-limits. I jumped at the chance to see what went on in here, but now..."

"You want out. Am I right?" Dr. Glover asked.

Edwards was about to continue, when a large report filled the lobby. Edwards head snapped back, and the back of his skull splattered the wall in chunky gobs of bone and brain matter.

More men charged inside and Boyd was driven to his knees as another soldier bounded into the lobby. Dr. Glover blasted him with the flame thrower, and the soldier was instantly enveloped in fire. The man unleashed a blood-curdling scream, howling, throwing his body forward, trying to dodge the flames that were enveloping him, and the M-16 released a burst of gunfire. The walls were filled with holes, and Cindy caught one in the stomach.

"No!" Boyd cried out. He picked up Edwards' M-16 and shot the burning man dead before he could do more damage. "This can't be happening!"

Boyd grimaced in pain when he saw her wound bleeding above her navel. She was prone on the floor, hands around the red circle, her lips frozen into a frown, panicky tears rolling down her cheeks.

"Hold on, Cindy. You hold on, damn it," Boyd pleaded.

"I can't get up, Boyd. It hurts so much," Cindy said as she went into shock.

"See to her, Doctor," Boyd said.

Dr. Glover went to Cindy to see what he could do to help as Boyd canvassed the area for anymore soldiers, finding none.

"We can't stop the bleeding, and the bullet will have to be removed, and we have nothing here I can use," Dr. Glover said when Boyd returned.

"No, I won't listen to that kind of talk, there has to be a way." Boyd raised his voice, insisting on a solution. "Come on, think about it. What can we do? I'm not giving up on her; you can go to hell with that talk!"

Before Dr. Glover could reply, bodies crashed into the post office and flooded the lobby, an entire assembly of the dead, each attracted to the post office by the gunshots and screaming.

As chaos ensured, Boyd quickly dragged Cindy to a storage room a few feet away. No sooner did he set her inside, then she pushed him out and locked the door.

"Cindy, what the hell are you doing?" Boyd yelled as he pounded on the door.

"Leave me, you can't go on with me," she yelled back, voice dimming with each word. "I can't walk, Boyd. Don't die on my account."

He slammed his fist into the door. "Please, don't do this. Don't do this, Cindy!"

Dr. Glover jerked the trigger, but the flame thrower coughed out nothing, it was empty. "*Shit*, it's out!"

"You have to run," Cindy reiterated. "You don't have a choice. Escape, promise me that, Boyd. Take your wife and kids and go to Mexico. Tell someone about this place that can do something about it."

Tears welled in his eyes, as he slid his hands down the door. "I can't just leave you."

The figures closed in, and Dr. Glover retreated, shooting a handgun taken from Edwards' body. He called to Boyd as he fled. "We have to go and we can't take her with us! It can't be helped. I have the key card, we'll get out of here and find a way to have this place destroyed and send help back for Cindy!"

"No, I won't leave without her!"

"I won't go with you," Cindy said, her voice growing softer and fading. "I'm too hurt to walk or even be carried. You have to go. You must!"

Clawing the door with his nails, Boyd grew desperate and begged her, "I'll carry you out; come on, give me a chance."

"I'm sorry. You're my friend, and as a friend, I'm telling you to run," she said, crying between words.

"Come on, Boyd, it's now or never!" Dr. Glover yelled as he shot another being in the head.

Seconds from reaching Boyd, only Dr. Glover shooting and slowing them down, as the dead tried to grab Boyd. He literally had no choice but to run or be ravaged by them.

"I'll come back for you," Boyd promised Cindy, his heart filled with guilt and emotions he couldn't decipher at the moment. "Stay quiet and keep pressure on your wound. I'm not giving up on you! I'll be back with help!"

He left it at that. There was no choice, and he hated himself for doing it. His limbs were weighed with guilt, the feeling growing stronger with every stride away from Cindy and closer to the rear exit.

Dr. Glover shot the last of his ammunition, and threw the empty gun at the head of a woman with a patchwork of flesh for a face, the butt of the weapon breaking her nose, then he was running with Boyd by his side.

Upon reaching the back door, they dashed through it, Dr. Glover jamming the handle with a pipe found on the ground.

Seconds later, the door shook as the dead tried to break it down but so far the door was holding.

"Is there another way out of here?" Boyd asked.

Dr. Glover's face went slack. "It's at the far end of the base, and it's heavily guarded. This isn't just a research facility; artillery and weapons are stored here for safe-keeping. The front entrance is also under surveillance, but you know that already. But I do have an idea how we can still successfully escape."

"And what would that be?"

"Just follow me."

Dr. Glover guided Boyd away from the post office, without another word of explanation.

CHAPTER 36

Hayden wandered into the street, convinced the band of armed men had dispersed. They were looking for him, and from what Boyd had explained, they wanted him alive.

You couldn't interrogate a corpse, Hayden reasoned, planning on killing himself if he was forced to leave.

A huddle of the dead beings surrounded the middle of the street. He stood among them and watched scalpels and knives sever the skin from the chest down to the belly button of one of the fallen soldiers. The long intestines were uncoiled and pulled free, slithering between many hands before a winner came of it. The limbs were then wrenched from the dead body with the awkward pop and dislocation of bones.

Finished, the group dispersed into alleyways, into buildings, and down into gutter crawlspaces to utilize their new body parts.

The echo of gunfire attracted his eyes to the bowling alley at the end of the street. The orange flickers revealed two men in black suits back-to-back as they shot at their attackers. A pair of the dead charged towards the two men, each one clutching a coil of barbed wire as the rest of the crowd stood back. They drew the barbs taught between each other, the distance between them the length of a car. The horde of bodies parted to allow the wire carriers through. One of the men ran out of ammunition, and soon after, the other soldier's rifle came up empty.

Each man drew a knife from their belts. Their faces were glued in dismay; they knew their final moment approached and that they would suffer greatly.

The wire-carriers closed in, gaining momentum the last few yards, and looped the barbed weapon around the men's midsections. The men howled in agony, unable to maneuver a step without slicing or cutting themselves deeper. The men were wrapped five times over, their faces bleeding in horizontal slashes, their arms and midsections locked into place.

Hayden skirted from the scene just as the entire group charged in at once, picking and choosing what they could of the two men through the pool of shifting bodies.

The truck at the end of the street was now disassembled and a slumped over body remained in the driver's seat, its arms and legs missing. As Hayden watched, a set of hands reached out to drag the rest of the corpse onto the street. Another soldier was impaled through the chest onto a street pole, the red **STOP** sign missing.

Hayden considered returning to the grocery store to tend to the body in the meat locker, but he caught a flicker of movement from behind the bowling alley.

His eyes went wide to see that it was Boyd and another man, but he couldn't tell who from his vantage point.

Hayden gave chase, the cleaver and skinning blade ready to execute his will. He ran along the side wall of the bowling alley, keeping out-of-sight. The two men were moving out of the town center and as he followed, the minutes passing, he saw them closing in on a bricked police station. They had good cover; none of the dead beings had spotted them.

But not for long. The dead crowd shifted their focus. Heads turned up at the two runners when they darted into their line of vision. The stares soon turned into a mass exodus up the street. Hayden clutched the bulge in his side pocket, the grenade taken from the man he'd slaughtered in the grocery store. The idea of lobbing it at Broman sent pleasant images through his mind, but it wasn't good enough; he craved torture.

Broman would be alive for weeks on end, while Hayden removed his toes, fingers, genitals, and ate them before the man's horrified eyes. The grenade would kill Broman or render him dead within moments, so he put it away, dissatisfied.

He closed in, but stopped when the man at Broman's side turned around.

And what the man did halted Hayden in his tracks.

Dr. Glover already knew where he was going. Boyd struggled to keep up with him, carrying the wounds and regrets of his time inside the perimeter, unable to forget Cindy was locked in a closet at the post office, bleeding. If she died, then he would never be satisfied with the outcome of this night and how he'd left her, no matter the reasons for his hasty departure.

"This place is locked down tight," Dr. Glover said, out-of-breath, breaking Boyd from his thoughts. "Beyond the barrier gate, there are more gates and clearance check areas. I have the key card, but they won't let us just walk out. No way in hell."

"Then how do we escape?" Boyd asked.

Dr. Glover rested against the police station wall. They'd been running for a time without a break. Boyd peered over his shoulder, back down to the town center, and saw the dead crowd now moving in their direction.

"Shit. They see us."

"I know," Dr. Glover replied, the alarm absent in his words. "We have to draw them through the gates. We must let them out. It's our only cover. Those things will be one huge distraction while we escape. Don't you see that we can't just walk out of here on our own?"

"But what if they escape and reach innocent people? We can't!"

"The guards will take care of them, Boyd. They're trained, and they're prepared for a breakout. They're professionals. Besides, we have no choice! Think about it."

Acid rose in Boyd's throat, and his mouth tasted like he'd been chewing on aluminum foil. A plan had been brewing in the doctor's mind long before he had arrived here, Boyd finally understood. He wanted to escape, but Boyd couldn't avoid weighing the consequences, whether the doctor had a point or not about them escaping.

"You can't do this, and you know it," Boyd protested.

"There's no other choice. I'm not staying in this place forever." Dr. Glover glared at the dead who approached in collecting numbers. "You don't understand what I've been through here. Maybe it's because we desecrated human life that those things are the way they are, or those brains we built, we built them from scratch. Those parts were untouched by God. I've considered this many times, Boyd, for years. Their thoughts, their memories, their ambitions, their brains were empty of those things, but maybe not. Maybe someone or something else put them there. Maybe God didn't like what we were doing, and maybe *He* decided to intervene. Now I'm intervening. In a way, we're doing God's will by throwing a wrench into the project." He threw his hands out, frustrated and confused. "Stapleton won't let them escape, Boyd, I assure you, but we need to get the hell out of here. We can't without help. We must have a distraction, or else the guards will simply gun us down." Lowering his eyes, he whispered, "I need to see my family before I grow too old to remember them. And so do you."

The pressure to make a decision crippled Boyd's resolve to hash it out. Boyd aimed his M-16 at him, but Dr. Glover was a step ahead of him, and he swung the tip of the flame thrower at him, the end striking Boyd on the forehead, stunning him.

Boyd lost his vision for a moment, everything blinding white, and then he collapsed, feeling everything supporting him go limp.

Dr. Glover looked down on Boyd, his face set in stone. "It ends my way. I'm leading them through the gates."

CHAPTER 37

Hayden watched as Boyd collapsed to the ground after being struck by the man with the flame thrower, leaving him behind.

Hayden quickened his stride as he heard the man start shouting and waving his hands wildly in the air, calling for the dead to chase him. "Follow me! I'm right here! Come after me! I'll let you out! I have the goddamn key!"

Bloodlust sparked the advances of the dead crowd. They were about to close in on Boyd's body, but Hayden couldn't let them kill Broman. He wouldn't suffer as he was unconscious. And if Boyd did wake, yes, he would die in agony, but it would be too fast. And the crazy bastard charging towards the barrier wall was trying to lead the dead out. Hayden recognized him as the man from the hospital. Hayden couldn't let him herd the dead from the facility. They were Hayden's barrier, his protection, his way of life, and it was all about to be snatched away.

Now was the time to use the grenade.

He pulled the pin.

Three seconds and counting.

Hayden tossed it, the grenade disappearing into the night sky. It blew up before it hit the ground, yards from the shouting man's position. The man was thrown to the ground, struck in the back by shrapnel, pushed down. The tank on his back, though empty, still contained flammable fumes, exploded when shrapnel hit it. The yellow burst produced a solid ball of smoke; the acrid fumes carrying to Hayden's position.

The man didn't get up as he burned, the corpse charred and black.

Hayden rushed to Boyd's fallen body, lifted him into his arms, then retreated back into the town center.

When Boyd woke, his face was pressed against a cold surface. Metal. His hands were bound with cloth and so were his ankles. He couldn't budge.

Dr. Glover had administered the blow that made him unconscious, abandoning him out among the dead beings and leaving him to be murdered. But if that was so, then why wasn't he torn to pieces and dead? The answer didn't matter, all that did was that he was still alive.

But Boyd's relief ended quickly. There were two possibilities why he was still alive, neither promising. One of the government-sent operatives had captured him, bound him in place, and was about to question him *or* Hayden had *saved* him.

The figure wreathed in shadow at the opposite end of the room answered his question. Hayden was hunched over a table, arranging knives, and when Boyd's eyes were able to focus hard enough, he discovered there was another body with him, this one very dead.

The legs of the corpse were removed and were laid out on a table, the wounds splattering blood onto the floor. The mess was smeared on the walls, dried flecks covering the glass display cases, and coloring the ceiling in random spatters. A man's severed head, shaved of hair, had been propped inside one of the glass display cases, the sight curling Boyd's stomach.

Boyd glanced at the aisles beyond the space he occupied; he was in a grocery store, though the aisles were all empty.

Hayden was studious in his work, obsessed. And he had changed his appearance again. Flesh hung from his back like a cape, and his head was encapsulated in new skin with two holes crudely carved for eyes. His mouth and nose were open to the air, making him look like a strange beast of flesh. He didn't wear a shirt, his skin dyed with dried blood. His hands were caked in red, the fingers dripping with crimson gore.

Hayden's lips shifted into a macabre grin, pleased to see that Boyd was awake.

"So, here we are, Broman."

Boyd didn't know how to reply. He studied the implements on the table, not wanting to think about what they would be used for. He wondered what was worse; to have his limbs severed or to experience prolonged torture?

Prolonged torture in itself was enough to consider suicide, but if it was done by Hayden it belonged in a different category of death wishes.

"You see that pot at the end of the table?" Hayden pointed at the stew pot on the floor. "It's catching blood. I might turn it into a soup. I'm not sure what else I'll find in this damn grocery store, most of the shelves are bare. I guess the produce truck didn't roll into this place anymore after the barriers were built. Oh well," he sighed, "this place belongs to us. At least we have that."

"Us?" Boyd asked, knowing Hayden was trapped in his warped world of insanity. He'd been delivered into a place where his crimes were unknown to anyone lawful or sane. The man was lost in his morbid desires. "You're not one of them, Hayden. You might've dressed yourself up to blend in, but you're still a human being. You're a living cannibal; those dead people have an excuse. They need spare parts to keep living, but you don't."

"This civil servant, this soldier, whatever you want to call him, he tried to attack me." Hayden pointed at the legless body on the table. "I was defending myself, and since nobody's sending me rations in this place, I have a right to take whatever means necessary to survive. I've eaten from rotten bodies for long enough; it's about time I enjoyed some *fresh meat.*"

The longer Hayden talked, the more time Boyd would have to locate a way to escape. "You've merely survived; that's nothing special."

"This place is special," Hayden argued, hammering the cleaver upon the torso, channeling his anger and culinary zest into the strike. Digging his hands inside the chest cavity, he parted the broken sternum, then wrenched out the heart. "They send you to capture me, and when you do, they bring in more people to kill you and to take me. Why would anyone go through all the trouble of sending men to their possible deaths unless there was something special here?"

"This is a failed project the government refuses to cut their losses on," Boyd countered, growing colder on the table, shivering now. Hayden hadn't heard the explanation about the town from Dr. Glover, so Boyd divulged the truth. "This used to be a real town, and then the government bought it up after a sewage leak of some kind. That's why there are grocery stores and post offices and a bowling alley. I guess they thought keeping a part of the town as it was would give the military residents a sense of home as they were being trained to handle the dead. They were built to be soldiers in war-time, those things out there, to take suicide missions and fight wars to avoid human causalities, but as you can see, it hasn't worked out too well. They can't be controlled. And the entire place is monitored, and I'm sure we're another part of the research. They send people in here for the purpose of maintaining the things, giving the dead the fresh body parts they need to survive. They won't scrap the project. But you, Hayden, they don't want you to stay. You're killing their investment, burning the bodies, and the police want answers from you for the other bodies they've found. You're a liability in the real world and in this place. As I see it, you're position is getting worse by the hour."

"And so is yours, Broman," Hayden sneered, shaking the blood off his hands. He didn't lose focus on the body he cleaved, returning to the job.

The solider was now down to an emptied torso, the rest scattered on the floor in wet vestiges. It was a half hour before Hayden paused from his efforts to finally rekindle words again, every second agonizingly prolonged. Any minute, the cannibal would focus on Boyd with that cleaver.

Done chopping, Hayden collected the bones from the floor and tossed them into a garbage bin; it was useless refuse.

"So, Broman, did you see the helicopters swoop overhead to put out that hospital fire? Those things are very important. Very deadly too. I'd like to imagine what would happen if they escaped."

"Everyone would be dead." Boyd tried to loosen the bonds over his limbs, but there was no slack. "Dr. Glover wanted to let them out. He considered it our only way of escaping from here, but it's not worth the consequences. He would be sending those murderers out there among the innocent, including his family, my family, too."

Hayden threw back his head and laughed. "Then it's a good thing I threw a grenade at him. He's dead now. I don't want this place to be vacated. This is the happiest I've ever been. I want things to stay as they are forever."

The table used as a chopping block was cleared except for pools of blood and Hayden sprayed it down with an overhead hose. He traced his finger over the knives on the counter and picked up the smallest one. "A simple kitchen knife will do for tonight."

Boyd's stomach dipped. Torture gleamed in Hayden's eyes, and in the gloom of the room, the man's eyes were liquid black, his smile animated by strange contortions—a man on the verge of horrific actions.

Hayden would extend the process of death for days, perhaps a week, maybe more. It would be useless to call out for help. Dr. Glover and Cindy were the only two people who had survived for so long, and now they were probably both dead. Everything they'd planned had turned against them, and it was because of the man standing before Boyd

"Your toes and feet will go first," Hayden whispered to Boyd, audibly mapping out his demise. "Then, you can't run from me. Next, I'll sever your testicles and cauterize them. Yes, yes, possibly with a hot frying pan, that's the best I can do here." Then he began to look off into the distance as he spoke. "Yes, I know Richard, I'll make sure he stays restrained, I know that. I'm ready to do this, all right? I've thought about this so long, Richard; we've both had good ideas on how to dispose of Broman."

Hayden grabbed Boyd's left foot and removed the shoe, twisting it off. Boyd resisted, but then the man jammed the knife into his ankle. Lances of pain sprang up Boyd's leg, and he unleashed a loud scream, as there was nothing else he could do to channel the agony.

"Voice your pain!" Hayden laughed as he removed the shoe and sock from Boyd's right foot, the man's body shuddering.

Boyd's breathing doubled, the blood in his veins stocked with lances and sharp edges, every inch of him radiant with warring nerves. A new coat of sweat draped his skin, a bitter heat that streamed down his flesh in heavy torrents. Hayden would have his way, and there was nothing Boyd could do about it. Hayden would survive here, in fact he would thrive in this environment, this was the lunatic's niche.

Hayden ripped the knife out of Boyd's ankle, a gurgle of blood spilling from the wound. "This is what I've waited so long to do. I'll find Cindy's body next. She must still be in the post office as I never saw her leave. I can't have her alive, so I'll kill her, pleasure myself with her corpse, then chop her up for stew. I have so much time. Nobody can evict me from this place. It's too hard to get me back into custody when I'm among a pack of bloodthirsty killers. You failed and so did that group of soldiers."

The knife's blade circled around Boyd's big toe. Hayden's grin branched out, no longer distracted by talking, wishing to enact his next torture. He touched the tip of the knife to the big toe, resting the point a moment. "This one goes first."

Hayden raised the knife to slice, and Boyd closed his eyes, waiting for the pain to come.

CHAPTER 38

From behind Hayden came quick footsteps and before the man could turn around, he was struck from behind, dropping to the floor unconscious, his legs going limp.

Cindy dropped the two-by-four she'd used as a club, hunched forward in her last moments of life. She was sweating profusely and her breath came in ragged gasps as she struggled to remain standing.

She worked at Boyd's restraints with shaking hands, and once they were undone, she stumbled a few feet and collapsed into a metal chair, spent. She leaned her head back, and her breathing became deeper and harder, labored and fluid-choked. Her lower torso was soaked in blood and she pressed her hand to her wound.

"Those creatures left the post office in a hurry. I heard a loud explosion, and I wondered what had happened. I crawled out of the closet to search for help, and I got lucky and spotted Hayden carrying you inside this place, so I came after you."

"Thank God," Boyd said, kneeling beside her. He put his hand under her chin, lovingly. "That was very brave of you."

Her eyes were slow connecting to his. "Where's Dr. Glover?"

"Hayden said he killed him. I got worried when Dr. Glover claimed we couldn't escape without a distraction, a diversion to keep the guards on the other side of the facility busy. Dr. Glover wanted to release those things, free them so the guards would be too busy dealing with them to worry about us. He promised me they wouldn't escape, but I wasn't so sure he could guarantee that. The key card is lost now. Maybe later we can look for it."

Cindy closed her eyes and nodded, a wave of weakness crippling her, limiting her awareness. "I'm not going to make it. I've gone as far as my body will take me."

He kissed her quivering lips, sincere, speaking against what he knew to be true. "I'll go out for supplies. I'm sure there are parts of the hospital that weren't burned. You have to give me a chance. You're all that's left. I can save you."

"No, you can't. You have to leave this place," Cindy instructed, her voice losing strength. "You've survived this long; you can't let it be for nothing. I don't have a husband or a family of my own to go home to, but you do. *You do.*"

The bullet wound in her side was bleeding heavier now. Cindy shuddered in pain, tears rolling down her cheeks. "I'm glad you were with me for as long as you were. I would've gone crazy in the library all alone. Maybe if you hadn't found me, I'd still be in there, but I wouldn't be happy. I'd be like a rat hiding in a hole, waiting for death to come sooner or later. At least now I've done something good for someone else, at least my life meant something in the end..."

Cindy closed her eyes, her breathing growing lighter until finally, she expelled a final breath.

Boyd couldn't leave her. Where would he go? Outside, the dead clamored for more destruction, and inside, Cindy's body was a reminder of his failure. Hayden's actions had cost them the one chance to leave the facility and turn the tables on the people who had put them inside the perimeter.

How he would escape now, he didn't know. He couldn't think; his brain became a blank slate.

Not wanting Cindy to be found by the scavenging dead, he carried Cindy's body to the meat locker. As he carried her, he dodged Hayden's body, still unconscious on the floor, shiftless. The sight of him was difficult for Boyd to take in, the dead flesh that had congealed to his face making him look like the dead beings outside. Boyd gritted his teeth at the pain in his legs and feet from Hayden's torture, leaving bloody streaks behind him as he walked.

After returning from the meat locker, a voice called out from the aisles, causing him to freeze.

"Your job is finished here, Broman." There were two men standing in the center aisle. One kept a gas mask over his face and had an M-16 aimed at Boyd. The other removed the mask so he could make eye contact with Boyd. He was pudgier around the midsection, and about five feet tall. His bald head had small, brown liver spots dotting its pate. His thick silver mane of a beard disguised the bottom half of his face; Boyd couldn't read the man's intentions, but he could see that the man's eyes were cunning.

When the man had spoken, the voice sounded familiar to Boyd. "So you're the one who's been calling me on the phone the entire time I've been here," Boyd accused, anger channeling at the recognition. "Commander Stapleton, right?"

"In person. I'm the head of security," Stapleton nodded, affirming Boyd's observation. "Green's End has been locked down for the better part of twelve years. You did well in here, Broman, better than most, especially considering that my creations out there had military training, and that they're already dead."

Boyd searched the kitchen for a weapon, but the closest was a knife and that was on the floor slathered in blood. "Did those soldiers you sent in here know what they were up against?"

"Who, my 'body shields'," Stapleton laughed, blithely removing a cigar from his pocket and lighting it. He puffed three times, the smell of balsa wood and cherry striking Boyd's nose as the smoke drifted through the store. "They were a distraction for us to sneak inside undetected. Causalities for the sake of the project are feasible. We can write them off as KIA in the Middle East. We're good at making up shit like that. In war time, any law or legislation we want to enact, Americans lap it up like warm breast milk. We could re-write the Constitution if we chose, and hey, maybe one day we will."

"What does that matter?" Boyd challenged, desperation for a weapon growing stronger. "Aren't you just here for Hayden?"

"Of course, but he has nothing to do with any ongoing criminal investigations in the real world. Nobody found body parts of his victims. I made that up. I told you, I'm good at making shit up. This is purely to protect the Green's End Project. He was eating our subjects and burning the rest. He was supposed to be used as their supplies, not vice versa. He should have been dead long ago after first arriving here."

Boyd rubbed his head; his migraine was tear-inducing and his foot was throbbing. What were they going to do with him now that he was cornered? The way Stapleton calmly smoked his cigar and his sidekick kept the M-16 aimed at him ensured Boyd he wasn't safe. He could run, but he'd complete two steps before being cut down by gunfire. What choice did he have but to keep talking? The same tactics he used on Hayden when sitting on the chopping block waiting to be tortured.

"What are those corpses out there really? You're going to kill me anyway, so at least answer that question."

Stapleton arched his bushy white eyebrows in delight. "Nice try stalling, Broman." He turned to his partner. "You can shoot at will, Gregson."

Boyd registered the threat before it was born. He lunged across the kitchen, rolled across it, and crawled into the meat freezer, bullets spraying in his wake.

He forced the door shut and blocked it with crates and stacked them high, but there was no way to lock it from the inside. The bullets pierced the outer steel shell but not the inner one until an entire clip had been emptied. Boyd waited, breathing hard, shocked by the cold, and shivering in the freezer. Cindy's body was slumped in the corner, her blood congealing across her midsection. Her eyes were closed and the flesh was pale.

He waited for the door to be opened.

"They're coming now, Broman!" Stapleton announced with a hearty cheer. "They heard the gunshots. You'll feed them soon enough. You'll keep them alive. You're doing your country a great service. Uncle Sam thanks you! Oh, and thanks for incapacitating Hayden. It saves us trouble. I have to admit, he's been a slippery bastard since arriving here."

Boyd heard muffled voices echo throughout the store, ensuring him that Stapleton was leaving. A barrage of moans filtered in from all sides. He wouldn't know if the commander made it outside alive, but Boyd knew the dead were coming for him, and that's all that mattered now. They smelled blood, and spotted the body parts of the late Dale Edwards on the floor outside the freezer. And moments later, the dead dismantled the bones of the body and fashioned them for their use, the auditory sounds jarring with the promises of what they'd do to Boyd. He piled more boxes in front of the door to double the barricade when fists began to bang against the door.

Seconds later, it was wedged open, hands and heads poking through the widening opening. One was over the boxes, two more behind it, the eyes wide with hunger their mouths open in gruesome smiles.

A pale hand grabbed Boyd's shoulder as another hand pulled out a tuft of his hair, ripping it away. Two hands attempted to unlock his arm from its socket, blinding pain causing him to lose focus as more bodies swarmed into the freezer, until the dead could barely move. Another attacker seized Boyd's neck and began to twist, and Boyd looked down to see Cindy's corpse being ripped apart, her body pulled from all sides as her parts went to the scavenging dead.

He screamed in pain and terror, feeling his neck about to snap. With tears rolling down his cheeks from his failure, he closed his eyes, knowing there was nothing else he could do but die.

CHAPTER 39

*I*n the warm bed, Boyd cuddled up against Karen, their bodies naked and half-wrapped up in the sheets in a post-coital pose at Cold Creek Bed and Breakfast, their honeymoon spot, in southern Arkansas. They had visited the town fair, a favorite past time of Karen's. She'd visited fifty town fairs in her lifetime, and he'd gone to seven with her, going as far out as six hundred miles to enjoy a day of greasy funnel cakes, balloon animals, and demonstrations of teen hormones and drunk adults having a cheap but good time. Today was a playful afternoon of tilt-o-whirl's, ring tosses (he'd won her a stuffed alligator the size of his Kawasaki dirt bike), house of mirrors, and the viper pit, a spinning cage going too fast for his taste, but she loved every second, laughing and hollering and holding his hand, urging him to share in the thrill. After a stint of silence in bed, he prodded her, asking his famous question. "Did anybody ever tell you that you have the blondest bush I've ever seen?"

The question always got her to giggle; it was the comment that had slipped out when they first had sex when he was still in the police academy. The question was ridiculous, and it stayed a running joke between the two of them ever since.

"How blonde?" she whispered, kissing his shoulder tenderly. "Blonde as angel food cake?"

Boyd played along, enjoying the game. "Or maybe blonde as horse hair."

"Eww." She rolled her eyes at the bad comparison. "How about blonde as lemon squares?"

"That's yellow, not blonde."

"Okay, forget it."

"But it's the blondest I've ever seen," Boyd said, adding in a random Irish accent. "These here hills are full of gold."

They relaxed, falling into nap mode, but they came out of it twenty minutes later when Boyd opened his eyes at Karen's question. He braced himself after taking in the introspective query: "We need rules for marriage."

"Rules? Huh?" he said.

"Yeah, because we're married, and it's hard, right? We need rules to keep each other happy. Boundaries. Understanding. Communication."

Boyd sighed, not understanding what she was getting at. After a nap/post-sex, Karen always came up with something different to talk about, and it was coming out and there was nothing he could do but take it head on. "Okay, give me an example."

"What would you do if I died?"

Boyd stared at her, trying to master the awkward question. "How romantic, dear. If you die, what would I do? That's the question."

"Just humor me."

"Okay, I'd be very sad. I probably take a leave from work. Be with family and friends. Polish off a nice collection of whiskey bottles and Gambino's pizzas. Howl at the night, I guess, I don't know. I don't think about you dead. That's good, right?"

"I just want you to be happy if I was gone. Live life to the fullest. Find yourself a new gal. Enjoy her. I'd want the same for myself. I don't picture myself growing old alone."

"You'd have so many suitors after you, you know that? Me, I'd have to canvas the country. Personal ads and on-line websites."

"You wouldn't have to look very long, Boyd. You're a good looking man."

Karen kissed his cheek, intertwining his hands into hers. "Okay, good, so we've got one rule settled."

Boyd kissed her neck, right under the ear. "We don't need rules. I'm confident we'll know what to do no matter what anybody throws at us..."

"Jesus, this guy stinks," the driver gasped, pinching his nostrils. "It's like he took a bath in flesh and shit and God knows what else."

"He'll be dead soon," the other man replied, dismissing the complaints. "At least he can't harm the things inside the facility any longer. He's costs us millions, the bastard."

Hayden blocked out the conversation, training his eyes on the back window of the military Jeep. The sun rose in the background, the dawn's light shining bright. A set of barbed gates parted, and the Jeep cleared the exit. Barracks surrounded the outside of the gate as did towers manned with armed soldiers. The vehicle parked after a short drive, braking hard. Hayden was then carried by one man holding him under the arms and the other his feet.

They had him secured in cuffs; no way to slip free.

Thrown down onto his knees, he was kicked hard in the back, as one of the men said, "You like that, asshole? You sick fucker. You're finished, man."

The two stepped in front of him, dressed in black—like the other men in the facility. They were both young, mid to late twenties, with smug expressions playing over their faces, conveying to Hayden that he was beaten.

"Stay on your knees and turn away from us," the first man said, the muzzle of an M-16 leveled at his head.

Hayden did as he was told. He couldn't fight back; he was helpless. They'd taken him from his home, and now he was about to be shot in the back of the head.

"Aren't I supposed to be interrogated first?" Hayden asked sarcastically.

"Nope," the other soldier replied, laughing snidely. "All that shot was just made up to convince Broman to find you. You're killing too many of them inside, and the people in charge wanted it to end. Broman's dead by now, but you're privileged, not that you deserve it. A bullet is merciful compared to being ripped apart while you're still alive. We could have left you for those things but Stapleton wanted to make sure we got the job done right. We couldn't chance you magically escaping or eating your way to safety yet again." Hayden kept his eyes on the woods and the way the branches were set ablaze by the sun. A breeze blew across his face, and he sucked in a breath of air, relishing it. It would be his last, he thought. *I guess this is it, Richard.*

Hayden waited for the soldier to pull the trigger.

CHAPTER 40

Dr. Glover's legs were torn into ribbons and a piece of burning hot shrapnel was lodged into his back. More than seventy percent of his flesh was burned beyond ever saving and his hair was gone, his face resembling a piece of beef jerky. The red of muscle glistened through the cracks in his charred flesh and he was so burnt he could feel no pain, the nerves burned off as well.

But he still considered lucky to be alive, though barely holding on.

The dead beings left him behind after a short series of automatic gunfire burst from the town center hours ago. Free of the threat, he crawled to the front gate, every limb and muscle working against him. Reaching his goal, he pulled himself up, leaving bloody smears in his wake, and unlocked the gate with the key card. He pulled his mangled body through and then closed the gate behind him.

He shouted for the dead to come to him, calling out with what was left of his lungs, his voice more of a ragged growl than actual words.

Within minutes, arms of hundreds reached through the grates for him. He turned away from them, and every inch he crawled down the stairs towards the final gate was agony, as he bled more and more, his life spattering upon the walkway. He couldn't stop the flow, and Dr. Glover understood he'd be dead soon. He'd spent too much time in this living hell, and now, he was terminating the project.

Dr. Glover swiped the key card at the second gate, the final egress that led out of the perimeter. It swung open, and he left it open.

He crawled back up the stairs, bits and pieces of his flesh sloughing off to land on the steps like dry leaves. He dragged himself back to the first gate where the dead reached for him through the bars, wanting to tear him apart, pounding the gate, begging in animal grunts and growls, wanting to be unleashed.

With his last ounce of life, he swiped the card reader, and upon unlocking it, the barrier was thrown open. Dr. Glover was immediately pummeled against the concrete stairs, his corpse picked to pieces, and when they were finished with him, there was nothing left but one bloody foot and an empty sternum.

Trudging on, the dead continued deeper into the facility and forded the perimeter gates.

"It can't be them," the first solder said, his voice shaking in fear.

"Jesus Christ, they're coming up over the hill!" the second man yelled.

"Shit, they've breached the perimeter!"

"What the fuck do we do?"

"We have to call for help, now!"

The soldier reached for his radio, but it was shattered by a random stream of gunfire.

"Duck!"

"Holy shit, they're firing on us! They're armed!"

From his kneeling position, Hayden viewed the dirt road a few yards outside the final gate of the perimeter. The pounding of footsteps grew louder, a growing stampede, resounding in an incredible throng of the approaching undead crowd. Armed corpses raced through over the hill, incensed and covered in fresh blood. Explosions rattled across the facility, turning the outside of the perimeter into a war zone. Flames swarmed from within the walls, a row of hanger buildings igniting as if fire-bombed. Jeeps and military vehicles sped about in confusion, many of the soldiers running alongside gunned down and before being able to commit to the war effort.

Hayden's captors were attacked by thirty beings at once. He couldn't witness the death of the first soldier as he was buried underneath a dog pile, though a severed head bounced free, soon to be stolen by eager hands. The other solider was shot dead center in the chest, but he never felt the bullet as another being smashed a rock over his skull, killing him instantly. The corpse was dragged deeper into the dead crowd to be lost from sight.

INSIDE THE PERIMETER

Hayden expected to be attacked next, but the dead bypassed him.

He'd forgotten he looked just like them, his flesh mask still on his face, his arms coated in blood and gore.

Many jumped the final gate barrier, but some were entangled in the barbed wire, while some sawed off their limbs or ate them, cutting their losses in order to escape, but in the end, they all reached the other side, mobile and on the hunt.

You're one of them now. Richard's voice emboldened Hayden as he walked into the booth that controlled the gates. The booth was drenched in blood, the attendant missing. He studied the panel and pulled back a lever that opened the main gate. The bodies shifted forward when the gate slowly began to open. Up the dirt path, the dead beings screamed and shouted nonsense and garbled words, their war cries floating on the wind.

Hayden smiled for Richard was with him, and he would stay as he always had, talking to him as they completed the arduous trek back to civilization, back to the *real* world.

Taking the first steps away from the perimeter, Richard spoke to him once more. *They're yours to guide, Hayden. You'll never run out of bodies. Fresh meat is better, warm from the bone. Out there shall be your new sanctuary.*

Hayden joined the dead crowd, venturing into the horizon as one of the living dead.

DEAD RAGE
by Anthony Giangregorio
Book 2 in the Rage Virus series!

An unknown virus spreads across the globe, turning ordinary people into bloodthirsty, ravenous killers.

Only a small percentage of the population is immune and soon become prey to the infected.

Amongst the infected comes a man, stricken by the virus, yet still retaining his grasp on reality. His need to destroy the *normals* becomes an obsession and he raises an army of killers to seek out and kill all who aren't *changed* like himself. A few survivors gather together on the outskirts of Chicago and find themselves running for their lives as the specter of death looms over all.

The Dead Rage virus will find you, no matter where you hide.

CHRISTMAS IS DEAD: A ZOMBIE ANTHOLOGY
Edited by Anthony Giangregorio

Twas the night before Christmas and all through the house, not a creature was stirring, not even a. . . zombie?

That's right; this anthology explores what would happen at Christmas time if there was a full blown zombie outbreak. Reanimated turkeys, zombie Santas, and demon reindeers that turn people into flesh-eating ghouls are just some of the tales you will find in this merry undead book. So curl up under the Christmas tree with a cup of hot chocolate, and as the fireplace crackles with warmth, get ready to have your heart filled with holiday cheer. But of course, then it will be ripped from your heaving chest and fed upon by blood-thirsty elves with a craving for human flesh! For you see, Christmas is Dead! And you will never look at the holiday season the same way again.

BLOOD RAGE
Book 1 in the Rage Virus series!
(The Prequel to DEAD RAGE)
by Anthony Giangregorio

The madness descended before anyone knew what was happening. Perfectly normal people suddenly became rage-fueled killers, tearing and slicing their way across the city. Within hours, Chicago was a battlefield, the dead strewn in the streets like trash.

Stacy, Chad and a few others are just a few of the immune, unaffected by the virus but not to the violence surrounding them. The *changed* are ravenous, sweeping across Chicago and perhaps the world, destroying any *normals* they come across. Fire, slaughter, and blood rule the land, and the few survivors are now an endangered species.

This is the story of the first days of the Dead Rage virus and the brave souls who struggle to live just one more day.

When the smoke clears, and the *changed* have maimed and killed all who stand in their way, only the strong will remain.

The rest will be left to rot in the sun.

The Zombie in the Basement
by Anthony Giangregorio
Illustrated by Andrew Dawe-Collins

The spooky house at the end of the street was the one all the kids avoided. With its overgrown shrubs and weeds, the place was a modern day haunted house. Especially at night. So when Ricky sneaks into the yard to retrieve his favorite ball, he comes across something he'd only seen in movies and bad dreams. He sees a zombie in the basement window of the old house, but when he tells his friends, no one believes him. Ricky knows what he saw, that something lurks in the old house, something that isn't supposed to exist.

With his best friend Eric by his side, Ricky will find out the truth and prove to everyone that zombies are real. And when the night is done, everyone will know about the zombie in the basement.

Note: This book is for young adults and for those who are young at heart.

DEADFREEZE
by Anthony Giangregorio
THIS IS WHAT HELL WOULD BE LIKE IF IT FROZE OVER!

When an experimental serum for hypothermia goes horribly wrong, a small research station in the middle of Antarctica becomes overrun with an army of the frozen dead.

Now a small group of survivors must battle the arctic weather and a horde of frozen zombies as they make their way across the frozen plains of Antarctica to a neighboring research station.

What they don't realize is that they are being hunted by an entity whose sole reason for existing is vengeance; and it will find them wherever they run.

VISIONS OF THE DEAD
A ZOMBIE STORY
by Anthony & Joseph Giangregorio

Jake Roberts felt like he was the luckiest man alive.

He had a great family, a beautiful girlfriend, who was soon to be his wife, and a job, that might not have been the best, but it paid the bills.

At least until the dead began to walk.

Now Jake is fighting to survive in a dead world while searching for his lost love, Melissa, knowing she's out there somewhere.

But the past isn't dead, and as he struggles for an uncertain future, the past threatens to consume him. With the present a constant battle between the living and the dead, Jake finds himself slipping in and out of the past, the visions of how it all happened haunting him. But Jake knows Melissa is out there somewhere and he'll find her or die trying.

In a world of the living dead, you can never escape your past.

DEAD MOURNING: A ZOMBIE HORROR STORY
by Anthony Giangregorio

Carl Jenkins was having a run of bad luck. Fresh out of jail, his probation tenuous, he'd lost every job he'd taken since being released. So now was his last chance, only one more job to prevent him from going back to prison. Assigned to work in a funeral home, he accidentally loses a shipment of embalming fluid. With nothing to lose, he substitutes it with a batch of chemicals from a nearby factory.

The results don't go as planned, though. While his screw-up goes unnoticed, his machinations revive the cadavers in the funeral home, unleashing an evil on the world that it has not seen before. Not wanting to become a snack for the rampaging dead, he flees the city, joining up with other survivors. An old, dilapidated zoo becomes their haven, while the dead wait outside the walls, hungry and patient.

But Carl is optimistic, after all, he's still alive, right? Perhaps his luck has changed and help will arrive to save them all?

Unfortunately, unknown to him and the other survivors, a serial killer has fallen into their group, trapped inside the zoo with them.

With the undead army clamoring outside the walls and a murderer within, it'll be a miracle if any of them live to see the next sunrise.

On second thought, maybe Carl would've been better off if he'd just gone back to jail.

ROAD KILL: A ZOMBIE TALE
by Anthony Giangregorio

In the summer of 2008, a rogue comet entered earth's orbit for 72 hours. During this time, a strange amber glow suffused the sky.

But something else happened; something in the comet's tail had an adverse affect on dead tissue and the result was the reanimation of every dead animal carcass on the planet.

A handful of survivors hole up in a diner in the backwoods of New Hampshire while the undead creatures of the night hunt for human prey.

There's a new blue plate special at DJ's Diner and Truck Stop, and it's you!

DEAD THINGS
by Anthony Giangregorio

Beneath the veil of reality we all know as truth, there is another world, one where creatures only seen in nightmares exist.

But what if these creatures do actually exist, and it is us that are only fleeting images, mere visions conjured up by some unknown being.

Werewolves, zombies, vampires, and other lost things that go bump in the night, inhabit the world of imagination and myth, but all will be found in this collection of tales.

But in this world, fiction becomes fact, and what lurks in the shadows is real. Beware the next time you sense you are being watched or catch movement in the corner of your eye, for though it may be nothing, it might just be your doom.

INCLUDES THE BRAND NEW DEADWATER STORY: **DEAD GRAVE**.

THE DARK
by Anthony Giangregorio
DARKNESS FALLS

The darkness came without warning.

First New York, then the rest of United States, and then the world became enveloped in a perpetual night without end.

With no sunlight, eventually the planet will wither and die, bringing on a new Ice Age. But that isn't problem for the human race, for humanity will be dead long before that happens.

There is something in the dark, creatures only seen in nightmares, and they are on the prowl. Evolution has changed and man is no longer the dominant species. When we are children, we're told not to fear the dark, that what we believe to exist in the shadows is false.

Unfortunately, that is no longer true.

SOULEATER
by Anthony Giangregorio

Twenty years ago, Jason Lawson witnessed the brutal death of his father by something only seen in nightmares, something so horrible he'd blocked it from his mind.

Now twenty years later the creature is back, this time for his son.

Jason won't let that happen.

He'll travel to the demon's world, struggling every second to rescue his son from its clutches.

But what he doesn't know is that the portal will only be open for a finite time and if he doesn't return with his son before it closes, then he'll be trapped in the demon's dimension forever.

SEE HOW IT ALL BEGAN IN THE NEW DOUBLE-SIZED 460 PAGE SPECIAL EDITION!
DEADWATER: EXPANDED EDITION
by Anthony Giangregorio

Through a series of tragic mishaps, a small town's water supply is contaminated with a deadly bacterium that transforms the town's population into flesh eating ghouls.

Without warning, Henry Watson finds himself thrown into a living hell where the living dead walk and want nothing more than to feed on the living.

Now Henry's trying to escape the undead town before he becomes the next victim.

With the military on one side, shooting civilians on sight, and a horde of bloodthirsty zombies on the other, Henry must try to battle his way to freedom.

With a small group of survivors, including a beautiful secretary and a wise-cracking janitor to aid him, the ragtag group will do their best to stay alive and escape the city codenamed: **Deadwater**.

DEAD END: A ZOMBIE NOVEL
by Anthony Giangregorio
THE DEAD WALK!

Newspapers everywhere proclaim the dead have returned to feast on the living!

A small group of survivors hole up in a cellar, afraid to brave the masses of animated corpses, but when food runs out, they have no choice but to venture out into a world gone mad.

What they will discover, however, is that the fall of civilization has brought out the worst in their fellow man.

Cannibals, psychotic preachers and rapists are just some of the atrocities they must face.

In a world turned upside down, it is life that has hit a Dead End.

BOOK OF THE DEAD 2: NOT DEAD YET
A ZOMBIE ANTHOLOGY
Edited by Anthony Giangregorio

Out of the ashes of death and decay, comes the second volume filled with the walking dead.

In this tomb, there are only slow, shambling monstrosities that were once human.

No one knows why the dead walk; only that they do, and that they are hungry for human flesh.

But these aren't your neighbors, your co-workers, or your family. Now they are the living dead, and they will tear your throat out at a moment's notice.

So be warned as you delve into the pages of this book; the dead will find you, no matter where you hide.

ANOTHER EXCITING ADVENTURE IN THE DEADWATER SERIES!
DEAD SALVATION
BOOK 9
by Anthony Giangregorio
HANGMAN'S NOOSE!

After one of the group is hurt, the need for transportation is solved by a roving cannie convoy. Attacking the camp, the companions save a man who invites them back to his home.

Cement City it's called and at first the group is welcomed with thanks for saving one of their own. But when a bar fight goes wrong, the companions find themselves awaiting the hangman's noose.

Their only salvation is a suicide mission into a raider camp to save captured townspeople.

Though the odds are long, it's a chance, and Henry knows in the land of the walking dead, sometimes a chance is all you can hope for.

In the world of the dead, life is a struggle, where the only victor is death.

The Lazarus Culture
by Pasquale J. Morrone

Secret Service Agent Christopher Kearns had no idea what he was up against. Assigned on a temporary basis to the Center for Disease Control, he only knew that somehow it was connected to the lives of those the agency protected...namely, the President of the United States. If there were possible terrorist activities in the making, he could only guess it was at a red alert basis.

When Kearns meets and befriends Doctor Marlene Peterson of the Breezy Point Medical Center in Maryland, he soon finds that science fiction can indeed become a reality. In a solitary room walked a man with no vital signs: dead. The explanation he received came from Doctor Lee Fret, a man assigned to the case from the CDC. Something was attached to the brain stem. Something alive that was quickly spreading rapidly through Maryland and other states.

Kearns and his ragtag army of agents and medical personnel soon find themselves in a world of meaningless slaughter and mayhem. The armies of the walking dead were far more than mere zombies. Some began to change into whatever it was they ate. The government had found a way to reanimate the dead by implanting a parasite found on the tongue of the Red Snapper to the human brain.

It looked good on paper, but it was a project straight from Hell.

The dead now walked, but it wasn't a mystery.

It was The Lazarus Culture.

DEADFALL
by Anthony Giangregorio

It's Halloween in the small suburban town of Wakefield, Mass.

While parents take their children trick or treating and others throw costume parties, a swarm of meteorites enter the earth's atmosphere and crash to earth.

Inside are small parasitic worms, no larger than maggots.

The worms quickly infect the corpses at a local cemetery and so begins the rise of the undead.

The walking dead soon get the upper hand, with no one believing the truth.

That the dead now walk.

Will a small group of survivors live through the zombie apocalypse?

Or will they, too, succumb to the Deadfall.

LOVE IS DEAD: A ZOMBIE ANTHOLOGY
Edited by Anthony Giangregorio
THE DEATH OF LOVE

Valentine's Day is a day when young love is fulfilled.

Where hopeful young men bring candy and flowers to their sweethearts, in hopes of a kiss...or perhaps more. But not in this anthology.

For you see, LOVE IS DEAD, and in this tome, the dead walk, wanting to feed on those same hearts that once pumped in chests, bursting with love.

So toss aside that heart-shaped box of candy and throw away those red roses, you won't need them any longer. Instead, strap on a handgun, or pick up a shotgun and defend yourself from the ravenous undead.

Because in a world where the dead walk, even love isn't safe.

ETERNAL NIGHT: A VAMPIRE ANTHOLOGY
Edited by Anthony Giangregorio

Blood, fangs, darkness and terror...these are the calling cards of the vampire mythos.

Inside this tome are stories that embrace vampire history but seek to introduce a new literary spin on this longstanding fictional monster. Follow a dark journey through cigarette-smoking creatures hunted by rogue angels, vampires that feed off of thoughts instead of blood, immortals presenting the fantastic in a local rock band, to a legendary monster on the far reaches of town.

Forget what you know about vampires; this anthology will destroy historical mythos and embrace incredible new twists on this celebrated, fictional character.

Welcome to a world of the undead, welcome to the world of Eternal Night.

BOOK OF THE DEAD
A ZOMBIE ANTHOLOGY VOL 1
ISBN 978-1-935458-25-8
Edited by Anthony Giangregorio

This is the most faithful, truest zombie anthology ever written, and we invite you along for the ride. Every single story in this book is filled with slack-jawed, eyes glazed, slow moving, shambling zombies set in a world where the dead have risen and only want to eat the flesh of the living. In these pages, the rules are sacrosanct. There is no deviation from what a zombie should be or how they came about. The Dead Walk.

There is no reason, though rumors and suppositions fill the radio and television stations. But the only thing that is fact is that the walking dead are here and they will not go away. So prepare yourself for the ultimate homage to the master of zombie legend. And remember... Aim for the head!

REVOLUTION OF THE DEAD
by Anthony Giangregorio
THE DEAD SHALL RISE AGAIN!

Five years ago, a deadly plague wiped out 97% of the world's population, America suffering tragically. Bodies were everywhere, far too many to bury or burn. But then, through a miracle of medical science, a way is found to reanimate the dead.

With the manpower of the United States depleted, and the remaining survivors not wanting to give up their internet and fast food restaurants, the undead are conscripted as slave labor.

Now they cut the grass, pick up the trash, and walk the dogs of the surviving humans.

But whether alive or dead, no race wants to be controlled, and sooner or later the dead will fight back, wanting the freedom they enjoyed in life.

The revolution has begun!

And when it's over, the dead will rule the land, and the remaining humans will become the slaves...or worse.

KINGDOM OF THE DEAD
by Anthony Giangregorio
THE DEAD HAVE RISEN!

In the dead city of Pittsburgh, two small enclaves struggle to survive, eking out an existence of hand to mouth.

But instead of working together, both groups battle for the last remaining fuel and supplies of a city filled with the living dead.

Six months after the initial outbreak, a lone helicopter arrives bearing two more survivors and a newborn baby. One enclave welcomes them, while the other schemes to steal their helicopter and escape the decaying city.

With no police, fire, or social services existing, the two will battle for dominance in the steel city of the walking dead. But when the dust settles, the question is: will the remaining humans be the winners, or the losers?

When the dead walk, the line between Heaven and Hell is so twisted and bent there is no line at all.

DEAD HISTORY: A ZOMBIE ANTHOLOGY
Edited by Anthony Giangregorio

The history of the walking dead is a long one.

Since before man walked the Earth, the dead have been with us. Rotting, decrepit animated corpses have existed, and in many places, have helped create the evolution of the very history we all know as fact, but yet they have always remained hidden from mankind as the sands of time flowed through the hour glass.

From Egypt, to London, to the first moon landing, to the old West; zombies have been a part of our culture, our very lives, though each time it has been erased, eradicated from our history.

Perhaps in these lost tales of our past is the hope for our future. In these stories might very well be the answers of what to do when the zombie apocalypse finally arrives. So read these tales quickly and learn from them. For even in the past, the dead walk, and if they did once before, it's a fact they will do so again.

The only question is: When will that be and will you be prepared?

THE CHRONICLES OF JACK PRIMUS
BOOK ONE
by Michael D. Griffiths

Beneath the world of normalcy we all live in lies another world, one where supernatural beings exist.

These creatures of the night hunt us; want to feed on our very souls, though only a few know of their existence.

One such man is Jack Primus, who accidentally pierces the veil between this world and the next. With no other choice if he wants to live, he finds himself on the run, hunted by beings called the Xemmoni, an ancient race that sees humans as nothing but cattle. They want his soul, to feed on his very essence, and they will kill all who stand in their way. But if they thought Jack would just lie down and accept his fate, they were sorely mistaken.

He didn't ask for this battle, but he knew he would fight them with everything at his disposal, for to lose is a fate worse than death.

He would win this war, and he would take down anyone who got in his way.

THE WAR AGAINST THEM: A ZOMBIE NOVEL
by Jose Alfredo Vazquez

Mankind wasn't prepared for the onslaught.

An ancient organism is reanimating the dead bodies of its victims, creating worldwide chaos and panic as the disease spreads to every corner of the globe. As governments struggle to contain the disease, courageous individuals across the planet learn what it truly means to make choices as they struggle to survive.

Geopolitics meet technology in a race to save mankind from the worst threat it has ever faced. Doctors, military and soldiers from all walks of life battle to find a cure. For the dead walk, and if not stopped, they will wipe out all life on Earth. Humanity is fighting a war they cannot win, for who can overcome Death itself? Man versus the walking dead with the winner ruling the planet. Welcome to *The War Against Them*.

DEADTOWN: A DEADWATER STORY
BOOK 8
by Anthony Giangregorio

The world is a very different place now. The dead walk the land and humans hide in small towns with walls of stone and debris for protection, constantly keeping the living dead at bay.

Social law is gone and right and wrong is defined by the size of your gun.

UNWELCOME VISITORS

Henry Watson and his band of warrior survivalists become guests in a fortified town in Michigan. But when the kidnapping of one of the companions goes bad and men die, the group finds themselves on the wrong side of the law, and a town out for blood.

Trapped in a hotel, surrounded on all sides, it will be up to Henry to save the day with a gamble that may not only take his life, but that of his friends as well.

In a dead world, when justice is not enough, there is always vengeance.

END OF DAYS: AN APOCALYPTIC ANTHOLOGY
VOLUMES 1 & 2

Our world is a fragile place.

Meteors, famine, floods, nuclear war, solar flares, and hundreds of other calamities can plunge our small blue planet into turmoil in an instant.

What would you do if tomorrow the sun went super nova or the world was swallowed by water, submerging the world into the cold darkness of the ocean? This anthology explores some of those scenarios and plunges you into total annihilation.

But remember, it's only a book, and tomorrow will come as it always does. Or will it?

THE PLACE TO GO FOR ZOMBIE AND APOCALYPTIC FICTION

LIVING DEAD PRESS
WHERE THE DEAD WALK
www.livingdeadpress.com

Blood of the Dead
A.P. Fuchs

Bits of the Dead
edited by
Keith Gouveia

Axiom-man
The Dead Land
A.P. Fuchs

Now Available From Pill Hill Press

Coming Soon From Pill Hill Press

Visit Pill Hill Press online at
www.pillhillpress.com